*For all of you
who reach out
in compassion
every day*

Church of the Old Mermaids

Also by Kim Antieau

Novels
The Jigsaw Woman
The Gaia Websters
Coyote Cowgirl
Mercy, Unbound
Broken Moon
Ruby's Imagine

Nonfiction
Counting on Wildflowers: An Entanglement

Short Stories
Trudging to Eden

Chapbook
Blossoms

Blogs
www.kimantieau.com
www.oldmermaids.com

Church of the Old Mermaids

Kim Antieau

Church of the Old Mermaids
by Kim Antieau

Copyright © 2009 by Kim Antieau

ISBN-10: 1440452245
ISBN-13: 9781440452246

http://www.oldmermaids.com
http://www.kimantieau.com

A production of
Ruby Rose's Fairy Tale Emporium
PO Box 1100
Stevenson WA 98648

One

Get the starfish outta your eyes, sister.
Sister Sheila Na Giggles Mermaid

Myla walked the wash looking for trash in the dirt. She looked for treasure too. One man's trash was another woman's treasure. And vice versa, she always said. She carried two bags over her right shoulder. Into the plastic bag, she dropped garbage; into the ruby-colored cloth bag, she put those bits of refuse she believed she could sell on Fourth Avenue, at the Church of the Old Mermaids. It was not a real church. At least not how most people defined that word. It was the space where she put her table, chair, and wares on Saturdays, shine or shine. She called it the Church of Old Mermaids because her mother told her when she was a child that the desert had once been a vast sea. She liked imagining that the mermaids had not dried up when the sea did; they merely changed their attitudes. And maybe their skin and fin-ware.

Myla's feet slip-slided over the sand as she went around a palo verde tree whose bare branches stretched out over the wash. Dry rust-colored bean pods dangled from the green twigs, like offerings from the skeletal fingers of a Catrina doll enticing her to snatch up a couple. So she did. She dropped them into the ruby bag.

"Thank you," she murmured. Wasn't about to say she wouldn't be able to get a nickel for them. Unless she came up with a particularly good story. Like how these pods came from the wash that used to be a river where the Old Mermaids were stranded when the Old Sea began to disappear; or these pods came from a tree hanging over the wash where the Old Mermaids were first stranded, where they finally came to shore, and the first thing they did, these Old Mermaids, was to plant themselves a palo verde, all green, just like Mother Star Stupendous Mermaid's tail had been, you know, before she had to leave the sea, the river, the wash.

Normally Myla did not take anything organic from the wash to sell. She removed only that which humans made, except for an occasional feather. She knew she could sell the latticed skeletons left by cacti—especially the cholla bones that grayed into exotic desert art—but she did not feel she had the right, not yet. Perhaps after she had lived on the land a bit longer. After all, ten years was only a drop in the proverbial time bucket. Sometimes she asked permission to snag an animal bone or cholla joint which she then stored in a room next to her studio apartment in the modular barn near the Crow house. She was not certain what she was going to do with these bits and pieces of the desert, but she felt as though she was retrieving pieces of long ago dismembered desert creatures. Or sea creatures. One day she would reassemble them.

But now, today, she needed to finish her walk and check on the houses in the Old Mermaid Sanctuary. Gail would be at the Crow house soon to pick her up. Myla was caretaker for the houses and land of five families while the owners were away, which was most of the year. The Wentworths usually came for the week between Christmas and New Year; the Castillos visited every spring for a couple of months; the Martins and Fords stayed most of the fall, and the Crows usually took up residence in October and again in March. Now in late January none of them were home.

All of the families wanted the houses to look as though they were lived in while they were away, and Myla did what she could to accommodate their wishes. The Crows encouraged her to use any part of their house since she lived on their property. They told her to watch television, swim in the pool, sit in the spa, use the library, or cook in their deluxe kitchen, but she rarely went into the house. Once or twice she had used the kitchen when she needed an extra oven.

She did like sitting by the Crow's peanut-shaped pool. It was a deep dark indigo blue with patches of lighter blue here and there, creating the impression that one had stumbled upon a curvature in the bedrock where a natural spring pooled. The palm tree growing next it, along with other desert flora, helped further this nature fiction. Or maybe it wasn't a fiction. The house was surrounded by the Sonoran desert. At midday sometimes, Myla sat on one of the lounge chairs and listened to the quiet and watched the cactus wrens hurry along the chest-high earth-colored wall that enclosed the pool area. Or at dusk, she stood at the edge of the pool and listened to the great-horned owl in the palm tree awaken and try to solve its daily identity crisis, "Who? Who?"

She especially liked seeing the mermaid at the bottom of the pool. David Thomas Crow had painted it when his parents drained the pool soon after Myla arrived. The mermaid was beautiful, with black eyes, a peach-colored tail, and tiny multicolored starfish in her wild black hair. She was quite voluptuous and had an uncanny resemblance to Myla, a fact everyone was too polite to mention. Everyone in the Crow family, that is. As soon as the family left that year, Myla showed the mermaid to Theresa, Gail, and George. Theresa and Gail asked her when she had posed for David Crow, a man nearly young enough to be her son. George said, "He got the chimmychangas wrong. Yours are more life-like." Myla couldn't really argue with him. He was right. Hers were more lifelike.

Myla had started working at the Old Mermaid Sanctuary ten years earlier after she left her husband—or he left her. After she answered an ad in the *Tucson Weekly*. The owners came to town and interviewed Myla collectively. They talked with her for fif-teen minutes, give or take, and then they offered her the job—pending a reference check. She had to get bonded too. They prom-ised her a monthly stipend, studio apartment, and use of a car; she promised to care for their land and houses.

She moved in almost immediately. Soon she was walking the wash every day, many times a day. In the beginning she felt a bit like La Llorona, weeping and wailing for her lost children. Only she did not have children. So she wailed for her lost life. Not that she thought about her life. She did not think about much of any-thing then: She felt. She felt sad, angry, lost, lousy. She felt the sand beneath her shoes and tried to keep her balance so she would not fall left into a prickly pear stand or right into a cholla tree, or the other way around. Sometimes she let David Thomas Crow walk with her. When she cried, he did not tell her everything would soon be all right; he did not tell her to look on the bright side or say time heals all. He never seemed uncomfortable with her sorrow—or anything else about her. Every once in a while he would put his hand on her back, lightly; this gesture steadied and relieved her, either by drying up the tears or causing them to flow more profusely.

She drank too much then. She hadn't been a drinker before, and she wasn't one afterward. But for a month or more, she used alcohol as her medicine, like someone with a cough taking cough syrup. That was how she thought about it. Just to stop the hacking ache.

Then one night the Old Mermaids came to her in a dream. They swam the wash, which was filled with sea water, and motioned to her to join them. One of them reached down to the sandy bottom and pulled up an old glass bottle and held it out to her. When she awakened the next morning, she stumbled into the wash and found the same glass bottle—or one that looked like it. Her life changed in that instant. She felt as though she had heard the call of the wild—or the call of the Old Mermaids. The Church of the Old Mermaids was born that morning. She stopped drinking, and David painted the mermaid at the bottom of pool.

David left soon after she stopped drinking, and Myla hadn't seen him since. His mother, Sarah, gave her updates on him now and then, but Myla did not ask a lot of questions about his life. She remembered that month only vaguely, and she was afraid she might find out she had done something embarrassing to drive him away. Besides, he was out of her life, and she did not like to dwell on the past. That was long gone.

Myla leaned over and picked up a piece of gray metal from the sand. It looked like the top half of a shepherd's staff. She dropped it into the ruby bag and kept walking. She passed several pieces of concrete in the sand. She had not yet figured out how so many blocks of concrete ended up in the wash. Even when the arroyo became a river again—temporarily during the monsoons—concrete could not float. Could it? She supposed the force of water could move just about anything.

She stepped over a mesquite log with an orange plastic rope

wrapped around it. She did not feel like unraveling it now. Maybe one day. She had been considering that orange rope for many days now—maybe even years. She shrugged. It must be that no one needed it yet.

The wash split, and she followed the left branch. She had not been here for a while. No horses and few other creatures had traveled this way either, judging from the lack of tracks. She stopped in the shade of an old mesquite. She always overdressed on these chilly mornings. Now the cool blackness of the mesquite felt good. Several prickly pear pads had draped themselves over the mesquite trunk that bent toward the ground a bit before curving up. The prickly pear pads looked wrung out, as though they had been traveling a long distance and had finally succumbed to exhaustion and thirst. The cactus had found a good companion in the mesquite. Very grounded. Rooted. Mesquite had the deepest root system of any tree, she knew. Someone had once found a live mesquite root 160 feet beneath the surface, in a copper mine. Myla put her hand on the mesquite trunk. Mesquite trees knew how to hold their ground. Old souls, she thought when she saw one like this, crouched toward the desert floor yet still reaching out to the world around it. Its yellow leaflets appeared almost fluorescent next to its dark branches and trunk.

In the sand near the base of the tree and the prickly pear was a piece of rusty metal; about a foot long and six inches across, it looked vaguely like a skeleton of the push part of a miniature lawn mower. Not that she had seen a mower in a long while. The Wentworths had a square of grassy lawn in the front of their house when Myla first moved into the Old Mermaid Sanctuary. They gave her detailed instructions on how to keep it living and thriving while they were away. She read the instructions and watched each day as the lawn shriveled and then died. She had George pull out the sod and let the desert floor be again. Eventually she talked George into helping her plant some prickly pears, chollas, and a young palo verde. By the time the Wentworths returned, the land looked like desert again. Mr. Wentworth asked her what had happened. She told him, "Putting sod like that on the desert is like putting a bad toupee on a bald man." He frowned, not understanding. "It covers up his beautiful bald head which was what was attractive about him in the first place," Myla said. Mr. Wentworth smoothed his hand over his shiny head and nodded. They never mentioned the lawn again.

Myla picked up the piece of metal and slipped it into the ruby bag. "Thank you, Mesquite," she said.

She walked out of the shade and went to the main artery of the wash. A crow called out. She looked up as it flew over her, its wings whooshing-whooshing against the dry desert air.

"Good morning, crow," she said. Sometimes she wished she was a crow. At least when she was walking the wash. Crows could spot treasure in the dirt even if they were looking down from the moon.

She looked away from the flying crow and at the ground and saw the metal loop to an earring sticking out of a dent in the sand made by a horse's hoof. She reached for it with her cotton-gloved fingers and pulled it out of the dirt. Hanging from the bent metal was a tiny red dreamcatcher with a metal feather at its center. She could get a good price for this with the right story, but maybe she would keep it for a bit, to see if anyone had lost it. She slipped it into the left pocket of her slacks.

Myla glanced up again. "Thanks, Crow. I owe you."

The wash continued across the road, but Myla did not follow it. The road marked the end of the Old Mermaid Sanctuary. She turned around, walked a few yards, then started up a path to the Wentworth house. She had memorized the paths to each house, but she never traveled the desert thoughtlessly. It was too prickly for that. Besides, the desert moved. Like a glacier. She was convinced. Well, she shrugged, maybe not exactly like a glacier. Maybe like a slow dance troupe. When the moon came up, the mesquite, palo verde, saguaro, and prickly pear did the two-step. Or maybe yoga. She shook her head. She was getting a bit too fanciful; Gail would say she was spending too much time alone.

Not too much, really.

Myla walked around the outside of the Wentworth house to see if anything was out of place. Her feet crunched over the pebbly dirt. This house looked similar to other houses in the sanctuary, made from adobe or fake-adobe, this one with a tiled roof. A small covey of quail scurried across the dirt drive, whimpering and cooing, reminding Myla—as quail often did—of a group of nuns bustling from sight, worried they might become tainted if they did not hurry, hurry, hurry away.

Myla pulled a ring of keys out of her pocket, searched for the Wentworth key, put it in the lock and turned it. She stepped inside the dark, quiet house and closed the door behind her. She paused in the foyer for a moment and wiped her feet on the mat. She looked down to make certain she was not bringing in any dirt or cactus thorns. Then she walked to the living room and called, "*Buenos días! Es Myla.*"

A moment later, a five year old girl came running around the corner from the hallway, her arms outstretched, her long black ponytails bouncing on her back. Myla bent over and enveloped the girl in her arms.

"Oh, Lily my Lily," Myla said in Spanish. "You are the most beautiful flower in this desert. I'll have to take you home with me and never let you go."

Lily kissed her daintily on the cheek.

"Ahhh, stingy with the water are we," Myla said.

Lily turned her cheek to Myla, and Myla gave her a wet kiss.

Lily laughed and wiped it away.

"Oh! You don't want my kisses? Okay. The kiss is on your hand now, so if you want it back, you can touch your cheek any time."

Lily put both hands up to her cheek and smiled. Her mother walked into the room.

"*Hola*, Maria," Myla said. "*Cómo estás?*" She embraced the thin young woman.

"I am well," Maria said, running her hands through her short black hair. "Lily had another nightmare."

"I was in the water," Lily said. "I couldn't breathe."

"We had to cross a river coming here," Maria explained. "It was higher than we expected. Below her knees, but the current was too strong for her. She started screaming. It was nearly dark. Everyone started running, afraid they'd be caught. She fell and the water grabbed her." Maria squinted, remembering. "But I got her right away. Didn't I, Lily?" She looked down at her daughter. "I would never do anything to put her in danger." She looked at Myla again. Both women knew she had risked her daughter's life by crossing *la frontera* and bringing her into the desert. "I couldn't leave her behind," Maria whispered.

"Did you eat?" Myla asked.

Lily slipped her hand into Myla's as they walked into the darkened kitchen.

"We made the oatmeal like you showed us," Maria said.

Microwaved. Less chance of them catching anything on fire.

"Then I washed the dishes and put everything away," Maria said. "It is very kind of these people to let me use their house."

"Yes, well," Myla said, "tonight we will have dinner at my place, when I get back from the Church of the Old Mermaids. Will you be all right until then? If anything happens, remember you can walk out onto the road and the second house on the right is where I live. There's a phone in my apartment in the barn. I will leave my door unlocked."

"I remember," Maria said. "You showed us."

"By the way, you can leave these kitchen curtains open if you like," Myla said. "No one could see you from here."

"Any news on my husband?"

Myla shook her head. She had discovered Lily and Maria in the desert a few miles from the border several days earlier, after their *guia* had deserted them. Myla had been searching for items for the Church of the Old Mermaids in a wash that ran through a stand of cottonwoods when she heard a child crying. She followed the sound until she discovered Lily, alone. A few moments later, Maria seemed to appear out of nowhere. She took Lily into her arms and explained to Myla that she was looking for her husband Juan who had come to the United States three months earlier. She had not heard from him since. Could Myla help her, Maria wanted to know. Finding Maria's husband would be like finding a particular thorn in the desert, Myla thought at the time—and she still thought so—but she did not say that to Maria then or now. Besides, maybe Theresa would find him.

Myla looked from the mother to the child now.

"I need to get going," Myla said. "I'll see you both later."

"Thank you, Myla," Maria said.

"Don't go," Lily said.

Myla crouched down. "I'll be back. I'll tell you another story tonight."

Lily turned her cheek to her. Myla bent over to give her another wet kiss. Lily laughed as though tickled.

Myla left the house. She stood outside for a moment until she heard the door lock behind her. Then she walked down the dirt street to the Martin house. She went around the outside of the building, then inside. All appeared to be as it should, although she needed to take down the Christmas lights sometime before the next holiday. She locked the house up again and walked back across the wash to the Castillo place. It looked as though the javelinas had been trying to dig up something near the palo verde by the master bedroom. No harm done though. Javelinas did what javelinas did. She went inside the house, stood in the semidarkness, then called out, "*Hola!* It's Myla, Ernesto." No answer.

She walked across the living room and looked out the sliding glass doors at the enclosed patio. Ernesto lay on one of the chaise lounges in the shade of a tall conifer. He was covered from head to foot. Myla nodded. This was good. He needed the rest. He had gotten sick picking cotton, probably from pesticide poisoning. His friends had taken him to the hospital emergency initially, but he wouldn't go back after the first visit. He was afraid someone would report him to *la migra*. He had not been able to work for two months, he had no money for rent or food, and he hadn't been getting any better. That was when Theresa heard about him from a friend of a friend. She told Myla about his situation. Two weeks at the Old Mermaid Sanctuary and he was almost back to his old self.

Myla opened the sliding glass door and went outside.

Ernesto looked up, took off his sunglasses, and started to stand.

"No need to get up," Myla said. "You've been eating the soup?"

Ernesto stood despite her protestations. He looked far older than his thirty-five years, fragile, his body slightly bent.

"I have been eating your soup, *señora,*" he said. "It is a miracle soup! You are a miracle worker!"

"Just thank the Old Mermaids," Myla said.

Ernesto smiled.

"I will be gone until dark," Myla said. "But we will have dinner at my place tonight. Should I have Stefan come get you?"

"I can come on my own," he said.

"Still, wouldn't his company be nice?"

"That is true," Ernesto said.

"Until then," Myla said. "I'm late so I have to go."

"I will see you out," he said.

"It's all right," she said. But he followed her anyway. They slowly walked to the door together. She said good-bye again, stepped outside, and listened for the door to lock behind her. She hurried down the path to the wash, then headed toward the Crow house.

Cathy and her teenaged son Stefan were at the Ford house, but Myla would not have time to stop there this morning. They would be fine without her looking in now. At least she hoped so. She did not normally have this many people at the Old Mermaid Sanctuary—and never anyone except migrants. Until now. Theresa had vouched for Cathy, an old acquaintance of hers who was fleeing an abusive husband. She could not stay with her, Theresa had pleaded, because Theresa was still a newlywed. It would only be a few days, she had promised. It had been ten days so far. Myla was not sure why she had agreed; maybe it was because Theresa never begged and she was so desperate for this second marriage to work. In any case, Myla had let Cathy and Stefan come to the Old Mermaid Sanctuary.

Myla hurried by the Crow house and empty horse corrals to her apartment on the north side of the barn. She went inside and dropped the plastic bag full of trash in the garbage. She added the contents of the ruby bag to a cardboard box. Then she put that box onto another cardboard box and carried them outside just as Gail drove up. Myla waited for the dust to settle, and then she went to the back of the car. The hatchback opened as Gail got out of the car.

"Good morning," Myla said.

Gail looked irritated, but she often looked irritated. Myla was convinced she would be a beautiful old woman: her face a net-work of wrinkles—like arroyos on a mountain—from a lifetime of frowns.

Gail pushed her curly brown-hair out of her eyes and asked, "The table inside?"

"Yep," Myla said. She put the boxes in the back of the car, then followed Gail into the apartment and picked up two more boxes and carried them to the car. Gail got the table. They packed the car, closed the hatchback, and both got in.

Gail started up the car. "You been rushing around this morning?"

"Of course," Myla said. "Saturdays are busy."

Gail turned the car around and drove down the dirt drive. She glanced at Myla. "Someday you're going to have to take me on one of your walks in the wash, so I can see exactly what you do."

"Nothing exact about it," Myla said. "And you know the Old Mermaids like me to walk the wash alone."

"Yeah, right." Gail turned out onto the road, and they headed for the main road that would, eventually, lead them into town. "I'd think you'd have all the alone time you'd need out here."

"You'd think," Myla said.

Two

Go with the flow—and watch out for waterfalls.

Sister Sophia Mermaid

Gail helped Myla unload her table and boxes in front of Antigone Books. Then she left. Myla set up the old card table on the sidewalk near the far end of the bookstore picture window. She smoothed a blue oilcloth with red and yellow flowers on it over the table. Pietra rolled out a comfy chair from the bookstore for Myla.

"Good morning, Myla," Pietra said.

"Thank you for this wonderful chair, Pietra!" Myla said, as if it were the first time Pietra had ever brought her a chair. "It makes the day much more pleasant."

Pietra smiled. "What goodies do you have this morning?"

"We shall soon see," Myla said.

She put one of the boxes on the chair, took the top off, and began pulling out items and arranging them on the table. Near one corner of the table, she placed a broken kitchen tile with a peach at its center. Next to it, she put a red piece of cloth, then a small white feather, a half blue marble, a baseball ticket from a Mariners game on June 5, 2001 (Section: 113, Row: H), an empty orange plastic lighter, a red brick, a yellow T-shirt with the word "Who?" on it, several glass bottles without labels, a smashed beer can, and a few other odds and ends. Closer to her, she laid out the items she had found today.

When the first box was empty, she opened the second box and took out the old pieces she had not sold yet but was not quite ready to throw away. In the middle of it all, she placed a small wooden sign with the words *Church of the Old Mermaids* and *Myla Alvarez, Novice* painted on it in yellow. On the far side of the table, she set an old cigar box with an orange-tailed mermaid painted on the lid. The mermaid held a sign over her breasts that read: donations. Myla put the empty boxes under the table, then sat on the chair.

"It all looks fine," Pietra said. "And I could use one of those bottles actually. My sweetie Ellie brought me in a yellow rose this morning, and I don't have a good vase for it."

Myla picked up a tall empty bottle.

"You might try this one," Myla said. "I found it near where the old kitchen used to be in the Old Mermaid Sanctuary. I can't be certain, but I believe this was the one that used to have a place on the window sill in the kitchen. It had a teardrop-shaped stopper. Oh, it was beautiful, that top, but it was off as often as it was on because you'll never believe what precious liquid was contained in this bottle."

Pietra said, "I would believe it if you said it was so."

"Ahhh, well, no one can know for sure, but they say it was filled with water from the Old Sea where the Old Mermaids made their home before it dried up. And before it all went away, Sister

Bridget Mermaid had the presence of mind to fill a couple of empty bottles they found along the shore with sea water. This one they put in the kitchen. Sometimes when the Old Mermaids were aching for the Old Sea, they came into the kitchen to gaze at the bottle, sometimes hold it. When the longing became too much, they took the stopper off and smelled the sea and remembered their lost friends and the life they had had to leave behind. They would even dab a drop behind their ears and on their wrists, as though it were perfume, and of course, it was, to them. Sometimes their grief overwhelmed them and they wept as they held the open bottle. That was why the bottle remained full for a long time, no matter how often they used it or how much time went by."

"Why?" Pietra asked. By now, two women and a man had walked up to the table and were listening.

"Because the tears of the Old Mermaids fell into the bottle and kept it full," Myla said. "And no one ever knew the difference because Old Mermaid tears are really sea water. Gradually the Old Mermaids realized they carried the Old Sea within them, always, just as you and I do. Did you ever notice when you cry, the grief begins to subside once you taste your own tears? That's because that sea water reminds the deepest truest part of you that you are always home, you are always with yourself, and that truth is comforting, even in the darkest times, even when you feel as though you are far from home, the way the Old Mermaids felt."

Myla held the bottle out to Pietra, and she took it.

"A gift," Myla said. "For the chair."

"No," Pietra said. "I want to help out the church." She pulled a five dollar bill from her pocket. "This feels so inadequate for a bottle that once held the tears of the Old Mermaids!"

"I'll give you ten dollars for the bottle," the man said. The other woman elbowed him and smiled at Myla.

"It's his first time," she said.

Pietra lifted the top of the cigar box and dropped in the money.

"I gotta go to work," Pietra said. "Thanks! It's just what I needed."

Myla nodded.

"What did I do?" the man whispered. "I thought you wanted the bottle."

The woman shook her head. "This is my husband, Bob. He's not been before."

"It's all right," Myla said. "I love having novices. As you can see"—she pointed to the sign—"I am a novice as well. We generally don't barter at the Church of the Old Mermaids. Each gift of the wash—and therefore a gift from the Old Mermaids—is exactly what a particular person needs and he or she leaves an exhange."

"Are you a nonprofit?" Bob asked.

Myla glanced at the woman with Bob. Then she smiled and said, "Do you mean have I registered with the government as a nonprofit and filled out the paperwork? No, I have not. No paperwork on anything here. Except maybe that baseball ticket."

Bob looked down at the ticket. He stared at it for a moment and then looked away. The woman picked up an amber glass bottle.

"You said Sister Bridget Mermaid filled a couple of bottles with sea water?"

"You have a good eye, Dolores," Myla said, remembering the woman's name as it came out of her mouth. "The bottle you hold is one of those bottles. Of course, it was lost for a long while. Sister Bridget Mermaid put the one bottle on the kitchen window sill, and she hid this one in the pantry, way in the back so that no one would find it. She figured it would be there should they need it one day. As it happened, Sister Ruby Rosarita Mermaid decided to make a pot of chili. She got anasazi and pinto beans from the Old Man who lived with the Old Woman in the mountains. Sister Ruby Rosarita Mermaid talked to the beans all the while she cooked. She always talked to the food. 'Beans, beans, we're Mermaid Queens. Make this stew a healing brew.' She stirred in various chiles from the garden, along with fresh tomatoes, and onions and garlic. She added a pinch of this and a pinch of that. Then she tasted it. It didn't quite taste the way she wanted it to. Didn't quite have the spark she wanted. So you can guess what happened. She went into the pantry and looked around for something special to put in the stew. She found that bottle you're holding. She thought it was beer. Who can blame her? It looks like a beer bottle. She smelled it, and it didn't smell bad. It didn't exactly smell like beer, but she shrugged and dumped the sea water into the pot of chili.

"There are plenty of stories about what happened next. Some say the chili began boiling and bubbling like a great witch's brew. Others said it began thundering and lightning outside. That seems a bit silly to me, doesn't it to you? Why would it suddenly start thundering and lightning because Sister Ruby Rosarita Mermaid poured a little Old Sea water into the chili? Then again, why wouldn't it? One person even claims the earth trembled. Someone else said that the birds on the kitchen tiles flew out of the tiles to get nearer to the pot of chili because everyone agrees that the chili gave off an aroma that woman or beast could detect for miles. And a funny thing happened. All sorts of animals and people began showing up at the Old Mermaid Sanctuary. And they were all hungry! The Old Mermaids began feeding everyone from that pot of chili. Not the animals, of course, since the Old Mermaids knew it wasn't good for wild animals to eat people food. The wild animals didn't seem to mind. They wandered around for a while, watched what was going on, and then left and began eating each other, as is Nature's way.

"The interesting thing is, the chili did not run out. Not until every last person had a bowl, including the Old Mermaids who ate after everyone else had eaten and gone on their way. The Old Mermaids sat in the kitchen eating the chili and looking out at their garden. All of them wanted to know what Sister Ruby Rosarita Mermaid had done to make the chili taste so good.

"'It was that old bottle of beer in the pantry,' Sister Ruby Rosarita Mermaid said. 'That really made it perfecto.' She put her fingers together and kissed them. Sister Bridget Mermaid got up, went to the pantry, and looked for the bottle of sea water. As we know, it was not there. She asked Sister Ruby Rosarita Mermaid to show her the bottle of beer. 'But it's empty,' Sister Ruby Rosarita Mermaid told her. Sister Bridget Mermaid insisted. So Sister Ruby Rosarita Mermaid went to her bedroom and got the bottle. You see, she had dropped several dried sprigs of lavender into it and then set it on the table next to her bed.

"'That was not beer,' Sister Bridget Mermaid said quietly. 'It was the last of the water from our Old Sea. Now it is empty.'

"The Old Mermaids got very quiet. Especially Sister Ruby Rosarita Mermaid. Then she apologized profusely. Sister Sophia Mermaid gently took the bottle from Sister Ruby Rosarita Mermaid. She put the bottle up to her ear. Who knows why? You know how Old Mermaids are."

The small group of people listening laughed.

"Then Sister Sophia Mermaid said, 'It is not in my nature to be contrary,' she said, although they all knew it was in her nature to be contrary. 'But this bottle is not empty. I can hear the sea.' And she passed it around to all the other Old Mermaids. They were astonished and so happy. Mother Star Stupendous Mermaid nodded, as if she had known it all along, and she said, 'Of course. It is good you emptied the bottle, Sister Ruby Rosarita Mermaid.

Because of the emptiness, we are now able to find again what we lost.' All the Old Mermaids nodded in agreement, even though not all of them understood what she meant. The Old Mermaids were not hierarchal, but they were respectful. And Mother Star Stupendous Mermaid was older than many of them. Sister Sophia Mermaid liked a good discussion, however, so she said, 'Was it because of the emptiness that we heard the Old Sea or because of the bottle? One could argue that in order to hear what we long for in the emptiness, we need a container. Like this bottle. Or our ears.'"

"She has a point," Dolores said. "Without the bottle, they wouldn't have heard the Old Sea."

"Unless they went to the ocean," the other woman said.

"So what did Mother Star Stupendous Mermaid say?" Dolores asked.

"She didn't say anything," Myla said, "for the longest time. She went down to the wash—the wash where I found all of these treasures—and she listened and listened. She heard the wind through the bushes and trees. She heard the woodpeckers tapping away on the saguaros. She heard the beating of her heart. She heard the rivers of blood within her pulsing, washing through her body. As the sun went down, she thought she could hear it sizzling in the west, as though this giant ball of heat was dropping into a vast ocean. She heard the quail and the owls and the coyotes at night. She followed this routine for many days.

"Then one morning she took the bottle with her out to the wash. This time she put the bottle—the one you are holding—up to her ear and listened. She heard the Old Sea, or something which sounded like it. She went back to the Old Mermaids and said that Sister Sophia Mermaid was correct: a container helped. Just as the chili pot contained the chili. 'Just as our bodies are containers of the sea we lost,' Mother Star Stupendous Mermaid said. 'In our grief over the loss of the sea, we sometimes forget that our bodies are containers of that sea. Our bodies are home.' The Old Mermaids agreed that this was a good thing to remember. By the way, everyone had pretty much forgotten about Sister Ruby Rosarita Mermaid dumping out the last of the sea water into a pot of chili. The Old Mermaids ate dinner, jumped in the pool, and life went on as usual. That was the way they settled their differences.

"They kept that bottle because they liked listening to the sea sometimes. And also, and this is just a rumor, some say that Sister Ruby Rosarita Mermaid continued to cook using the bottle. She'd fill it up with water and leave it sit until she needed it. If she wanted to feed a lot of people—or if the dish did not taste the way she wanted it to no matter how she tinkered with it—she would get out the bottle. It worked every time: the dish was magnificent. And every time, people came from miles around to eat with the Old Mermaids."

Dolores nodded as she put money in the cigar box. "I do need to remember that I have everything I need right here," she said, tapping her chest with the fingers of her right hand. "Don't need to be pining for the good old days. And I could really use a little help with my cooking. This bottle is just what I need."

Dolores and Bob moved away. Others came up to the table. Most of them greeted her by name.

"Every item is from the Old Mermaid Sanctuary wash today," Myla said. "It is a very special day!"

Red, one of her regulars who had long bushy red hair, picked up the broken sheep staff.

"Now this is different," Red said.

Myla nodded. "Yes. When the Old Mermaids first came onto land, they were not used to walking, and in the desert, as you know, one has to have shoes! They eventually figured out shoes,

28

but they still kept bringing in cactus thorns on the bottoms and sides of their shoes. You know how that is. Well, one of the Old Mermaids, I think it was Sister Laughs A Lot Mermaid, found this piece out in the wash, just like I did. She liked hunting around for lost things too. When she started to go back into the house at the Old Mermaid Sanctuary, she held it like this." Myla stood and took the staff from Red. She grasped it by the curved edge and then held up her foot. With the straight end of it, she picked off a stone on the bottom of her shoe. "Sister Laughs A Lot Mermaid held it like this and was able to get the cactus thorns off her shoes."

"That's exactly what I need!" Red said. "I'm always poking myself with things I've brought in from the desert." She dropped some dollar bills into the cigar box. Then she opened up a captain's chair she had brought with her and moved out of the flow of people traffic.

Dolores brought Myla a *limonada* from Maya Quetzal, the Guatemalan restaurant a couple of doors down. They made it especially for her, no sugar, touch of honey. Fresh lemons. Her lips puckered when she drank it.

"Thank you, Dolores!" Myla said after she took a sip, as though it was the first time anyone had brought her lemonade. "I think this is the best limonada I have ever had."

James walked up to the table with his son Trevor. They had been coming to the Church of the Old Mermaids since Trevor was a small boy. Today they each carried a folded captain's chair. As usual, Trevor held a lined record book in one hand. Across the cover in bold lettering were the words: TREVOR'S JOURNAL. PRIVATE.

"Trevor and James!" Myla said. She leaned over and kissed each one on the cheek. "Anything you need today from the Old Mermaid Sanctuary?"

"Just one of your smiles," Trevor said.

"You've always been a charmer," Myla said, smiling. "With a sincere heart, of course."

"How is everything at the sanctuary?" James asked.

"Everything is as it should be," Myla said. "And yourselves?"

"We're doing great," James said.

"I'd like a present for my girlfriend," Trevor said. His face reddened when his father glanced at him.

"What's she like?" Myla asked.

"What would she like or what is she like?" Trevor asked.

Myla shrugged. "Whichever."

"She's funny," Trevor said. "I mean she has a good sense of humor. She's pretty. She'll do practical jokes and then pretend she didn't have anything to do with it. Nothing harmful. Just funny. Kind of artistic."

"Sounds like a peach of a girl," James said.

Trevor looked over at him. James nodded toward the broken tile with the peach at the center of it.

"This is a very special tile," Myla said. "It comes directly from the kitchen of the house in the Old Mermaid Sanctuary. You've heard me talk about this kitchen. It was an amazing place. This is where they did all their cooking, of course, and oh could the Old Mermaids cook. The kitchen was open to the outside, at least during the day time, so they could walk straight out to the garden, which was enclosed, of course. They were Old Mermaids and they knew it was in their best interest to live with the wildlife but maybe not in the same room. You know what I mean.

"Anyway, when they were building the house, they wanted tile in their kitchen," Myla said. "That goes without saying. The Old Mermaids were very creative, but none of them knew how to make tile. That's a very solid, earthy art, and the Old Mermaids were still a bit watery then, so they hired a young man from town to come out to the sanctuary. Sister Magdelene Mermaid—they called her Sissy Maggie Mermaid—volunteered to work with the man once he got to the house. She thought artistic men were quite attractive, you see. Sissy Maggie Mermaid and the young man, Carlos, worked together for many days. Soon they were painting the tiles to go around the kitchen. They painted seashells and saguaros. Even a couple of mermaids. Carlos liked to paint birds. He told Sissy Maggie Mermaid that he liked painting birds because he felt like he was flying when he painted. When he worked with the earth to actually create the tiles, he felt like a lizard. Lazy and warm and comfortable. It was a nice feeling. But when he painted, he flew! And he loved that feeling. So he painted birds.

"Sissy Maggie Mermaid loved to listen to Carlos talk. And to be truthful, he worked with his shirt off a great deal of the time, and he was a young man, and he was nice to look at. Brown, sweaty. You know. Sissy Maggie Mermaid began painting peaches on the tiles. No other fruit. Just peaches. The sweaty man said, 'You must really like peaches.' 'Indeed I do,' she said. She had not known about peaches until the Old Sea dried up. One day someone brought a basket of peaches to the Old Mermaid Sanctuary. At first, Sissy Maggie Mermaid did not like the fuzz. She was supposed to eat this? They didn't have fuzz in the sea. But then she put the peach up to her face and rubbed it across her skin. 'Oh my,' she whispered that first time. As she ran the peach along her cheek and over her mouth, she couldn't resist taking a bite. All the other Old Mermaids did the same. They gasped as the juice went down their chins. And they laughed. It was the finest fruit they ever had. Since then they hardly ever ate any other fruit. If it was out of season, they waited. Old Mermaids are very patient, even when they are impatient. Sissy Maggie Mermaid explained all this to Carlos. As she talked she noticed he had a little peach fuzz on his cheeks. She wanted to rub her cheek against his, but she felt a bit awkward. After all, she was an Old Mermaid and he was a young tile maker. She wasn't quite certain how that would work.

"On the tile maker's last day, Sissy Maggie Mermaid decided to let him know how she felt. Sissy Maggie Mermaid was artistic, as you know, but she was not always good at expressing herself verbally. She made a peach tile—this peach tile—and then she tried to break it in two so that she could give Carlos one half and she'd keep the other."

"Like two halves of a single heart," Trevor said.

"Exactly," Myla said. "As you can see, it didn't quite break in two. When Carlos was leaving, Sissy Maggie Mermaid ran out to give him the broken tile. She kept the little piece for herself. She held it out to him and said, 'This is how I feel about you.'

"As you may have guessed, Carlos was an artisan. To him, a broken tile was a broken tile. It was shoddy work. He held up the tile and said, 'This is how you feel about my work?' 'No, no, not about your work.' Carlos dropped the tile into the wash and walked away. Sissy Maggie Mermaid was stunned and a bit peeved. She pulled the smaller piece of tile out of her pocket and threw it into the wash. And that's where I found it, right where Carlos had dropped it." Myla shrugged. "The bottom of a wash is like the bottom of the sea. Things shift. A legend grew up around this broken tile, however. Can you imagine what they believed would happen if someone could find both pieces?"

Trevor said, "That they'd find true love?"

"Okay, that's good, but no, the legend was that if someone found both pieces a good tile maker was in their future."

"What about Sister Maggie Mermaid?" Trevor asked. "Was she brokenhearted for long?"

"Oh no," Myla said. "You know what Old Mermaids say about

love, don't you?"

She paused. Trevor shook his head.

"There are always more fish in the sea," she said. When the laughter subsided, she added, "And the other Old Mermaids endeavored to teach Sister Magdelene Mermaid how to communicate more directly. In the sea, the Old Mermaids didn't talk much. A little wiggle of the tail here, a little wink and a nod there. But on land, they had to learn to be more direct. In a charming way, of course."

Trevor reached into his pocket and pulled out some money. He slipped it into the cigar box.

"It's just what I needed," he said. "I'll be direct with her, in a charming way."

Myla laughed. James winked at her, and the father and son moved away to set up their chairs.

And so the day went. At one point, Myla looked up and thought she saw David Thomas Crow for an instant. Then he was gone. She chuckled. Had she conjured up his lookalike because she had been thinking of him earlier?

For lunch, Trevor brought Myla *vegetal tacquitos* from Maya Quetzal.

"These are the best tacquitos I have ever tasted," Myla said. "I think you must have asked Sandra to do something special to them to make them so tasty, Trevor."

"Maybe I let him borrow the chili sea bottle," Dolores said.

Myla nodded. "I bet something like that did happen," she said.

Near the end of the day when most everyone had wandered away, Dolores's husband Bob came up to the table. Bob put a finger on the Mariners ticket.

He looked at Myla. "Do you have a story about the ticket?"

She said, "I can't quite remember it yet. But it will come back to me. What about you?"

"My college roommate's name was Robert too," he said. "When we first met, he decided I would be Bob and he would be Robert. He didn't really like Robbie. Or Bobby. So he became Robert. Which made him sound a little stuffy. But he wasn't stuffy. I was. I told him it should be the other way around, but he insisted. He told me I'd grow into it." He laughed, quietly. "I don't think I ever did. Maybe when I was around him. He saw things differently than most other people. We went to a baseball game together not long ago. Someone had hit a line drive and Ichiro— yes, it was a Mariners game—Ichiro caught it. It was the third out, so Ichiro tossed the ball to an outfielder, the way they do as they all run off the field toward the dugout. That slow run. And as Robert watched Ichiro, he said, 'He's so beautiful.' I laughed at him. But he said, 'Look at him. He's relaxed. He's completely in his body. It's beautiful to watch him. He's always right there, in the game.' I watched until Ichiro disappeared into the dugout. And Robert was right. It was beautiful. Robert was like that, like Ichiro, at least most of the time. He was present in his life." Bob picked up the ticket. "I don't mean he was perfect because he wasn't. He drank way too much. He cheated on his wife. But he wasn't cruel."

Bob was silent. Trevor cleared his throat and then said, "That date. Does it mean something to you? Was that the game you went to see with him?"

Bob looked over at him, kind of dazed. "What? No." He shook his head. "No, it's the day he died."

Dolores came and stood next to him.

Myla nodded. "The Old Mermaids sometimes played baseball. They did. I know it's difficult to believe. As you can imagine it was a bit tricky with all the prickly things growing around them in the desert. You have to really pay attention when you're playing ball in the desert."

34

Bob smiled but kept looking at the baseball ticket.

"They played in the wash, mostly," she said. "They liked games. They're a playful lot, the Old Mermaids. They liked baseball because it's not a fast paced game. They couldn't hurry anyway, especially when chasing the ball through the cactus, mesquite, and palo verde. The best player was Sister Faye Mermaid. You remember her. She knew more about plants, animals, and the ways to talk to the wind and the earth and the clouds and the sun than you could shake a stick at. I've never been sure what that expression means, but you get the idea. She knew a great deal. She was organized. She understood methodology. She was very focused. And that was exactly what made her a good baseball player. It wasn't because her head was in the game, as they say. But her entire being was in the game. Whatever she was doing, she was there: mind, body, and soul. Or however you want to split it up. She was there. Once, a neighbor of the Old Mermaids stopped by to borrow a cup of sugar. This particular neighbor could get irritated if the sun was shining one day and the next day be irritated because it was finally raining. Sister Faye Mermaid irritated her most of all. Sister Faye Mermaid was the only one around on this particular day, so the old neighbor had to ask her for the sugar.

"'We only have honey,' Sister Faye Mermaid said. 'I'll get you a cup of that.' And she went into the pantry to get her some honey. This irritated the neighbor. Who knows why? Just then, Sister Sheila Na Giggles Mermaid walked through the kitchen. 'Well, hello,' Sister Sheila Na Giggles said to the neighbor. 'How are you this fine day?' 'Oh, I wish you had been here when I arrived," the old neighbor said. "Sister Faye Mermaid won't get me any sugar!' Sister Sheila Na Giggles Mermaid said, 'We don't have any sugar.' 'Exactly,' the neighbor said, 'but oh, she's just so full of herself! I can't stand it.' Sister Sheila Na Giggles Mermaid frowned. 'I'm confused, old neighbor. Who should she be full of if not herself?' Sister Faye Mermaid returned with a cup of honey for the neighbor. 'Enjoy,' she said. 'This honey was made by the best desert bees. The finest! They made this honey just for you. For you and their babies, but you will do. It's great medicine. And it'll taste good in your cookies. Have a grand day.' The neighbor took the honey and stalked away, madder than a hornet."

Bob nodded. "Yep, Robert was full of himself."

"I don't know anything about your friend Robert except what you've told me," Myla said, "but maybe he took the name Robert because he wanted to be more like you, not because he thought you should be more like him."

Dolores said, "Bob is full of himself too." She smiled and patted his arm. "That's a good thing."

Bob looked up from the ticket. He reached into his pocket, pulled out some money, and put it in the cigar box. "He used to tell me he wanted to be more like me, but I just couldn't imagine that was true." He dropped the ticket into his shirt pocket. "Thanks. This is just what I needed."

Myla held out her hand to him, and he shook it. "Nice to meet you, Bob. I'm Myla. I hope to see you again."

"I'm looking forward to it," he said. He and Dolores linked arms and walked away.

Late in the afternoon when Myla decided it was time to leave, Trevor returned the chair to the bookstore while she began putting the few remaining items back into the boxes. She folded the oil cloth and slipped it into the side of one of the boxes.

"I don't know how you do this week after week, Myla," James said as he turned over the table and began unlocking the legs and pushing them down. "It's just wonderful."

"I've been telling you for years that I'm not doing anything," she said. "It's the beauty of the Old Mermaids flowing through me."

"I'm starting to believe you," James said. "I remember you told me once you studied to be a teacher. Why didn't you ever teach?"

"I don't know. My ex and I started the business. Then after the divorce, the Church of the Old Mermaids was born, and the rest is...mystery!"

James laughed. Myla smiled.

"Do you remember when I first started coming?" James asked. "I was so angry about my divorce."

"You listened to me for one afternoon, and then you came up and told me I was making these stories up."

He smiled.

"I thought you were some kind of charlatan," he said. "A trickster."

"And now?"

"You're a trickster all right," he said.

"I don't remember what you needed that first day," she said.

James laughed. "Yes you do!"

She grinned.

"After practically accusing you of stealing from people," James said, "I looked around and saw there was nothing on the table I needed."

Myla nodded. Trevor came out of the store and stood with them. Myla put her arm around his waist as he stood next to her.

"I agreed with you," Myla said. "Then I reached over and took a hair from your shirt."

"And you said, 'You don't need anything from the church because you already have everything you need. See, you're even wearing a reminder of that on your shirt.' And you handed me this long black hair. Your hair was very long when you were seven years old, Trevor."

"I remember," he said.

"I took the hair from you and looked at it," James said. "And I knew it was Trevor's hair, and I knew you were right. I had everything I needed. I think I started to cry."

"Just a few tears," Myla said. "The next week, you brought Trevor to the Church of the Old Mermaids."

"And I put the hair in this," he said, pulling on a string around his neck until it came out his shirt. At the bottom of it was a tiny glass vial, like a pendant on a necklace. "To remind me of what was important when he wasn't around."

"He put one of my baby teeth in there too," Trevor said.

Myla nodded. They had shared this story before, and it was good to hear it again.

"That scared away women for a long time," Trevor said. "Thank goodness he's got a girlfriend now. Maybe he'll put her hair in the vial now."

James laughed. "Now that seems a little weird, son."

A car pulled up to the curb. It was Gail's. James carried the table to the car, and Trevor lifted the boxes into the back. Gail waved to them from inside the car. Myla thanked them. Trevor leaned over and kissed her check.

"I needed a little sugar today. Thanks, Trevor. See you boys next week."

Myla got into the car, she waved, and Gail pulled the car out into traffic.

Three

Step lightly. Dance hard. Eat your vegetables.
Sister DeeDee Lightful Mermaid

"Did you have a good day?" Gail asked Myla as they drove down Speedway.

"Yes, it was wonderful. You?"

"I got a lot done," Gail said. "By the way, Sarah Crow left a message on my voice mail that she's been trying to reach you."

"My phone must not be working again," Myla said. "Did she say what she wanted? Anything wrong?"

"She asked me to ask you to call her," she said.

Myla said, "Okay. You coming to dinner tonight?"

Gail never came to the Saturday dinners even though Myla invited her every week. It was just as well. If Gail ever found out what she was doing, Myla wasn't sure how she would react. Gail had come to the Church of the Old Mermaids only a couple of times, and Myla didn't think she was impressed.

"Don't you ever feel guilty selling people that junk?" Gail asked. "You can't need the money that much."

"I don't feel a bit of guilt," Myla said. "People know exactly what they're buying."

"Fairy tales," she said. "They're trying to buy fairy tales. And life isn't about stories."

"What is it about then?" Myla asked.

Her friend looked at her and said, "I don't know what it's 'about.' I do know it's hard."

"Life is shit and then you die?"

"Exactly."

Myla laughed. "I wish you had stayed today. I had just what you need."

"I doubt that," Gail said. Myla glanced out the window. Gail was driving too fast. She always drove too fast.

"I had lemonade from Maya Quetzal," Myla said. "It was so good. No sugar."

"It must have been sour," Gail said.

"No, they put honey in it. Not too much. It was still tart but not sour."

"Why are you talking about lemonade?" Gail asked. "You know, since your divorce, you've gotten a little strange."

"That was ten years ago," Myla said. "But you're right. I have gotten a little strange. I'm going with the flow of the rest of the world. And you, sugar, you could use some flow—and sweetening. You're getting a little sour."

"I don't understand half the things you say," Gail said.

"That means you understand half? That's progress."

Gail laughed.

"Are you coming tonight or not?" Myla asked.

"No, I can't," she said. "Too much to do. Although I'd love to meet your friends. Is Theresa going to be there?"

"I hope so."

Gail made a noise.

"What?"

"She's so...she just seems so full of herself."

Myla laughed.

"What are you laughing about?"

She shook her head. "I'm not sure you'd understand. Do you ever wonder why we're still friends?"

"Because my husband is a sonofabitch and I need an excuse to get out of the house every Saturday."

Myla nodded. "And I'm just what you need."

Gail laughed. "Yes, you're just what I need. I'll show up to your strange Saturday night dinners one of these times. You wait."

"I'm waiting." Myla sighed.

"What's that sigh about?" Gail asked.

"Tomorrow is the anniversary," Myla said. "George is coming over."

"You and George still perform that stupid ritual?" Gail deftly wove them in and out of traffic as they traveled down Speedway. "Don't you think it's a little strange?"

"Of course it's strange," Myla said. "But George and I went through this together. He's the only one who understands—at least a little bit. Remember my husband was having an affair with his wife."

"Of course I remember," Gail said. "But they've moved on. You should too. It's been ten years. He was not such a great man, you know."

Myla nodded. Gail glanced over at her.

"He wasn't. You had an inflated view of him."

"I'm over it," Myla said. "Him."

She could not explain how she felt to Gail. Or to anyone. She allowed herself to mourn her lost life once a year: on the anniversary of the day she walked into her bedroom and found her husband on top of her next door neighbor, George's wife Nadine. She no longer loved her ex-husband, but she still missed something about their life together. It was as though he had been imprinted on her being when they got married and she couldn't change that. Just like she couldn't change the color of her eyes or the DNA in her cells.

He had promised to love her for life, and she had promised to love him for life. It was a pact they made together, and she never doubted it. It was not as if she had not been loved during her life. Her mother loved her. Her father probably loved her, but he spent more time with his second family than with his first, so she could not swear to that. And the sister and brothers from the second family may have loved her. They were family, though, and that did not feel like real love.

True love was being loved for herself, not because she happened to share chromosomes with someone. Wasn't that what everyone wanted? Someone to listen to them, to see them, to curl up next to them at night, someone who would want them always? Her ex-husband had told Myla often that she was the best person he had ever known. She had had no hint that he no longer loved her. Even in those instants after she found him on top of George's wife—George's much younger wife—she thought he must still love her.

But then he took her aside, away from George and Nadine, and he said, "You are still the best person I know, but I don't love you any more. Not in that way."

For a long time afterward whenever she closed her eyes, she would see her husband's mouth moving and hear his words, "I don't love you any more. Not in that way."

Richard. That was his name, but she tried to avoid saying it out loud if she could.

Tomorrow was the anniversary of that day, the same day she and George walked in on their spouses, the same day she learned her husband did not love her any more.

"Maybe this year we won't go to the house," Myla said.

"What?" Gail said. "You mean you go back to your old house?"

Myla didn't say anything.

"Woman, you need to get laid," Gail said.

"That'll happen too," Myla said. "I don't know why George's wife left him. He's a much better lover than my ex ever was."

Gail laughed. "Myla Alvarez!

"I'm speaking truth," Myla said. "But saying George is a better lover isn't saying much."

Gail laughed. After a moment of silence, she said, "I know it was a bad time for you, Myla. But you got through it. You proved you don't need him. I went by the shop the other day, on my way to something else, and it doesn't look like it's doing well. Shabby imports from Mexico. Not like the stuff you used to bring in."

"I wish them all the best," Myla said.

"No, you don't."

"Sometimes I do. Today has been a good day. What do I care about them?"

"So ignore that stupid anniversary," Gail said. "We could go to a movie or something. Call me."

"That reminds me," Myla said. "I need to make sure my phone is on."

"Don't change the subject," Gail said.

"Hey, I thought I saw David Crow today," Myla said. "Isn't that strange? I was thinking about him this morning."

"Whatever happened to him?" Gail said. "When you first moved there, you two were together all the time."

"We weren't together all the time," Myla said. "He was a nice boy. We kept each other company."

Gail laughed. "You keep telling yourself that, Myla. That's what you used to say back then—and I didn't believe you then either. You were attracted to him."

"Maybe a little," Myla said. "But I didn't act on it. I knew I was just lonely."

"Didn't keep you from acting on George."

"George wasn't nearly fifteen years my junior," Myla said. "I'm not my husband."

"If I had had a choice between George and David Crow," Gail said. "I would have eaten crow."

"Gail!"

Gail laughed. Myla smiled.

"I did not have a choice," Myla said. "And George isn't that bad. He's easy. I don't ever have to worry about him leaving me."

"Because he's already gone," Gail said.

"That's right," Myla said. "He doesn't care whether he ever sees me again. I don't care either. That's fine with me. Better than living a lie, I can tell you that much."

Myla hurried into her apartment after Gail dropped her off. It would be dark soon, and she needed to make dinner. She diced two onions and several handfuls of shitake mushrooms, then sautéed them in olive oil. She added dried oregano, basil, and four large cans of crushed tomatoes. She diced a garlic bulb and dropped the pieces in, too.

"There," she said. "Instant spaghetti sauce. Thank you, everything in this pot. We appreciate your nourishment."

She looked in her cupboards for the big pot to cook the pasta in but couldn't find it. "Must have left it in the big house." She stirred the bubbling sauce. "Cumin." She had almost forgotten her secret ingredient: cumin. She shook some into the bubbling sauce.

"Are you decent?" Theresa asked as she knocked on the screen door.

"Hardly," Myla answered. "Come on in."

Theresa opened the door and came inside, carrying a grocery sack. She set it on the counter and then took from it a covered bowl of salad and two loaves of bread.

"I left apple juice and water on your table outside," Theresa said. "Guess who came with?"

"Who? I've got to get a bigger pot," she said.

"Luisa," Theresa said.

Theresa's teenaged daughter had been living with her father in Los Angeles for the past year.

"So I didn't stop and get Maria and Lily," Theresa said. "I didn't want Luisa asking all kinds of questions."

Myla looked at her. "Luisa? I thought she was still in California."

"She showed up on my doorstep two days ago," Theresa said. Myla handed her a serrated knife from the silverware drawer. Theresa began cutting the bread. "And she's dyed her hair blond."

"You haven't told her anything?" Myla asked.

"No!" Theresa said. "I never told her before. Why should I now? Nothing has changed. She and Del Rey still fight all the time, so I brought her along tonight."

"Have you found out anything about Maria's husband?"

"Do you know how many Juan Martinez's there are?"

"I can guess," Myla said.

"She said he came with his cousin, so I'm searching both names," Theresa said.

"I need to go make the noodles over at the Crow house. I'll be back in a few." Myla grabbed three boxes of spaghetti pasta and went out the door. She stopped and looked at the Catalinas and

Rincons. The fading sunlight created distinct shadows on the mountains. She loved this instant of the day—before night fell. Everything seemed more alive than at any other time. A moment later, the sharp, black shadows disappeared. Myla stepped off her porch—which was just several planks of wood raised off the dirt—and went across the drive and down a bit, toward the house. She passed by Theresa's car and waved to Luisa who sat in the passenger seat talking on the phone.

Maria, Cathy, and Lily were walking up the drive toward her.

"Myla, Myla!" Lily said. She ran toward Myla.

Myla crouched and opened her arms to the girl. They embraced.

"How are the Old Mermaids today?" Lily asked in accented English as they hugged each other.

Myla laughed. "They are great!"

Myla hugged Cathy and then Maria. The young woman looked tired.

"I'm sorry I couldn't come to the house this morning, Cathy," Myla said. "You and Stefan do all right?"

"I'm good," Cathy said. "I worked on my resumé today. Stefan cleaned the house."

"He doesn't have to clean every day!" Myla said.

"We're trying to do our part," Cathy said.

Ernesto and Stefan walked up the drive toward them. Stefan was tall and gangly, his fifteen year old body trying to grow into a man overnight it seemed. Ernesto walked a bit more sprightly than he had earlier in the day.

"Good evening, Ernesto and Stefan," Myla said in Spanish when they reached them. "How are you?"

"I am well," Ernesto said.

Stefan nodded. "I had to hurry to keep up with him."

"Good, good," Myla said. "Theresa's daughter Luisa is joining us tonight."

"That means we should all keep our mouths shut about where we're staying," Cathy said. "Right?"

"Yes," Myla said. "That would be best. Now I'm going to make the noodles in the house. Theresa is at my place. I'll meet you there."

Myla left the group and went up the steps to the long porch in front of the Crow house. This was a good spot to watch the sun come up over the mountains in the morning. She had done so once or twice, wrapped in a blanket and curled up in one of the chairs. It had been a while since she had watched a sunrise. When she first moved here, she had felt so tired and battle-scarred that she had needed the comfort of watching the sun come up and go down every day. She needed to feel the rhythms of this place. Any place perhaps. But this place, this land, was what had rocked her back to sanity.

She took out her keys and unlocked the door to the Crow house and went inside. She wiped her shoes carefully on the mat, then looked at the soles to see if they were clean. She walked down the short hall, through the living room, and into the large kitchen. She hummed as she opened the cupboards and took down a large stainless steel pot. She filled it with water from the sink, put a bit of olive oil in it—"I owe you, Sarah Crow," she said—and then she put the pot on the stove to boil.

"I wonder if it's true," she said, "that a watched pot doesn't boil."

"Why don't you ask the Old Mermaids?"

Myla started and turned around. A man stood several yards from her. She must have looked frightened because he immediately put up his hands.

"Myla, it's me, David Crow," he said. "Don't you recognize me?"

"Of course!" she said. "I thought I saw you today, but I decided it was only wishful thinking."

She went to him, and they embraced.

"I'm sorry, David," she said. "It's been a few years. You're all grown up."

He laughed. "I think I was grown up last time you saw me."

"Weren't you just out of college then?"

"Still a grown-up," David said. "And I finished college late."

"Well, you've grown into an even more handsome man," Myla said. She walked back to the stove.

"Thank you, Myla," David said. "You, too."

Myla laughed. She had forgotten how shy he was. "I am a handsome young man?" She looked over at him. In the kitchen light, she saw him blush.

"Now I feel like I'm twenty-five again," he said.

"I'm sorry," Myla said. "I shouldn't tease you. By the way, I would have knocked if I'd known you were here. Ahhh, is this why your mother called me? To tell me you were coming? I just got the message that she wanted me to call her. I think my phone isn't working."

"You used to leave it off the hook because you didn't want anyone to be able to get a hold of you," he said. He sat at one of the stools at the counter. His curly black hair was short, his face neatly unshaven. And he looked tired.

"I did that?" She shrugged. The water began to boil. She opened the pasta boxes and tipped the spaghetti noodles into her hand. She broke them by the handful and dropped them into the water. "After my divorce I was a little crazy. I was reminded of that today. You only knew me as that crazy woman. I'm different now. I'm much crazier." She laughed. "So you're just visiting?"

"I'm visiting," he said. "For a while."

"You and your wife, kids?" No, it was too quiet in the house. He must be alone.

"No wife, no kids. Just me."

"I thought you got married." Myla took a wooden spoon from a container near the stove and stirred the pasta.

"That was my sister Susan. She's the well-adjusted one."

Myla set the spoon on the stove and looked at David.

"You've come to the Old Mermaid Sanctuary for some sanctuary then?" she said. "That's good. You are welcome."

David laughed. "Thank you, Myla. It's good to see you. I've missed the Old Mermaids."

"I understand," she said. "Where's your car?"

"I don't have one," he said. "I've been in Chicago for the past few years."

"Have you been living *la vida loca*?" She leaned against the counter and looked at him.

"Interesting question, Myla," he said. "As always. I have been having a life. Better than most people, I suppose."

"A bunch of us are having dinner at my apartment. You'll join us?"

"I'm not really up for a party," he said.

"You don't have to entertain anyone," Myla said. "Just sit, eat, breathe."

"All right. When?"

"As soon as the pasta is finished," she said. "You'll bring it when it's done, and then we'll eat. You do know how to cook? I know your mother. She would not have let her children go out into the world without showing them how to cook."

David nodded. "You throw the noodles at the wall, right? And if they stick, they're ready?"

"See, you're feeling better already! Wait, I have an idea, David. Why don't you invite us here? We can all sit at the table on the patio. It's bigger than mine and everyone will get to see the mermaid in the pool."

"Uh, okay."

"I'll go tell the others. What a perfect way to end the day! I'm so glad you're here, David." She smiled at him. "And not just because you have a bigger house!"

"I'm glad too," he said.

Myla went out the door nearest the kitchen and hurried across the drive to her porch where the others had gathered. Luisa stood a bit a part from the others.

"Change of plans!" Myla said in Spanish. "David Thomas Crow is visiting and he's invited us to eat at his house. Everyone grab a dish, and we'll go over there. Theresa, did you hear that?"

"Yep," came her voice from inside the apartment. "I'll bring the sauce. Luisa! Come help."

Luisa's face seemed to close down, or harden, as soon as she heard her mother's voice.

"Hello, Luisa," Myla said. "It is nice to see you. How have you been?"

"Hi, Myla," she said. "I better go see what my mother wants."

Lily gently took Myla's hand, and they led the others across the drive and into the kitchen of the Crow house where David stood over the boiling pot of pasta.

"David Crow, I would like you to meet Cathy, Ernesto, Maria, Lily, and Stefan."

"*Buenas tardes*," David said.

"*Buenas tardes*," the others said, awkwardly, suddenly shy.

"Hello, hello, hello," Lily said, letting go of Myla's hand and clapping.

"Hello, hello, hello," David said. He smiled.

Myla crossed the kitchen and living room and turned on the light to the patio. "We'll eat at that table next to the pool," she said. "David, can you wet a towel and give it to Stefan? The table and chairs might have some dust on them. It is the desert, you know, and no butts have sat in those chairs for a long while."

David pulled a tea towel from the drawer and dampened it with water. He held it out to Stefan who shyly took it. Neither looked the other in the eye.

Myla opened the door to the patio and most everyone went outside. Lily, David, and Myla stayed in the kitchen. Lily stood a few feet from David watching him, her face a portrait of intense fascination. Myla crossed her arms and watched them.

"The noodles are just about done," David said. "Would you like to try one and tell me if they are?"

Lily glanced at Myla; Myla translated what David had said. Lily looked at David again and nodded. David dipped a fork into the pot and pulled out several strands of pasta. He bent over and held the fork out to Lily.

"*Picante*," David said.

"*Caliente*," Myla corrected.

Lily pursed her lips and blew on the spaghetti strands. Then she lifted two of them off the fork and put them in her mouth. She chewed and breathed through her mouth at the same time, trying to pretend it wasn't hot.

"Okay," Lily said.

"Okay. I'll take your word for it," David said. He handed Lily the fork, and she ate the few remaining strands as she watched him. Myla came into the kitchen and opened an upper cabinet door and pulled out a colander. She held it over the sink. David turned off the burner, then carried the pot over to the sink.

"Got it?" he asked.

Myla nodded.

He carefully poured the water into the colander as Myla held it until the pot was almost empty; then he let the pasta fall into the colander. He reached over Myla—"Excuse me," he said—and turned on the cold water. She shook the colander to let the cold water go all through the noodles and drain out.

"Make room," Theresa said, coming through the kitchen door. "I think the sauce is ready. Where's the meat, Myla? This sauce has no meat. Ernesto needs some meat on his bones."

"There are mushrooms," Myla said. "Besides I have him on the Old Mermaid diet."

Theresa made a noise as she set the pot on the stove. "What kind of diet is that? Seaweed and vegetables?"

"It's a bit more than that," Myla said.

"We'll have the spaghetti family style?" Theresa asked.

"Sure," Myla said.

"Hello, I'm Theresa," she said to David. She turned around as Luisa came into the kitchen carrying a bowl of salad. "This is my daughter Luisa. You're David Crow."

"I like your name," Luisa said. "It's so dark and mysterious."

"David?" He shrugged. "Never seemed that mysterious to me."

Myla laughed quietly. Theresa rolled her eyes.

"I meant crow," Luisa said. "Do you have any tattoos?"

"Not any that you can see," Theresa said. "Luisa, take the salad out to the table. Did they get the bread and drinks?"

"Take Lily with you, please," Myla said. "Lily, will you go with Luisa?"

Luisa sighed loudly. She smiled at David, then went out onto the patio, with Lily bouncing next to her. Myla heard Lily exclaim, "There's the mermaid in the pool!"

Myla nudged Theresa, and the two women laughed.

"I hope I wasn't that obvious when I was Luisa's age," Theresa said.

"Her age? You're still that obvious."

"Please," Theresa said. "I'm a married lady."

"David, you watch out for that girl tonight," Myla said. "She's looking for trouble."

"What kind of trouble?"

The women looked at him. He stared back. Theresa and Myla glanced at each other and shrugged.

"She was flirting with you," Theresa said.

Myla put the pasta into a large glass bowl. Theresa ladled sauce over it.

"Flirting with *me?*" David made a face. "She could be my daughter."

"Oh?" Myla said.

"I mean age-wise. If I'd procreated when I was young. Which I didn't do."

Myla and Theresa stared at him.

"I think maybe I'll go to bed," he said. "I'm kind of tired."

"Oh, honey," Myla said. "I'm sorry. We're just two old women giving a handsome young man a hard time. No one has flirted with either of us for a long time. Please, I'll be good." She put her hand on his arm and smiled. "I promise."

David frowned. "It's not you. I am tired."

"Please," Myla said. "We've invaded your house. Have a meal with us. Then we will let you sleep. Go sit with the others. We'll serve you. Be with all that young energy. It'll do you good."

David started to say something, stopped, started to leave, hesitated, then went through the living room and out onto the patio.

"You have some history, you two?" Theresa said as she lifted the spaghetti with two forks to cover it with sauce. "You seem very familiar with each other. Won't it be a problem that he's here? We've got so many people at the sanctuary right now."

"I've known him since he was a boy," Myla said. "He's all right. His mother is a good woman."

"You knew him before you moved here?"

"No, why?"

"You've been here for about ten years? That man is in his mid-thirties. He's not a boy! If he finds out all these people are living here—illegally, might I add—he might not be too happy about it."

Myla shrugged. "Don't worry so much. It will all work out."

"So you say," Theresa said. "Maria and Lily were too much. I knew that."

"No, Cathy and Stefan were too much," Myla said. "But where would they be without us? And I had to help Lily and Maria. They have been deserted too many times. You'll find Cathy a job in California, and they'll be moving on."

"It's getting to be too much," Theresa said. "With the business, Del Rey, now Luisa. Del Rey thinks I'm cheating on him."

"Where is Del Rey?" Myla asked. "He's welcome to our Saturday dinners. I told you we could change it to a different night if that was better now that you're a married lady again."

Luisa came into the kitchen. "Mom, we're getting hungry."

"We're coming."

The two women went outside and set the spaghetti on the table. Someone—must have been David—had turned on the pool light. The mermaid undulated on the bottom of the pool.

Myla sat next to Lily and David. Theresa sat between Luisa and Stefan. They began passing around bowls of salad, a plate of lightly steamed pea pods, a basket of bread, and the spaghetti.

Before they began to eat, Myla looked around the table and said, "I am so glad we are all here together. This is a beautiful place made all the more beautiful by the company. I would like to thank the spirits and beings of this place, especially the Old Mermaids who have made all this possible."

"A-men," Theresa said. "Now let's eat."

They ate in companionable silence for a while.

"Ernesto, did you want to phone your wife tonight?" Myla asked in Spanish, then in English. "That reminds me, I need to call your mother, David."

"It is so dark now," Ernesto said. "I should call earlier."

"The phone is at the little market in her village," Myla explained to David. "When someone gets a phone call, the boy at the store tells the person calling to call right back—or to hang on—and then he gets on his bike and goes to the house of the person wanted on the telephone. Then that person either rides the boy's bike or walks to the store."

"Why not just get a cell phone?" Luisa asked.

"Why not indeed," Theresa said. "Child, these things cost money."

"I had a cell phone in LA," Luisa said.

"Until you ran up an enormous bill," Theresa said, "just like I told your father you would."

"I'd have figured out a way to pay it," Luisa said.

Maria whispered something to Lily. Lily nodded.

"If we speak English, we leave out half of the table," Myla said. "If we speak Spanish, we leave out the other half."

"Yeah, I don't understand much Spanish," Luisa said.

"It's your father's language," Theresa said. "You should learn it better."

"I can understand some of it," David said. "Besides, I don't mind. Hearing a language that isn't your own, that you don't quite understand, is like listening to music. I imagine that's what the sailors used to hear when they passed the mermaids at sea. The mermaids were talking in a different language."

"You believe in mermaids?" Luisa asked. She sounded disgusted.

"Mermaids, mermaids, mermaids," Lily said.

"This is the Old Mermaid Sanctuary," Stefan said.

"The what?" Luisa said.

Stefan glanced at Myla.

"Remember, Luisa," Myla said. "I sell things on Fourth Avenue on Saturdays. I call it the Church of the Old Mermaids."

"Church of the Old Maids?" Luisa asked.

"Luisa!" Theresa said sharply.

"This spaghetti is very good," Stefan said.

"Kiss ass," Luisa murmured.

"Luisa Ann, I brought you into this world, and I can take you out. Don't doubt that."

Ernesto said, in Spanish, "The one with the straw hair should not throw insults."

The women laughed. Ernesto shrugged. "That is a saying in my village, at least."

Luisa blushed. Myla nodded. So the girl understood more Spanish than she let on.

Lily tapped Myla on the arm. Myla leaned over so her ear was close to Lily's mouth. She whispered in Spanish, "Did the Old Mermaids eat spaghetti like this?"

Myla smiled and said in Spanish, "That is a very wise question, Lily." To the rest of the group, she said, "She wondered if the Old Mermaids ate spaghetti."

"Yes, do tell us about the Old Mermaid diet," Theresa said. "How did the ol' mermaids stay slim and fit."

"Oh no," Myla said. "It wasn't about staying slim. Fit, okay, yes. But Old Mermaids came in all sizes and all colors. They understood that image wasn't everything, but it was a great deal and their image of themselves was very clear: they loved their Old Mermaid bodies, even after that Old Sea dried up and they had to lose their tails and walk on land. Yes, those Old Mermaids loved, Lily my Lily. They loved themselves, they loved each other, they loved the sea and they loved the dried up wash. They loved the cacti and the quail and the coyotes and the mesquite and the Old Man and Old Woman of the Mountains. They loved their neighbors. And guess what else they loved?"

Lily said, "Butterflies?"

"Yes, Lily. They loved butterflies! They loved so many things. And they loved food. They loved to eat. They were glad they had enjoyed the bounty of the Old Sea and now they enjoyed the bounty of the New Desert. But I'm rattling on and you wanted to know if they ate spaghetti. And I'm sure they did. They spent a lot of their time growing food, preparing food, eating food. They talked to the plants they grew, and they talked to everything they ate."

"Did they get tired of talking?" Lily asked.

"Or tired of listening to the talking," Luisa said.

"I don't know," Myla said. "It was just the way they were. It was like breathing to them. They held conversations with the trees and animals and clouds and wind."

"Like crazy people," Luisa said.

"Maybe," Myla said. "Maybe some crazy people have a bit of Old Mermaid in them and no one understands. The Old Mermaids were very thankful for what they had. So when they prepared the spaghetti, they would thank the tomatoes and the herbs and the water and the onions. Thank you, thank you, thank you."

"So what was the Old Mermaid diet?" Luisa asked.

Myla glanced at Theresa. She wondered if she realized that Luisa was listening; she was listening carefully to everything everyone said.

"Part of it was that they honored every ingredient," Myla said. "And they ate plants that had been treated well before they were harvested. And the land they grew up from was treated well."

"How do you treat a plant well?" Luisa asked. "Give it a hug every day?"

Stefan smiled. "Or kiss it maybe."

"That would work," Myla said.

"Unless of course they eat prickly pear pads," Luisa said. "When I was a kid Mom took me on some outing where the Indians showed us how they got things from the desert."

"The Tohono O'odham," Theresa said.

"Maybe the plants would like to hear stories," Lily said in Spanish, "the way you tell us stories."

Myla nodded. "Ahhh, that is a good idea. I will have to remember that."

"I tried to teach Luisa to eat right," Theresa said, "but the experts keep changing their minds about what's good for you and what isn't. And it's hard cooking meals for two or three people. Eating in community is much nicer and more efficient."

"I think it is more natural for us to live and work in community," Myla said.

Cathy shook her head. "The communes in the sixties sure didn't work."

"I don't think you can make a blanket statement like that," Theresa asked. "Do you know that all the communes didn't work? And I hate that word. Commune."

"Mom's just an old hippy," Luisa said.

"I've been hearing about these squatter communities that are sprouting up all over the world," David said, "creating community from necessity I suppose. Worldwide one person in six lives in a squat now."

"What's a squatter community?" Stefan asked. "Is that where people move into empty houses that aren't being used?"

His mother glanced at him.

"I mean I've heard of that happening," Stefan said.

"Most often they're people from the country who come into the city because they need work," David said. "They'll find work but there isn't housing. Or they can't afford housing. They build these places on empty lots or on land that isn't being used. They build houses, figure out sanitation, have their own government."

"Doesn't sound easy," Cathy said.

"Why should things be easy?" Myla asked.

"Don't you have it easy here?" Luisa said. "You live in a beautiful place and all you do is look for junk in the wash."

"And you have such a rough life?" Theresa asked.

"I was just saying," Luisa said.

"We shouldn't judge people until we walk a mile in their shoes," Cathy said. "That's what my mother taught me. She also said that teenagers should be seen and not heard. Truthfully, she said they shouldn't be seen either."

"That seems pretty judgmental," Luisa said, her face red, her voice angry.

"All of us have a right to be seen and heard," Myla said. "That's what most of us want. To be seen, truly. To be heard. All of us. Whether we are younger or older."

"Yes, it's nice to think so," Theresa said. "But it goes both ways, Stefan and Luisa. When you see someone older—if you see someone with gray hair, for instance—do you just assume they're stupid or have nothing worthwhile to say to you?"

Stefan and Luisa glanced at one another.

Luisa said, "It depends upon whether it's a man or a woman. If it's a man, I might listen. If it's a woman, you're probably right. I just ignore her."

Silence pulsed around the table. Theresa put down her fork.

"That is a stunning statement," Theresa said.

"It's the truth," Luisa said. "I bet everyone here feels the same way." She looked at Stefan. "Don't you?"

"I don't think I notice whether people are young or old," Stefan said.

"Liar," Luisa said. "If a pretty girl and an ugly old woman came up to you, you wouldn't pay more attention to the pretty girl?"

"Why does the older woman have to be ugly?" David asked.

"I'd probably pay attention to the pretty girl," Stefan said, "because I couldn't help it. Hormones you know."

Several of the adults laughed.

"But that's not because I'd think she was smarter than the older woman or that she had more to say."

Myla had been translating to Ernesto and Maria. She now said to them, "Ernesto and Maria, what do you think of all this?"

Ernesto shrugged. "When I was a boy, we listened to our elders. They knew more than we knew. That was just the way it was. I felt honored that an elder would take time for me. Now I am becoming an elder. I am not certain I know much yet. But I would be glad to share not much with anyone who wants to listen."

"Maria?" Myla asked.

Maria smiled, painfully, shyly. Myla instantly regretted putting her on the spot.

"I don't understand much of what you are talking about," Maria said. "I was thinking that I miss my mother. She has very black hair, but she has shown me a few gray hairs. She told me she was glad to have lived long enough to have gray hair. My grandmother has gray hair. You could say she is an old woman. She knows more than anyone else. It's a fact. And if she doesn't know, her best friend knows. They are both beautiful women. Once I asked my mother if I would be beautiful like my grandmother when I was old. She said I was beautiful now. She told me I was sun beauty because I was young. Bright and shiny, she said. My grandmother was moon beauty. Old people, especially old women, were beautiful like the moon. Both sun and moon beauty were good, but those with moon beauty knew more secrets because they knew about things and places where the sun did not shine." Maria smiled.

Myla nodded. "Your mother is a wise woman."

"I like that," Theresa said. "Maybe I'll stop dyeing my hair and become naturally moon beautiful."

"It's getting a bit chilly out here," Myla said. "Time to go inside?"

"Sure," David said.

Everyone stood and began clearing the table.

"We never did find out what the Old Mermaid diet was," Luisa said.

"Myla, whatever happened to the Old Mermaids?" Stefan asked.

"Ah, well, that's a story for a different night," Myla said.

"I sure like these Saturday night dinners," Stefan said.

David said, "You do this every Saturday?"

"Not in this house, but yes, we have dinner at my place," Myla said.

"Last Saturday, we talked about art," Ernesto said.

"*Arte publico*, especially," Myla said. "Very interesting."

"Yeah, made me want to do a mural," Stefan said.

"David painted the mermaid in the pool," Myla said. "He might have some tips for a mural."

"Wow!" Stefan said. "You painted her? She's great."

David said, "It was a long time ago."

"She's held up well," Theresa said.

David glanced at Myla. She smiled.

"Oh Ernesto," David said. "I can turn on the spa, if you like." He pointed to the tiny pool next to the pool. "That water gets hot."

Ernesto shook his head. "Oh, too much trouble, *señor!*"

"No, really it isn't," David said. "Takes just a few seconds."

"Maybe another time," Myla said. "Some hydrotherapy might

be good for you, Ernesto."

"Very kind," he said. "Maybe the mermaid in the pool will come over and join me."

"You never know," Myla said.

Four

Things change. Get over it.
Sister Bea Wilder Mermaid

David and Maria did the dishes. Myla started to remind David
that the house had a dishwasher, but she watched the two of them
trying to talk to one another, and she decided to leave them alone.
Theresa and Cathy sat in the living room talking about job possibilities. Luisa and Stefan played cards at the kitchen table. Lily
watched.

"What are you playing?" Myla asked.

"Old Maid," Luisa said. She smiled as though she had said
something very clever. "You wanna play?"

"Yeah, it's kind of boring with just two players," Stefan said.

Myla sat at the table with them. "How do you play this game?"

"First you take away one of the queens," Luisa said. "Then
you pass out all the cards to the players. Every player puts down
all the pairs they have. Then you go around the circle and each

player takes a card from the player on the right. If you get a pair with that card you put it down. You do this until one person is left with the single queen. The Old Maid. That person loses because she's the Old Maid—she's a loser because she's all alone."

Myla made a face. "The person who ends up with the Queen is the loser? She should be the winner!"

"It's not the queen then," Luisa said. "It's the Old Maid. Get it. Everyone is in pairs except the queen. I mean, except the Old Maid."

"Maybe she is like the queen bee," Myla said. "The queen bee is not part of a pair. Or maybe she's an old maid goddess, or an Old Mermaid goddess. Atargatis was a mermaid goddess, you know. Yemaya too. There are many others. Sometimes they were alone, sometimes they were part of a pair. That makes me think of something. Where's the box the cards came in?"

Stefan handed it to her. She opened it and pulled out the joker.

"Let's play Old Mermaids instead," Myla said.

"Oh here we go!" Theresa said from the couch. She and Cathy got up and came over to the table.

"We need thirteen mermaids," Myla said.

"Why?" Stefan asked.

"It's a nice round number," Myla answered.

Luisa frowned. Theresa laughed.

Myla began pulling the face cards out of the deck. When she had them all, she spread them out on the table and added the joker. "Here are the Old Mermaids! It's played like Old Maid except whoever ends up with the most Old Mermaids wins. And the thirteenth Old Mermaid, if you get her, you get an additional thirteen points."

"Is she making this up?" Luisa asked.

"I'm remembering it as I talk about it," Myla said.

"She does that a lot," Theresa said.

64

"Shall we play?" Myla asked.

"These look like mermen, not mermaids," Luisa said.

"Where do you think baby mermaids come from?" Stefan asked.

Myla laughed. "That is a story for another night too." She picked up one of the cards. "We could decorate these and make them all into Old Mermaids."

"You mean draw on them?" Stefan asked.

"Why not?" Myla looked up at David who had come over to watch. "They're your cards, I presume?"

"Do whatever you like with them," David said.

"I've got crayons, pencils, and markers at my place," Myla said. "I think. David, you're an artist. What about your room? Do you still have anything here?"

"There might be something in the closet," he said. "I'll go look."

"I'll come with," Luisa said.

"Me, too," Stefan said. Luisa gave him a dirty look. Lily slipped her hand into Luisa's.

"I go," she said.

"We'll have an expedition then," David said. They disappeared down the hall.

"Wow," Theresa said. "I should have brought Luisa here earlier. She's actually playing well with others, sort of."

"My son was angry," Ernesto said in English. "He left home when he was fourteen."

"What happened to him?"

"*No sé. No sé.*"

"Uplifting story, Ernesto," Theresa said.

He shrugged.

A few minutes later, David returned with the children. Luisa carried a cardboard box. She set it on the table and took off the lid.

"Mom must have saved this stuff," David said. "I haven't done art in years."

"I thought you got a degree in art education," Myla said.

"Didn't pan out," he said.

"Look," Luisa said. "We've got colored pencils and pens. And glitter glue. Sequins. Beads. We can make these mermaids into babes."

"Some of these babes are going to have mustaches," Stefan said, holding up a Jack.

"Some of the best women I know have mustaches," Myla said.

Cathy and Theresa made coffee while everyone else sat around the table with the face cards. Luisa began coloring on a queen. Stefan took a Jack. Lily a king.

Lily asked her mother what she was supposed to do.

"We're making them into Old Mermaids," Maria said in Spanish.

"You too, Maria," Myla said. "David. You haven't done art in years? Now is the time. Your life is your art statement. Everything is about art!"

Soon, the table sparkled with glitter. Sticky glitter. Luisa used sequins to approximate the scales on the Old Mermaid's somewhat truncated tail. Lily glued sequins everywhere and then added glitter. Maria shredded ribbon David found in his mother's sewing basket and made it into hair for her mermaid. Ernesto drew in a hammer and nails. "Someone has to do the work around the sanctuary," he said. David's mermaid seemed to get darker and darker the longer he worked on the card. Stefan colored in the mermaid and then added more figures so it looked like a tiny mural.

"I wish these cards were bigger!" Luisa said.

Myla walked around the table and looked at the artwork.

"That one with the green tail, Luisa," Myla said. "She reminds me of Mother Star Stupendous Mermaid. She was very wise. You have a wisdom about you, too. That must be why you thought of her. She listened and thought about things a great deal."

"She was wise and beautiful," Luisa said.

"Of course," Myla said. "And yours, Lily. Ahhh, I think that might be Sister Laughs A Lot Mermaid. She is a happy glittery kind of Old Mermaid. Now Stefan, that must be Sister Magdelene Mermaid. They call her Sissy Maggie. She's very artistic. You'd like her. Maria, which Old Mermaid is that? I think it might be Sister Bridget Mermaid. She had long curly hair, a bit red. I know what you're thinking. All Old Mermaids have long hair, but that isn't actually so. Some do have short hair; some don't. Sister Bridget Mermaid knows all about poetry, herbs, plants, songs, healing. She and Sister Faye Mermaid plan the parties and ceremonies for the Old Mermaids. They know when the moon is full or when it is dark. They know the best sea chanties. Ernesto, that has to be Sister Sheila Na Giggles Mermaid. She is practical, too, and very handy around the house. She tells it like it is. If she thinks someone is getting too fanciful, she'll say, 'Get the starfish out of your eyes, Sister Mermaid.' And she knows the more colorful sea chanties." She walked over to David. "Ahhh, this must be the Grand Mother Yemaya Mermaid. She knows more about the oceans and seas than anyone. She knows more about the mystery of ourselves—our watery bodies—than anyone. She is like your grandmother, Maria. She is a moon beauty. When you feel as though you are drowning, she is the Old Mermaid who will save you."

"That's only six," Luisa said. "We've got seven more to do."

"Next week," Theresa said. "It's getting late. Some of us have had a long day."

Luisa looked disappointed. "We still haven't played Old Mermaids."

"David, can we leave this stuff somewhere here?" Myla asked. "Then they could finish it next Saturday."

"I don't know if I'll be here," David said, "but I'm sure my parents wouldn't mind."

"I'll take everyone home," Theresa said.

Myla glanced at Luisa who was putting the supplies back into the box.

"Oh, wait," Theresa said, understanding Myla's hint. "Um, I forgot. I'm not going that way."

"What way?" Luisa asked. "We can take them. Come on, Mom."

She was sharp as a tack, this one.

"I need the exercise," Ernesto said, "so I'll walk."

"Yeah, us too," Stefan said.

Luisa shrugged. "Whatever. See you later, gators." Her mother handed her the empty bowls.

"Sorry to leave you with this mess," Theresa said to David. "My husband and I are newlyweds, sort of. He misses me, so I better get home."

Luisa rolled her eyes. "Yeah, good old Del Rey. We should have had him here tonight. Hearing you all talk about communes would have given him a heart attack. He'd probably think you were communists or something."

"He's not like that," Theresa said. "Don't pay any attention to her. He'll come sometime, I promise. Night!"

Theresa and Luisa left.

"Can I say good night to the mermaid in the pool?" Lily asked.

"I'll take you out," Myla said. "We don't want you to go out to see the Old Mermaid in the pool without one of us going with you."

"Why?"

"Because the water is deep," Maria said.

"The Old Mermaids said they would teach me to swim," Lily said.

"Oh really?" Maria asked.

"The Old Mermaids come to me in my dreams. And they're teaching me."

"We'd feel better if you only went out to the pool to see the mermaid with one of us," Myla said. "And don't ever try to swim without one of us there, even if the Old Mermaids have taught you to swim."

Lily nodded. "Okay."

The girl took Myla's hand, and they walked through the living room out to the patio. The pool light was the only illumination. Myla opened the door, and the two of them walked to the edge of the pool and looked down at the mermaid. After a few moments, Lily began nodding, as if she were listening to someone speak.

Myla sat near the edge of the pool. Lily sat next to her.

"What are you listening to?" Myla asked.

"The Old Mermaids," she said.

"Oh? What are they saying?" Myla asked.

"Not to be afraid," Lily said. "They sing to me while I sleep."

"What kind of song?"

"A not-be-afraid song," Lily said.

"That's good," Myla said. "Then you probably don't need what they left in the wash for you."

"What is it?" Lily asked.

Myla carefully took the dreamcatcher earring from her pocket. She handed it to Lily.

"This is called a dreamcatcher, Lily my Lily," Myla said. "If you put it in your room, it'll take away all the bad dreams. A Native American healer gave one like it to the Old Mermaids when they first came to the sanctuary. It was all new to them, and some of them were afraid. Sister Laughs A Lot Mermaid, who was the youngest, had bad dreams. When the medicine man gave her this dreamcatcher, the bad dreams went away."

Lily nodded solemnly.

"Sometimes when I open my eyes in the dark, I see it all moving," Lily whispered.

"What's moving?" Myla asked.

Lily whispered, "Everything. Like when we crossed the river. The water pulled on me. And there were flashes of light in it. I couldn't keep a hold of Momma's hand."

"That must have been very scary," Myla said. "Have I told you much about Grand Mother Yemaya Mermaid?"

"A little."

"She is the wisest of wise," Myla said. "She is one of the ones who is a moon beauty, like your great grandmother. And her skin is as dark as night. Darker. She is so grand that she had two tails before the Old Sea dried up."

"The Old Mermaids don't have tails any more?" Lily asked.

"That's a good question," Myla said. "They do and they don't. If you were to see them most days, you would not see a tail. You would see only their legs. But other times, if the light is just right or if you are a bit sleepy, you might be able to see the glitter of their tales—as though they are wearing beautiful gowns—with flashes of color and light. In a good way, not like your scary flashes. And if you wake up and the darkness frightens you, remember Grand Mother Yemaya Mermaid is there with you. She is the darkness that protects you. Those flashes of color and light are just her mermaid tails."

Maria came to the patio door. "It is time for bed, Lily."

Lily waved to the mermaid in the pool. "*Hasta mañana!*" Then she threw her arms around Myla's neck and hugged her. "Good night, Myla Mermaid."

"Good night, sweetheart."

The girl let go and ran to her mother.

"Good-bye, Myla!" she heard the others call. Myla waved. She looked down at the mermaid in the pool and was suddenly very tired. She wasn't sure she was up for tomorrow — for her yearly sojourn with George.

The patio door opened and closed. Myla looked up. David. He sat next to her. She put her hand on his back.

"I'm sorry I sprung all this on you," she said. "You wanted to rest and I gave you us."

He smiled and took her hand in his.

"Oh!" Myla said. "I felt a spark."

"Sorry about that," David said.

"It's very dry in the desert," Myla said. They were silent for a moment. She laughed. "I suppose that's like saying the ocean is wet!"

David laughed. "You always knew how to draw me back into things," he said, "especially when I didn't want to be drawn in."

"That's an interesting choice of words, David. 'Drawn' into things. You gave up your art? Your mother didn't tell me."

"So many school districts have cut out all art programs," he said. "And I didn't want to teach anything else. So I got my MBA, and I've been brokering deals between small struggling companies and larger corporations so that the small companies can keep doing what they've been doing using the backing and capital of a big company."

"Sounds like it could be interesting," Myla said.

"Except most of the time it didn't work," David said. "At least not the way I envisioned it. If it was a small company doing business sustainably, the corporation would always put pressure on them to be more profitable. Even if they were profitable, the corporation wanted more profits. I kept wondering when is more enough?"

"So you've taken a break from all that?" Myla asked.

"I quit," he said. He rubbed his face. "I'm done with it."

"You look tired," Myla said. "I'll clean up. You go to bed."

"You're just about perfect, aren't you, Myla?"

"Don't you say that," Myla said. "You knew me way back when. You know I'm not perfect—whatever that means."

"You were always kind," David said. "And beautiful."

Myla laughed. "I was ragged from a bad divorce. I can't imagine I was nice."

"I didn't say you were nice," David said. "You always told me nice is overrated, but kindness is a gift. Kindness is acknowledging that we are all kin. Nice is a fake smile, trying to cover up the truth, which is often dark and painful."

"I said all that?" Myla said. "I don't remember. I don't remember a lot about that time."

"Do you remember all the time we spent together?"

Myla said. "I remember you painted this mermaid and everyone thought it was me. I remember we walked the wash together."

"Do you remember we talked about starting a school together?"

"Together?" Myla said. "Did we? Yes, now that you say that, I remember. What else? Have I forgotten anything important?"

"No, no," David said. "That was it. I think I'll go in now. You don't need to clean up. I'll do it in the morning. It'll give me something to do." He stood and reached a hand down to Myla. She took it and let him pull her up.

"If you say so," Myla said. "I'll see you in the morning."

"Good night, Myla Mermaid."

George knocked on Myla's door too early the next morning. When she didn't answer, he opened it and came in to the apartment. Myla covered her head with a pillow. George whistled.

"Come on, girl," George said. "The day is wasting. I brought bagels, croissants, coffee, and orange juice."

Myla sat up and pushed her hair out of her eyes.

"You really have got to stop this boozing, Myla," George said. "The hangovers are awful."

"Very funny," Myla said. "Any protein in that bag?"

George sat on the bed and opened the white sack. He reached in and pulled out two boiled eggs. He tossed one to her. She tapped it against the wall until it cracked and then began pulling the broken shell off of it.

"George," Myla said as she ate the egg.

"Yes, dear?"

"Do you ever think perhaps we're getting a bit too old for this? It has been ten years."

"Maybe," he said. "But I'm here. We might as well go."

Myla got out of bed and took off her red cotton pajamas. She didn't care that George watched while he ate a bagel and gulped coffee. He watched her like she imagined he watched a football game or an animal crossing the road in front of him: with interest but without enthusiasm.

"I like your curves, woman," he said.

Maybe she was wrong about the enthusiasm.

"Thank you, George."

She pulled on a pair of slacks and tucked her camisole inside them. Then she took a purple shirt from her small closet and put it on.

"He got that right," George said.

"Who got what right?"

"The guy who painted the mermaid in the pool got your curves right."

"What made you think of David Crow?" Myla asked.

"I saw him as I was driving up."

"You recognized him?"

"He looks the same to me. I remember him because he tagged along with you a lot then. You even let him walk the wash with you. You never let me do that."

"That's because you talk too much."

"He had quite a crush on you," George said. "Made me a little jealous."

"David? I think you're mistaken. I'm almost as old as his mother. Well, not quite."

George shrugged. "I'm telling you. Men know about this kind of stuff."

"Oh really?"

"About other men. Sure."

Myla snatched the paper bag from him. "George, you're talking nonsense. Let's go."

They drove to their old neighborhood. Brick houses predominated, making it look like a suburb in the Midwest. Or someplace like that. Myla had never actually been to the Midwest. She only knew these houses did not look like desert houses. She wondered why she had ever agreed to live here. Had she actually liked it? George slowed the car as they turned the corner onto their old street. He parked two houses away from his old house, three from her old house. Her ex-husband's car was in the drive. At least that was the car he had had last year. Several plastic children's toys were strewn around the yard. They had finally taken out the grassy lawn and replaced it with rock. About time.

George relaxed against his seat and lifted a cup of coffee from the paper sack.

"I heard the shop isn't doing well," George said. "I bet you're glad you took a lump sum."

Myla didn't say anything. She stared at the house. Would her ex look different this year?

The front door opened and George's ex-wife, Nadine, stepped

outside. A nine-year-old girl came out next. Or was she ten now? She had been born a few months after Myla and her husband broke up—a few months after Myla found her husband on top of Nadine, in Myla's bed. Nadine had been naked, her breasts heavy—when normally they were small—and her belly round. Myla knew then why this thin young woman had been wearing baggy clothes for months. Still, it had taken her a moment to grasp what she and George had walked into, so she said, "Congratulations. You look just like those pictures of the pregnant Madonna."

"Only the Madonna isn't naked," George had said. Something about George's voice had snapped her out of her stupor. She blinked and realized her naked husband was getting dressed, and Nadine was crying.

"It can't be mine," George said. "She hasn't let me come near her for a year or more."

Now Myla felt butterflies in her stomach.

"George, I think we should go home."

"Wait," he said. "Just a bit longer."

Then Richard—Myla's ex—stepped outside onto the steps and shut the door behind him. Nadine looked back at him and smiled. Myla could see his lips moving. He looked old enough to be Nadine's father. She was what now? Thirty-five? And he was fifty-five. Myla had been twenty-three when she and Richard married; he had been over thirty. Both old enough to know what they were doing.

The family got into the car. The girl laughed. Or whined. Myla couldn't be sure.

"The girl looks just like her," George said. "That could have been my kid."

"I thought you didn't want children," Myla said.

"That's beside the point."

The car backed out of the driveway. Then they drove by Myla and George. George stared right at Richard, but he was talking and looking ahead.

"God I hate him," George said.

Myla said, "I don't hate him. Or her. That can't be good for you to hate them." She sighed. "George, I'm going into the house."

"No you're not," he said.

She put her hand on the door handle. "I am. I want to see it. It was my house. The only house I ever owned. I feel as though I was evicted and never got a chance to say good-bye." She didn't know if any of that was true. Maybe she had said good-bye. She could not remember any quiet contemplative moments from that time, but that did not mean she hadn't had any. What she did remember was that it had been her home and then suddenly it wasn't. After she saw Richard and Nadine in bed together, the house felt contaminated, and she had to leave it.

"If you go in," George said, "I'm driving away."

"Oh you are not," she said. "I'll be right back."

Myla got out of the car. She crossed the street and went up the driveway and through the paved path between the carport and the house around to the back door. She stopped for a moment and breathed deeply. Then she went up the steps and opened the screen door. She put her hand on the door knob, turned it, and pushed the door open. She stepped into the cool semidarkness and quietly closed the door. The house pulsed with silence. On her tiptoes, she walked across the kitchen to the living room. Different sofa and chair. Same coffee table. The house looked familiar but different. Smaller. Stuffier.

She walked down the hallway. Four doors. Two closed. Two open. The first closed door was the bathroom. She carefully opened the door and looked inside. She didn't recognize anything. It had all been redone in red and white. She shuddered and closed the door again. The second closed door was what she and Richard had used as a guest bedroom. She opened it. Now it was a little girl's room. Pale blue and white. A small canopy bed. A little dressing table. One wall painted in pastel-colored stars. Myla smiled. It was a beautiful room—cluttered and messy—just like a young girl's room should be. She closed the door again.

Now she was at the end of the hallway. The master bedroom. The door was wide open. There was the bed. It looked like the same bed. Same headboard. Was that possible? Yes: Richard was so cheap. He never replaced anything until it broke. She guessed that Nadine had probably wanted to get rid of the bed Richard had shared with Myla for fifteen years, but he wouldn't do it.

Myla stepped into the room. Their old dresser was still here. She had found it at a garage sale. Beautiful old oak dresser. Richard hadn't wanted it. She insisted—one of the few times in her marriage that she had insisted. Ordinarily when they disagreed about something, she usually gave up—worn down by their "discussions" which usually consisted of him haranguing her until she came around to his viewpoint, or at least until she pretended she did so that he would shut up.

During their marriage, she had thought Richard was a great debater, a man with intellect. Myla shook her head. Had she really ever been that naive? She ran her hand over the top of the dresser. She should have taken this with her. But she had not taken much—only her clothes, gardening tools, books, and a few pots, pans, dishes.

She walked to the bed, put her hand on the mattress, and then gingerly sat on it, bouncing slightly. She lay back and looked at the ceiling. It was comfortable. They must have gotten a new mattress. She closed her eyes.

A toilet flushed.

Myla sat up quickly, her eyes wide.

Someone was in the master bathroom. Right behind her.

She jumped up and ran out of the room.

"Is someone there?" A woman's voice.

Myla ran through the living room and into the kitchen. Then she stopped. She couldn't help it. She stared at the tiled kitchen wall. Her tiled kitchen wall. When she and Richard had first moved into the house, they decided to put in a tile backsplash. She wanted to tile the whole wall beneath the cupboards and above the sink, but she couldn't convince Richard. He thought it would be too expensive.

One day he took her into the back room of the shop.

"I have a surprise for you," he said. He opened up a box of tiles. Myla began pulling them out. Some were indigo blue, others were light green, and others had seashore scenes painted on them: sea shells in the sand, clams, starfish in the ocean, sea gulls against a blue sky.

"These will be big sellers," Myla told him.

"No, they're for our kitchen."

"But these are ocean scenes," she said. "They're better suited to the bathroom. Or somewhere near an ocean. I want desert scenes. We live in a desert."

"This whole desert was once an ocean," he said. "And you can do the entire wall beneath the cabinets if you use these. I got a great price on them."

Myla had finally agreed. They tiled the wall themselves.

Now Myla walked closer to the wall, her hand outstretched. She walked until her fingers touched one tile over the sink, at the center, right above the faucet: a tile of a mermaid.

How could she have forgotten this? She had looked at this mermaid every day for years. This mermaid had made the ocean tiles work for her. She had loved seeing the mermaid every time she came into the kitchen, every time she did the dishes. Until—

Until she forgot to look?

"Who are you?"

Myla turned around. An older woman stood in the kitchen behind her, holding a phone.

"I'm going to call the police," she said.

Myla said in Spanish, "No *habla* English. I'm the housekeeper."

"On a Sunday?"

"*Es* Sunday? Oh! I've missed mass then! *Lo siento, lo siento!*" Myla hurried out the door. She ran around the house and across the street to George's car.

"Hurry!" she said as she got inside. "We've got to get away."

"Why? Did you steal something?" He started the car.

"No. Someone was there!"

George quickly drove them out of the neighborhood and onto a main street.

"Who was it?" George asked.

"I don't know!" Myla said. "Some older woman. Maybe Nadine's mother."

George laughed. "I hope so."

"Why?"

"Because her mother hated him," George said. "Believe it or not, she liked me. And she was very upset when we got divorced. She could be really mean. I hope she's living with them!" He laughed loudly. "Out into the desert then for our celebration?"

"No," Myla said. "I don't feel like it."

"Home then for some midday delight?"

"George, take a hint."

"Sorry," he said. "What was the house like?"

"It wasn't much different," Myla said. "He's still a cheap s.o.b. They're using some of our old furniture. Even our old bed."

"That's kind of creepy," George said.

"And us going over there once a year and me sneaking into

their house is normal?"

"Did it still feel like your house?"

"I'm not sure," she said. "But I started remembering some things."

"Like seeing them naked together, his—"

"George."

"Okay. Like what?"

"Like the kitchen tile. There was a mermaid."

"Huh," George said. "I don't remember that."

"Why would you?" she said. "It wasn't your house."

"So what if there was a mermaid?" he said.

"Take me home, George."

She closed her eyes and leaned her head against the window. She had had a mermaid in her previous life. How could she have forgotten that? For the last decade she had been certain that the Old Mermaids were part of her *new* life—conjured to save her, to give her a brand new life with a purpose.

When she first started the Church of the Old Mermaids—after the dream—she saved the money she earned. It wasn't much, but it was something, and she knew she would figure out what to do with it eventually. Then one day during a trip out into the desert searching for treasure, she saw a group of people in the sandy bottom of an old wash. She went over to say hello. Three men, a boy, and a woman sat on the dirt, too exhausted to move. She immediately offered water. They gave it to the woman, who was barely conscious. Myla wanted to take them to the hospital, but they refused. Once they drank the water and ate the food she gave them, they revived. They had crossed the border illegally, as she guessed, and had been deserted by their smuggler—the *guia*—soon after they crossed. Myla took them to her apartment in the Crow barn, fed them, and let them use her phone. The woman—Grace—was too ill to leave with the others, so Myla let her and her son, Roberto, stay. She didn't give it a second thought. She got her keys and took them over to the Ford place and let them sleep there. The Old Mermaid Sanctuary—in its present form—was born.

Two days later, using some of the money she had earned from the Church of the Old Mermaids, Myla bought Grace and Roberto bus tickets to Texas where Grace's husband worked in the fields. After she took them to the bus station, Myla came home and went to the Ford house to clean it, but the house was spotless, the garden tidy, the dirt raked. Myla believed the house felt better too. A house was created to be lived in. That was its purpose. When the Fords returned, they even remarked that the place had never looked better.

Myla kept making excursions to the desert, near *la frontera*. Sometimes she found people, sometimes she did not. She was very careful about who she brought home with her and even more careful about who she let stay in the houses. When she told Theresa what she was doing, Theresa offered to help. Myla was glad to have her as a partner, especially since Theresa was a private investigator and many of the migrants came looking for family, friends—and a job. After a while, Theresa and Myla began going into the desert together, mostly in the summer when it was so dangerous for those crossing. In recent years, they sometimes encountered other rescuers who left water or transported migrants to the hospital, all activities which had been deemed legal until recently. A few months earlier a couple had been arrested as they drove several people to an area hospital. They were charged with aiding and abetting illegal aliens. Or something like that. Myla knew if she got caught, she wouldn't be able to help anyone, so she and Theresa kept quiet about what actually went on at the Old Mermaid Sanctuary, and they avoided the other rescuers as much as possible.

In the winter, the Sanctuary was usually quiet, except for visits from the homeowners. Summer was busier. Myla made certain each house was not occupied often or for very long, and visitors always did work around the property in exchange for their room and board. One year a family retiled the Castillo roof. Another time, a man helped fix the gray water irrigation system at the Ford house. Myla told the migrants that if anyone happened to see them and ask what they were doing there, they were to say that Myla had hired them. After all, the homeowners had instructed her to keep up the yards, facilitate repairs, and make the houses looked lived in. Myla made certain all that happened—only the workers stayed in the houses while they did the work.

Myla kept an Old Mermaid Sanctuary binder. In it, she put photos of the visitors with their names, ages, which house they had stayed in and what work they had done. Almost always, the migrants sent Myla a postcard once they were settled, and she'd add those to the binder.

Myla understood that these niceties would not placate the owners should they ever learn of her venture. She knew they would view what she was doing as a betrayal. Criminal even. She knew she could not adequately explain her actions; she could not tell them that the Old Mermaids had come to her in a dream and that she was doing their work here on dry land. That would sound crazy. Or—at the very least—possessed. She had tried to figure out other ways to explain what she had done—what she was doing. It wasn't like she thought God had spoken to her, or that she was channeling Ramtha or that she'd seen a vision of the Virgin Mary. It was more like the Invisibles of the land—and the sea— had spoken to her. But that wasn't right either. The land and its occupants were always speaking and she just happened to be able to understand them one morning a decade ago. Now she always heard them, in the form of the stories that poured from her mouth like a wonderful kind of babel—or babble—which most people, fortunately, understood. (She had encountered the occasional visitor to the Church of the Old Mermaids who said something like, "I see your lips moving, but all I hear is nonsense.")

Now after seeing the mermaid tile in her old house, Myla wondered about her *raison d'etre*. Maybe the dream had only been a bit of undigested memory making itself a character in her vision. Maybe she had concocted the Old Mermaids as a way of hanging onto some shred of her former life.

George stopped the car. Myla looked up. They were home.

"You sure I can't come in?" George said. "It's tradition."

"Maybe sometime we can go on a real date," Myla said.

"A date? Now that's crazy talk."

Myla leaned over, and they kissed.

"See you later," Myla said.

"I could come in and we could just talk," George said. "You seem a little lost."

"Thanks," Myla said. "You're welcome to come to Saturday dinner though. You always are."

Myla got out of the car and shut the door. As George drove away, Myla stood in the drive and listened to the silence for a few minutes. Then she went to the edge of the wash, stepped down onto the sand, and walked unsteadily until she came to a wide stretch. She looked north, and she looked south. The wash disappeared into desert trees. She looked east, and she looked west.

What if it had all been a dream? No call to action. No cosmic message. Only a dream.

She heard crunching in the wash and turned in the direction of the house. A moment later Gail came around the palo verde bend; Theresa followed.

"I figured you'd be here," Gail said.

"David said he'd seen you go this way," Theresa said.

"You two together?" Myla asked.

"No!" they said at the same time.

"Thought you might need company," Gail said. "How about that movie?"

Myla turned around again and kept walking.

"I don't feel like a movie," she said.

"I'm glad to see you decided not to go to your old house," Gail said, following her. "Don't you get a lot of sand in your shoes when you do this?"

"Decided not to go where?" Theresa asked. "You need to wear walking shoes, Gail. Or something to protect your feet. You're in the desert, for chrissakes. A scorpion or rattlesnake would bite right through those tiny little things."

"I did go to the house," Myla said.

"What house?" Theresa asked.

"Her old house," Gail said. "It's the anniversary of her catching her husband doing the nasty with her next door neighbor."

"Why on Earth would you go back there?" Theresa asked.

"It used to be her house, too," Gail said. "I remember when she moved in there. Kind of a strange little house. Looked like it didn't really belong here—you know—in the desert."

"Do you remember we redid the kitchen soon after we moved in?" Myla asked. She stopped and turned to her friends.

"Vaguely," Gail said. "You used some strange tiles. Bathroom tiles or something."

"You remember that?" Myla asked.

"Probably just because I thought it looked stupid," Gail said.

"I was never at your house," Theresa said. "I met you right after you came here."

"Do you remember there was a mermaid tile?" Myla asked.

"A mermaid tile?" Gail said. "In the kitchen? No, why?"

Myla shook her head. "I had a dream, remember? The Old Mermaids came to me in a dream. I thought it was a message from the Universe. I thought they were telling me what I should do with my life."

"Why would you want anyone to tell you what to do with your life?" Theresa asked.

Myla made a noise and continued walking. "I don't mean like that. It was like a sign that I could go on, that I could make a difference. I mattered. I can't explain it!"

"I think I know what you mean," Gail said.

Theresa frowned. "A message from God? I don't believe in God."

"Theresa, we're talking about me," Myla said. "I didn't say anything about God. I said Universe. The Old Mermaids were about my new life. They had absolutely nothing to do with my old life."

"And because there was a mermaid tile at your old house, you're doubting your mission, or whatever it is?" Theresa asked. "Come on. There are mermaids everywhere. They're a ubiquitous symbol. You didn't make up mermaids."

"She did make up the Old Mermaids," Gail said. "They're pretty cool." Myla looked at Gail. Gail shrugged. "You don't think I pay attention, but I do. The Old Mermaids are interesting."

"I didn't make them up," Myla said. She did not like talking about the Old Mermaids like this. It seemed rather sacrilegious — gossipy. "I don't want to talk about it."

"You always want to talk about everything," Gail said.

"No, not the Old Mermaids," Theresa said.

"What are you talking about? She is always talking about the Old Mermaids. She spends every Saturday talking about them nonstop."

"That's not talking *about* them," Theresa said. "That's more like being with them. It's like remembering interesting stories about your family and then sharing them."

"Exactly," Myla said. Although not quite. She stopped abruptly and looked down. "This is why I don't let anyone walk the wash with me. If you're talking all the time, you don't see what's right in front of you."

Gail and Theresa came up beside her. Directly in front of them was a shoe in the sand.

"Looks like a dog gnawed it all to bits," Gail said.

"More likely a coyote," Theresa said. "Hardly anything left but the sole. Wow, Myla. You really do find things here. That's perfect. What a story you could make out of that. Someone must need a soul."

"No, I think it means someone should bare their soul," Gail said. "See, because it's been eaten down to the sole."

"It's more like someone lost their soul," Theresa said.

"Someone lost their shoe," Myla said. "And now it's a coyote plaything."

"You mean you aren't going to take it?" Theresa said.

"No," Myla said. She stepped over it and kept walking.

"I think it's a message for you," Gail said. "The Old Mermaids want you to bare your soul. To us. You can talk to us, Myla. We'll listen."

Myla groaned and turned around. Ordinarily, she was a patient and good-natured woman. Beyond her friends she could see the log wrapped in orange rope. Maybe it was time she unraveled that rope because she suddenly felt at the end of hers. Just then, David came into view. He stepped over the log. Luisa scrambled behind him.

"Hello," David said.

"I know you," Gail said. "You're David Crow."

"You remember him after all these years?" Myla asked.

"You were just talking about him yesterday," Gail said.

"Myla was talking about me?" David asked.

"You're the one who painted the mermaid in the pool," Gail said.

"You painted that mermaid?" Luisa asked.

"Myla said that last night," Theresa said.

"I didn't hear her," Luisa said. "That mermaid is naked and everything. And she looks like Myla. Not that I've ever seen her naked."

"The mermaid is not naked," Myla said. "She has a tail. David is an artist. He extrapolated."

"Technically, she is naked," Theresa said. "A tail doesn't constitute clothing."

"In any case," Myla said.

"What does extrapolate mean?" Luisa asked.

"I'm not sure," Gail said. "Could you use it in a sentence?"

"I just used it in a sentence!" Myla said.

"Could you use it in another one?" Gail smiled. Myla started to laugh. Soon the three women were giggling. Luisa and David watched.

"What?" Luisa asked.

"Nothing," Theresa said. "You had to be there."

"I *was* there," Luisa said. "Here. Are we going to a movie? Or would you like to paint another mermaid, David? I could be your model this time."

"I was not his model," Myla said. "Would you all please go away? I don't want to go to a movie. You go. Theresa and Gail, you need to get to know each other better. Learn to like one another. Get along together. Show Luisa how it's done. Luisa, you are not going to pose naked for this man or any other man. Or woman. Not today. Away!"

"All right," Gail said. She embraced Myla.

"Okay, okay, let her go," Theresa said. She hugged Myla. "I love you."

"I love you too," Gail said.

"Go away," Myla said. "Well, except David. You live here. You can stay."

The two women and girl walked away together. Myla stood still until she no longer heard their voices.

David looked down at the shoe.

"A sole," David said. "I wondered where I had lost that. Just what I needed." He picked it up. "See you later, Myla Mermaid." Then he turned and left Myla alone.

That was just what she needed.

Five

Fear has no sisters, but I have many.
Sister Lyra Musica Mermaid

On Wednesday, Theresa came to the Old Mermaid Sanctuary to pick up Maria.

"We'll go see if any of the places in town that help migrants have heard anything about Juan," Theresa said as she and Myla leaned against Theresa's car. Maria and Lily stood away from them, on the bank of the wash, looking up and down it, as if it were running with water instead of sand.

"If we still don't hear anything," Theresa said quietly, "I'll probably take her to the morgue so we can talk to my contact in the coroner's office, see if they remember anyone or we'll look at photographs of any of their unidentified dead."

Theresa glanced over at Maria and Lily.

"She's looking tired," she said.

Myla nodded. Most of those seeking sanctuary got better—

stronger—here. Maria seemed to be deteriorating.

"Are you ready, Maria?" Theresa called.

The four of them walked to Theresa's car. Maria hugged Lily good-bye.

"Are you going to find my daddy?" Lily asked Theresa.

Theresa said, "I hope so, Lily. But I don't know for sure."

Maria went to the passenger side of Theresa's car and got inside. Theresa opened the driver's door. "Hey, Myla, get your phone fixed. It wouldn't even let me leave a message for you. Said your voice mail was full or something."

Myla nodded. She kept forgetting to do that.

Lily reached up for Myla's hand as her mother and Theresa drove away.

"Do you want to look for treasure in the wash with me?" Myla asked.

Lily nodded, although Myla guessed she did not know what Myla meant. Myla picked up the plastic bag and the ruby bag from the picnic table on her porch and put them over her shoulder.

"First, the desert is very prickly," Myla said in Spanish, "so you need to watch where you are going. You need to pay careful attention. Can you do that?"

"Yes," Lily said. "We have prickles where we live too."

"Of course," Maria said. "Let me see your shoes. Those are good. All right. Let's go."

They walked across the drive and stepped into the wash. As they went by the house, Myla glanced inside. She had not seen David since Sunday. She hoped he was doing well. Maybe he was avoiding her. Maybe all that talk about her being a naked mermaid had embarrassed him. She smiled and turned back to the wash. She was beginning to sound like Theresa. The world did not revolve around her. She probably hadn't seen David because he was not around—not because of anything to do with her.

"Is this where the Old Mermaids live?" Lily asked.

"Well, Lily," Myla said. "They did live all around here. This used to be an ocean. Do you know what an ocean is? The sea?"

Lily nodded.

"Long ago this was the sea," Myla said, "and all kinds of creatures swam in the sea."

"Mermaids too?"

"That's what some people believe," Myla said.

"Look at the red bird!" Lily pointed.

"That's a cardinal. Isn't he beautiful? His mate is around here somewhere. She isn't quite as colorful."

"Do the Old Mermaids have fathers and husbands?"

They came to a wide stretch of the wash. Up ahead was the log and the orange rope.

"You know, Lily," Myla said, "I've been asked that question before. I wish I had an answer, but I don't really know yet."

"When will you know?" Lily looked up at her.

"Maybe I'll just remember one day," Myla said.

Lily let go of her hand and ran ahead to the orange rope.

"Look," Lily said. "A treasure!"

Lily started pulling on the rope, but it wouldn't come loose. She stopped and looked at it, her face smooth with concentration. A few moments later she began unwinding the rope from the log. Soon it was free. Lily wrapped it around her waist.

"Will you tie it?" Lily asked. Myla squatted and tied the rope loosely but firmly to the girl.

Lily danced around Myla and swung the end of the rope back and forth.

"Now you," Lily said.

"What do you mean?"

"Tie it to you."

"Darlin', there's not enough to go around my waist."

Lily grabbed her left hand. "Here! I'll tie it here."

Myla let Lily tie the rope to her wrist; Lily had not quite figured out the art of the knot, so Myla closed her fingers over it when it started to slip off.

"There! Now we can't get separated," Lily said.

"Like your momma and you did in the river?" Myla asked.

Lily nodded. "And in the desert."

Myla frowned. "When did you get separated from your mother in the desert?"

"You know," Lily said. "You were there. Can I have this rope or do the Old Mermaids need it?"

"You may have it," Myla said. "The Old Mermaids left all these things as gifts for us. They don't need them any longer."

"Was this their rope?" Lily asked.

"I can't be certain," Myla said. "But I think this is the rope Sister Laughs A Lot used to tie the crow so it wouldn't try to fly away."

"Why?"

"Well, it happened when they first got here," Myla said, "when the Old Sea first dried up, and they didn't quite have their land legs."

"What are land legs?"

"They weren't swimming in the Old Sea any more," Myla said. "They had to get accustomed to solid ground. It was different than the Old Sea, you know. One day, Sister Laughs A Lot Mermaid found a crow outside the house. Actually, it wasn't quite a house yet. The Old Mermaids were still building it, with the help of some neighbors. They used mud and straw and stone—all materials from the old dried sea. As they built the house, they let the mud and straw and stone tell them stories. They listened to what the cacti and coyotes and crows had to say too. The neighbors had more stories. The stories made the work easier, and the house seemed to like the stories. It shaped itself beautifully around them and this land. It was a piece of art. The Old Mermaids had tile in the kitchen and bathroom and in funny places in the walls all over the house, so you might look here and see a flower blooming from the tile or you might look there and see a cardinal flying. They painted scenes from the Old Sea on the walls. And scenes from the mountains. Valleys. The desert. These paintings on the walls were so realistic, Lily, that you would swear you could walk right into them and keep on going. Everyone liked to be invited to the Old Mermaid Sanctuary because it was so beautiful. Many people—even to this day—swear the house was alive. And it was a happy house. Care was taken with every bit of it. The Old Mermaids even asked the land before they built the house where would be the best place."

"And the land answered?"

"It did," Myla said. "The place answered. The Old Mermaids could feel where the house should be, where the house wanted to be. And they talked to the plants and animals all around and asked to be welcomed to this place. They intended no harm. So Sister Laughs A Lot Mermaid found the crow outside as they were finishing up the house. Sister Bridget Mermaid was working on getting water with Sister Sheila Na Giggles Mermaid while Sister Ruby Rosarita Mermaid and Sister Sophia Mermaid finished up work on the bathroom and Sister Maggie Mermaid painted the front room with Sister DeeDee Lightful Mermaid. Sister Faye Mermaid helped plant the garden with Sister Bea Wilder Mermaid. And the others were around, too, doing their share. You're being very patient, Lily, since I have wandered all around this crow who didn't fly away when Sister Laughs A Lot Mermaid walked toward him. And it was a him. He strutted a bit more than the female crows Sister Laughs A Lot Mermaid had seen. Plus he had a deep voice."

Lily laughed. "That's silly!"

"Yes, but it's true."

Lily pulled the rope tight between her and Myla. "See, Myla, we're still tied together. Even if I fell to sleep right here, we'd be tied together."

"That's right, Lily my Lily. Sister Laughs A Lot Mermaid watched the crow and realized he was hurt. She picked him up and carried him to Sister Faye Mermaid and Sister Ursula Divine Mermaid. Sister Faye Mermaid called to Sister Bridget Mermaid and together they made an ointment from Jimmyweed to reduce the swelling on the wing, and they made plaster from the same plant to hold the wing into place while it healed. They sang over the wing while they treated it. 'The Old Sea rolls in and washes away the pain. The Old Sea rolls in and washes away infection and inflammation. The Old Sea rolls out and washes away all disease. So say the Old Mermaids. Blessed sea.'

"Sister Ursula Divine Mermaid talked to the crow. She had a way with wild things. 'His name is Rochester of all things,' Sister Ursula Divine Mermaid told the other Old Mermaids. 'But we can call him Rocky.' Rocky was soon on the mend, but he couldn't fly right away. They all tried to explain this to Rocky, but he didn't seem to understand. Sister Laughs A Lot Mermaid got a piece of rope from the newly built shed—an orange rope because she knew the crow would like the bright color—and she carefully and gently tied the rope around one of the crow's feet. The other end she tied around one of the porch posts, which was the trunk of an old mesquite.

"Grand Mother Yemaya Mermaid saw what Sister Laughs A Lot Mermaid had done, and she said, 'I don't think Rocky likes that. He keeps looking at the sky. Do you remember what happened when you tried to tie the sea horses to the coral with sea-weed?'

"'That was different,' Sister Laughs A Lot Mermaid said. 'This is for Rocky's own good. He'd hurt himself if he flew away.'

"'At least take him into the house so he can't see the sky,' Sister Magdelene Mermaid said.

"'But he'll still know the sky is there,' Sister Sophia Mermaid said.

"'It'll become a distant memory,' Sister Laughs A Lot said. She took him indoors but kept the rope on him and tied him to her. That way, she said, she would always know where he was and she would take good care of him. And truth to tell, Rocky did seem to like spending time with Sister Laughs A Lot Mermaid — and all the Old Mermaids. He was fed and pampered, plus they found him shiny things to play with. Mother Star Stupendous and Grand Mother Yemaya Mermaids were skeptical, however.

"'He is a wild thing,' they said. 'He does not belong indoors.' 'We were once wild things,' Sister Bea Wilder Mermaid said. 'But now we sleep under a roof.' 'Things changed for us,' Grand Mother Yemaya Mermaid said. 'We had to go with the flow.'

"'Things changed for Rocky, too," Sister Laughs A Lot Mermaid said.

"Rocky's wing got better, but he no longer tried to fly away. In fact, he stopped looking for shiny things. He just waited for Sister Laughs A Lot Mermaid and the others to feed him. One day they took him outside again. Rocky the Crow did not even look at the sky."

Lily looked up at the clear blue sky. Three crows flew overhead.

"You know what Sister Laughs A Lot Mermaid did? She untied him right there and then. She said, 'Grand Mother Yemaya Mermaid was right. You're a wild thing. Now go be wild.' At first Rocky the Crow did not know what to do. Finally, the Old Mermaids all lay on the desert floor looking up at the sky. Rocky eventually followed their gaze and saw the sky again. He stared for a long while, and then he shuddered, as if he had suddenly been filled up with wonder or love for the sky. He flapped his wings and flew away."

"Was Sister Laughs A Lot Mermaid lonely after he flew away?"

"No," Myla said. "Well, maybe for a while. But she got over it, and she never tied up anything again."

"I like the Old Mermaids," Lily said.

"So do I," Myla said.

"Can I go see the mermaid in the pool now?"

"Sure," Myla said. "Are we finished looking for treasure today?"

Lily nodded.

They turned around—still tied together—and walked to the Crow house. No one answered when Myla knocked. She opened the screen door and leaned in.

"David?" she called. "Anyone home?"

No answer.

She took Lily's hand, and they went into the kitchen. She called out again as she crossed the kitchen and living room. She looked out on the patio. David lay on the chaise lounge reading. In the spa near him, Ernesto sat, his eyes closed, the hot water churning around him. Myla knocked on the patio door. David looked up. He smiled and motioned them outside.

"Lily wanted to see the mermaid," Myla said.

Ernesto waved. "Mr. Crow invited me to come sit in the spa."

"I saw him walking on the road," David said, "so I invited him over."

"I'm feeling better every day," Ernesto said.

"He said he works for you?" David asked.

"He's going to do some things around the place once he feels better," Myla said.

Lily tugged on Myla's hand, and they walked to the edge of the pool and looked down. "She looks like you, Myla."

"That's what I've been told," Myla said.

After a moment, Lily turned around and walked over to David. Myla followed—since she was attached to her.

"Did you paint the mermaid?" Lily asked.

"I did," he said. "A long time ago. Before you were even born. When your mother was still a girl."

"Do the Old Mermaids talk to you?" she asked.

David said, "Sometimes it seems like they do," he said. "Do they talk to you?"

"Sometimes," Lily said.

"Why are you two tied together?" David asked, looking at Myla.

"It seemed like a good idea at the time," Myla said.

"Myla!" Someone outside screeched her name. Cathy? "Myla!" Sounded like someone was torturing a cat.

"Lily, I need to go for a minute," Myla said. "I'm going to untie myself from you."

"No!" Lily cried.

"I'll be back," Myla said.

Lily looked panicked.

David said, "Lily, you can tie yourself to me." He leaned closer to her. "Okay?"

"Okay," she agreed.

Myla handed David the rope.

"I'll be right back," Myla said.

She pulled open the wooden patio door, went outside, and closed it again. Cathy stood near the picnic table by Myla's apartment trying to light a cigarette with shaking hands.

"Smoking is not allowed at the sanctuary," Myla said. "You

know that. What is wrong? Why are you here?"

"I'm bored," she said. She sat on the picnic table. "And Stefan is being a pain. He needs to be in school. I've gotta get out of here. There's nothing to do. It's been two weeks. The kid is going stir crazy."

"Have you been drinking?" Myla asked.

"No," Cathy said. "Just a little."

"Where did you get alcohol? Did you leave the house?"

"I went down the road."

"Cathy," Myla said, "we took a big risk letting you come here."

"You've got all these other people here," Cathy said. "It can't be that big of a risk. At least I belong here. I'm not breaking any laws."

"If you're talking about Ernesto and Maria," Myla said, "they're working for me."

"That's what you told me to say if anyone asked," Cathy said. "And I'm not working for you."

"With them it's true," Myla said.

"I just want to go out for a while," Cathy said. "I'll go someplace where he won't find me."

"You can go wherever you want," Myla said. "Whenever you want. But if you leave, you can't come back. We can't risk your husband coming here. You told us you were running for your life!"

"Mom!" Stefan hurried down the drive toward them. "She didn't sleep last night," he said to Myla when he reached them. "She's just tired."

Cathy put her arm across his shoulders. "That's my boy."

"She gets this way sometimes," Stefan said. "I'll take her back."

"You aren't prisoners here," Myla said. "You can leave any time. I'll give you a bus ticket to wherever you want to go. You said you had family in Oregon. You could go there."

Cathy shook her head.

"We're fine here," Stefan said. "Theresa will find her a job soon. Come on, Mom."

Myla shook her head. "No, Stefan. You stay here. Lily and Ernesto are out by the pool. You go on in. I'm going to take your mother back to the house."

"I can do it," he insisted.

"Go on, Stefan," Myla said.

He hesitated, then turned and went into the Crow house.

Cathy said little as she and Myla walked back to the Ford house. At the door, she turned around and faced Myla, "I'll go in. I just need to sleep."

"I'm coming in," Myla said.

Cathy went in first, then Myla followed. She looked around. The living room was tidy. Nothing amiss here. Cathy staggered past her and down the hallway. Myla went into the kitchen; she heard Cathy slam the door. Not a glass out of place. She walked back to the room where Stefan slept. The door was open. She could not even tell someone had been there. She stood in front of the closed door to Cathy's room.

"I'm coming in," Myla said. She opened the door.

The room reeked of liquor and cigarettes, and it looked as though Cathy had trashed it. Clothes were scattered everywhere. A plate of half-eaten food balanced on top of a glass precariously perched on the cluttered night stand. Cathy lay asleep on top of a pile of clothes on the unmade bed.

Myla went to the window and opened it. Then she picked up the clothes and stuffed them into the paper bags Cathy used for suitcases. While Cathy slept, Myla swept, vacuumed, and cleaned. To help get out the smell of tobacco, she put several bowls of vinegar around the room. She opened the closet. It was mostly empty except for some sheets and blankets. Myla would wash those as soon as Cathy and Stefan were gone. And they would be gone tonight.

When Myla finished, she walked back to the Crow house. Stefan came out to meet her.

"Don't make us leave," Stefan said. "She'll just go back to him. She walked down to the store the other night and called him."

"The store is two miles away," Myla said. "You weren't to leave the sanctuary."

"I didn't," Stefan said. "I stayed. I don't want to go back there. He's going to kill her."

"I'm sorry, Stefan," Myla said. "What she did has put us all in jeopardy. When Theresa comes back, you're going home with her."

"Please, Myla. Let me stay here. He hits me too."

"You didn't tell us that," Myla said. "Your mother knows he hits you?"

"She can't do anything to stop him," Stefan said.

"You'll be safe at Theresa's," Myla said. "And she can take you to social services. They'll find a place for you both."

"Let me stay here," Stefan said.

"You've seen how small my place is," Myla said. "And there is no other place."

"What about with David? Or Ernesto?" he asked.

"I can't risk your stepdad coming here," Myla said. "If I had known your mother was drinking, I would have never considered allowing you to come here. It's a dangerous situation."

"But David owns the house, right? If he says it's all right, can't I stay with him? We haven't finished the Old Mermaid cards."

Myla put her hand on his shoulder. Tears popped out of his eyes like tiny clear seeds, and he quickly wiped them away.

"I'm sorry," Myla said. "I know this is something you have no control over. You are welcome to come to Saturday dinner. You're always welcome to come to that. You can finish the cards then."

His shoulders slumped, and he walked away from her toward the Ford house.

David came outside.

"What happened?" he asked.

"It's a long story," she said. "They've been staying nearby, and now they have to leave. The husband is abusive, and Cathy was trying to get away from him and step out on her own. Stefan wanted to stay here. He wanted to ask you if he could stay with you."

"He can stay," David said. "I've got all this room. Why not? They can both stay."

Myla shook her head. "No, they cannot both stay. She is drunk, David, and she's been calling her husband. Can you imagine what her husband would do if he came here and found his wife and stepson living with you?"

"You could stay in the house with them and I could stay at your place," David said.

"Thank you," Myla said. "That is very kind. But frankly, I want her gone."

David looked at her. "How is it that you have a say in whether they stay or go? Where are they living?"

Myla sighed. "It's a long story. Let's just say that I don't want to be involved with them any more. They can stay with Theresa and she can take care of them."

"I don't really understand," David said. "But if it will help, Stefan can stay here for a few days. At least until they can finish the Old Mermaid cards. I heard him mention that."

Myla suddenly realized he was not tied to Lily.

"Did she let you go?"

"She's tied to Ernesto," David said. "He thinks it's very amusing. He's telling her stories about mermaids in Mexico."

Myla and David went back to the patio. Ernesto and Lily sat happily next to each other at the edge of the pool, feet dangling in the cold water, tied together with the orange rope. Lily waved to Myla.

"Shall I make you all some lunch?" David asked.

"Do you have any food?" Myla asked.

"I could cook that chili Sister Ruby Rosarita Mermaid made with the sea water, only I'll use pool water instead," David said. "We're going into the kitchen, you two." The man and girl nodded.

"You heard that story on Saturday?" Myla said. "You were there long enough? I only saw you for a moment."

"I'm good at being invisible," David said. "In case I can't find sea water for the chili, by the way, I do have other food. I used Mom and Dad's old car in the barn and went shopping. Don't you ever drive it? It hardly has any miles on it."

"I sometimes go out into the desert," Myla said, "or I go grocery shopping. But it is their car. They said I could use it, but I don't want to take advantage."

David opened the refrigerator and looked inside. Myla sat at the end of the counter and watched Ernesto and Lily out by the pool.

"He's getting so much better," Myla said.

"I noticed he seems even better than he was on Saturday," David said. "How about beans, rice, and wild salmon? I've got some leftover brown rice."

"I'm your guest," Myla said. "I'll eat whatever you serve." She looked at the clock. She hoped Cathy would sleep until Theresa returned. "Are you having a good visit?"

David took a glass dish with the salmon in it and put it directly into the oven. "Three-fifty sounds good, doesn't it?" he said as he turned the dial. "I'm feeling better every day too."

"Which reminds me, I have to make a phone call," Myla said. "I'll be right back."

"You can use the phone here," David said. "I had it turned on."

"I need to check mine anyway," Myla said. "I think I may have shut it off. I'll see if Stefan wants some lunch too."

Myla went outside and walked to her apartment. She sat on the bed and picked up the phone and looked at the side. Yes, she had shut it off. It was not her favorite mode of communication, but it was careless of her not to check her messages: What if one of the families decided to come into town unexpectedly? She called her voice mail. Twenty messages. How could that be? She barely knew twenty people. She began going through them. David's mother Sarah called three times. Theresa five times. Gail twice. Four hang-ups. Probably telemarketers. Her mother called once. George called three times. Her ex-husband called twice.

George called last Saturday to make certain she would be there Sunday—this past Sunday. And he called yesterday to see if she wanted to go out to dinner Thursday night.

"Answer your damn telephone, woman!" he said. "If you don't call me, I'm just going to show up and take you someplace you don't like. Call me!" He yelled the last part, as though she could actually hear him if he yelled loud enough.

She deleted all the messages as she listened, except for the last two from Richard. She saved those to listen to later.

First she called Theresa. She did not answer her phone, so Myla left a message. "As soon as you're finished, come back here. Cathy got drunk and trashed her room. She's going home with you tonight. I want her out."

She called Mrs. Ford next.

"Hello, Myla!" Mrs. Ford said. "I haven't heard from you in a while. Everything all right?"

"Yes," Myla said. "But I wanted to let you know that I had someone in to fix some things around the house, and I'm afraid they smoked in the back bedroom. I'm really sorry. I've cleaned it, and I'm going to wash down the walls. I'll wash all the linens and the things in the closet. Is there anything else I can do to make it all right for when you come?"

"We won't be there for another few months, Myla," she said. "I'm sure you've done all that can be done. Just make certain it is all aired out."

"I'm sorry, Mrs. Ford," Myla said. "I trusted this person to do as I asked."

"It's all right," Mrs. Ford said. "What work needed to be done?"

"Some tiles were loose," Myla said. Which was true. "And we were worried the roof might have leaked and it was right over that room." Which was also true. "So they were checking inside the house." Which was not true. Myla cringed. She did not mind lying every once in a while. Telling a friend she liked her new haircut when she didn't or saying she was tired and wanted to stay home even when she wasn't tired. She didn't even have problems with bigger lies. "No, sir, I haven't seen any illegal aliens. How do you know I'm not one?" She had actually had that conversation with someone outside a park near Arivica, minutes after she had given six people food and water as they hurried through a nearby wash. But she did not like lying to people who trusted her.

"Thank you for telling me, Myla," Mrs. Ford said. "I'm sure you'll take care of it, and it'll be fine. I heard David is there for a while. That'll be nice to have some company for you."

"Yes," Myla said. "It is nice having him here."

"We'll talk to you later, Myla," she said.

Myla said good-bye, and then she called Sarah Crow.

"It's Myla," she said when Sarah answered.

"You turned off your phone again, didn't you?" Sarah said.

"Yes, I'm sorry," Myla said. "I forget sometimes that you might need to get a hold of me."

"I talked to David," Sarah said. "He says you're quite busy. Everything all right?"

"Sure, why?" Myla asked.

"It's that time of year," Sarah said.

That time of year?

"You sometimes get a little down at this time of year," Sarah said.

"I'm fine," Myla said. "David seems good. I haven't seen him in such a long time that I almost didn't recognize him at first."

"Does he really seem all right?" Sarah said. "I wasn't sure about him coming. He had such a difficult time after last time."

"Last time?" Myla said. "Did something happen last time he was here?"

"You must have noticed he hasn't been to the house in ten years," Sarah said.

"None of you come to the house much," Myla said.

"Maybe he'll tell you about it," Sarah said.

Myla frowned. Tell *her*? Or *it*?

"In any case, I'm glad to hear he seems all right," Sarah said. "He wasn't doing well during the holidays. I might come in a couple of weeks to spend some time with him."

"It would be nice to see you," Myla said.

"Take care," Sarah said. "And be careful with my boy."

Sarah said good-bye. Myla cradled the phone in her hand. That was a strange conversation. She sighed. Speaking of strange conversations, it was time to listen to the messages her ex-husband had left.

In the first message, he said, "Were you at the house today? My mother-in-law said some strange woman claiming to be our housekeeper was there staring at the kitchen walls. Then George called and said he wanted the mermaid tile. What's going on?"

Myla felt her face flush. She had hoped Richard would not figure out that she had broken into his house. Maybe he wouldn't have if George hadn't called him. She shook her head and listened to the second message from Richard. "Myla, call me. I know it was you. I figured out what date it was. You and George should really get lives."

Myla's face flushed again. She breathed deeply. "What would the Old Mermaids do?" she murmured. "Find the nearest Old Sea and drown him, that's what."

She pressed in the phone number he left—her old phone number. She hoped Nadine wouldn't answer. She hoped no one answered.

"Hello?" It was a little voice. A girl's voice. Myla knew her name was Bethany, but she pretended ignorance.

"May I speak with—" She did not want to say his name out loud. She knew it was ridiculous. Silly. Juvenile. But she did not want to say his name. "May I speak with your father."

"Yes, may I say who's calling?" They had trained her well. Myla squeezed her eyes shut. No, she was not going to be bitter. She was not like that. The girl's parents taught her to be polite. To have common courtesy. That was a good thing.

"Tell him it's the housekeeper," Myla said.

The little girl didn't say anything, but Myla could hear her breathing as she walked. Finally she said, "Daddy. It's that housekeeper."

A moment later, Richard came on the phone.

"Hello?"

"Hello," she said. "How are you?"

"Fine," he said. "And you?"

She wanted to scream, "I do have a life! It's not the life you promised to have with me, but it is a life. And it's a good life."

"What is it you want?" Myla asked.

"I don't want you sneaking into my house," he said.

"I want the oak dresser," Myla said. "And I want the mermaid tile."

"That's ridiculous," he said. "It would ruin the entire wall if I took out that tile. It would ruin the tile. You can't just remove tile."

"When I left, you told me I could have anything I wanted," Myla said.

"You took what you wanted," he said.

"I took what was mine."

"And that didn't include the tile and the dresser," he said.

She sighed. "I'll pay you what we paid for the dresser," she said. "I'll pay for the new tiles."

He was silent. She could hear Bethany talking or singing in the background.

"We paid fifty bucks for that dresser," he said.

"And I bet she doesn't even like it," Myla said. "I can't believe you still have all of our things in the house. Even the bed."

"They're just things," he said. "You said that yourself when you left. What are you going to do with that dresser? You live in one room."

Myla cringed. He was still negotiating with her—still trying to control every interaction they had.

"All right," he said. "We were going to get a new dresser anyway. I can have it delivered. But I'm not going to give you that tile. I can try to find another mermaid tile in the shop."

Don't you dare!

"I want that mermaid," Myla said.

Why was she asking for the mermaid tile? She had forgotten all about it for a decade. Blocked it out, most likely. She had left that house and forgotten everything about it.

"You evicted me from that house, Richard," she said. "It was my home. What you did made it impossible for me to ever live there again. I want what was mine."

"I gave you quite a tidy sum of money," he said.

"You didn't give me anything," Myla said. "That was my money. It was my business."

"And you walked away from all of it," he said.

"I walked away from you," she said.

"I don't want to rehash all this stuff," he said. "I've got a life."

Don't say it. Don't say it.

"You need to get one too."

"I want the dresser and the tile," Myla said. "And throw out that bed!"

"Or what, Myla? What are you going to do? You have no power to do anything."

Myla thought about all the things she could do. She could call the IRS and tell them where he hid a second set of books. She could call all his suppliers and tell them he had been cheating them for years. Not that either of those things was true.

Besides she did not want to destroy him. She did not want to be a part of his life. Gail was correct in her assessment of him: He was a small man. She just wanted the dresser and mermaid tile.

"You're right, Richard," she said. "I have no power over you. And you have no power over me. I still want what is mine."

She pressed the off button on the phone and listened to the silence. She looked around her one room apartment. Yes, it was small, but it was beautiful. She surrounded herself with beauty. Every morning she stepped outside and chanted the Navajo prayer, "I walk in beauty before me. I walk in beauty behind me. I walk in beauty beside me. I walk in beauty above and below me. I walk in beauty." Her life was about turning trash into beauty. So why had she called her ex-husband? Why had she asked for a dresser she couldn't use and a piece of her kitchen she had forgotten?

Maybe Sarah was right. This time of year made her a bit...melancholy. Or crazy.

Myla went outside into the blue day again. She walked over to the Ford house. Cathy was still sleeping. She asked Stefan to have lunch with them. As they walked back to the Crow house, Myla slipped her arm through his.

"David said you can stay with him," Myla said, "but only if that is what everyone decides is the best thing. Your stepdad can't find out about this place. What happens in the Old Mermaid Sanctuary stays in the Old Mermaid Sanctuary. I trusted your mother because Theresa vouched for her. I should have listened to my instincts and never let the two of you come here. But then I would not have met you, and you would not have gotten the opportunity to meet the Old Mermaids. A man who abuses his wife and son is a dangerous man. I will do whatever I can to protect you. At the same time I cannot put Lily, Maria, Ernesto, myself, or David in danger. Do you understand?"

"Yes, I know," he said. "But I don't want him to hit me again. I don't want social services to take me away either. That happened once when I was a kid, and it was worse being with a foster family. They weren't mean, but I never knew where I was going next. If I stayed with you, I could see my mom whenever I wanted, but I wouldn't be around him."

"You're pretty sure your mom is going back to him?"

"She doesn't know how to be by herself," Stefan said. "She's always hooking up with some loser. She'll stay sober for a while and swear things will get better, but then they don't."

Myla and Stefan went into the Crow kitchen. Ernesto and Lily sat at the kitchen table. The orange rope hung from Lily's waist. She swung her legs and held a fork in one hand and a spoon in the other, both upright, a clear and present sign that she was ready to eat.

"Just in time," David said. He began spooning black beans onto plates. Myla got the rice pot from the stove and scooped rice onto the plates. David set the platter of salmon in the middle of the table. Then he and Myla sat at the table with the others.

"Thank you," Myla said, "for this lovely meal, David. And we thank this place for having us. We thank the fish and the beans and rice for giving their lives so that we might eat."

"And the salsa," Stefan said, nodding toward the jar.

"And the salsa," she said.

"And the Old Mermaids," Lily said. Her English was getting better every day.

"Yes, and the Old Mermaids."

"Do the Old Mermaids eat *pescados*?" Lily asked.

"Wouldn't that kind of be like cannibalism?" Stefan asked.

"*La Sirenas* are like people," Ernesto said. "Not *pescados*!"

"It depended upon the Old Mermaid," Myla said. "Some ate fish; some did not. Some felt more passionate about it than others. Sister DeeDee Lightful Mermaid did not eat any fish. She wouldn't even be in the house when they ate fish, so they didn't eat it often. Sister DeeDee Lightful Mermaid argued that they didn't cook fish when they were in the ocean, so why would they cook fish now? The other Old Mermaids agreed that this was a good argument. Sister Sophia Mermaid said, 'That is a good argument for not cooking fish, perhaps, but it is not a good argument for not eating fish. When we lived in the ocean we did indeed pop the occasional sea creature into our mouths and munch them.' Sister Bea Wilder Mermaid said, 'Sister DeeDee Lightful Mermaid, we must keep up with what is happening now. And now my body no longer craves what it once craved. And it craves what it once did not. We sing to the fish, and we are maintaining the Old Sea within our bodies when we eat fish. Equilibrium, sister.' Sister Bea Wilder Mermaid did not miss the ocean like the other Old Mermaids did, but she loved Sister DeeDee Lightful Mermaid best of all.

"Well, you see how the arguments went," Myla said. "Sister DeeDee Lightful Mermaid never did eat fish, as far as I know, but she accepted that some of her sisters ate sea creatures. Especially after Sister Sophia Mermaid told her, 'Have no fear, Sister DeeDee Lightful Mermaid, we will not suddenly wake up one morning and have a craving to gobble you up.'"

Lily laughed.

Myla smiled. "Yep, Sister DeeDee Lightful Mermaid laughed just like that. Now eat up!"

I am most at home where the wild things are.

Sister Ursula Divine Mermaid

After lunch, Myla tucked Lily into David's sister's bed. Stefan walked Ernesto home while Myla and David cleaned the kitchen. They worked side by side, mostly wordlessly. Then they sat at the table, each with a cup of tea in hand. Myla thought it was nice to be in the same room with someone and not have to talk. No awkwardness at the silence, no searching for the right words, just silence.

"When you were here before," Myla said after a time, "we often didn't talk, did we?" She laughed before he answered. "I mean we spent quiet times together too. We would walk the wash together, or sit on my porch. You had a sketch pad. And I had...what did I have? A drink in my hand, probably."

"We didn't talk," David said, "but we talked too. You were not always drinking, by the way. In fact, I never thought I'd seen you drunk, but then later I figured out I had. You were mostly sad and a bit frantic."

"I don't know why I'm asking you about then," Myla said. "I don't really dwell on the past much."

"Aren't the stories about the Old Mermaids all in the past?"

Myla laughed. "Now that is a story for another time."

"Do you remember when you first started the Church of the Old Mermaids, you didn't want me to come?" David asked.

"That's right," Myla said. "At first I didn't want anyone around who knew me! I had no idea what I was doing. And then the first person came and picked something off the table, and I told him a story about the Old Mermaids. After that, I was all right. After that, it was as if my old life was dead and I was on to a new one."

"That dead life included me," David said.

"What? No, you weren't part of my old life," Myla said. "You weren't part of my new life."

David flinched.

"I mean we were friends, David," Myla said. "But you were a young man off to find his way in the world! I couldn't imagine why you wanted to spend time with me in the first place."

"I went to the Church of the Old Mermaids a few times back then."

"You did?" Myla said. "I thought you were only here for a few weeks that winter."

"No," David said. "I was here for a while, but you didn't want to have anything to do with me after you started the Church of the Old Mermaids."

Myla tried to remember.

"I thought you left after you painted the mermaid. I stopped drinking. I started going out into the desert more. Was George around then?"

She looked at David's face. He gazed at her silently. She re-

114

membered George said David had had a crush on her back then.

"You know, David," Myla said. "I called your mother today, and she mentioned that something happened when you were here before which prevented you from coming back. I didn't think it was any of my business, but now as we're talking, I'm getting the distinct impression that something is going on that I don't know about. And then George said—"

She stopped. She did not want to embarrass herself. Not about this.

"What did George say?" David asked.

"George says a lot of stupid things," she said.

"I'm surprised he's still around," David said. "With you, I mean. The two of you."

"No more surprised than I am," Myla said. "I think we just got used to each other."

"That's a good basis for a relationship," David said.

"That sounded sarcastic. I don't remember you being sarcastic."

"But you don't remember a lot about that time," David said.

"I'm not senile," Myla said. "I don't understand subtle, David. Did I do something terrible to you back then? Am I the reason you never came back here?"

"No, you didn't do anything terrible," David said. "I was very fond of you. We spent a lot of time together and then one morning you didn't seem to want me around. That hurt."

"One morning?" Myla said. "You can pinpoint the morning?"

"Sure," David said. "It was after you had the dream—the vision of the Old Mermaids. We had dinner the night you had the dream. Everything was fine, as far as I knew. And then the next day it was as though you hardly knew me."

"I remember George was there that night," Myla said.

David laughed unhappily. "You remember George that night

but not me?"

Myla felt a bit off-balanced by this conversation. She was missing some piece of it. She had been drinking back then. She had never felt as though she had to apologize or explain herself because of anything she had done while drunk. After all, she had barely seen anyone during that period, and she hadn't driven anywhere. She hadn't robbed a bank or slept with some else's husband. She had walked the wash and had a vision. Her rotten behavior could not have affected anyone else—or so she had always believed.

David reached for her hand. "I can see this conversation is distressing you. I apologize. That's the last thing I wanted."

"All right," Myla said. She pulled her hand away. "We were friends, so I'll tell you something. I hope you won't laugh at me. I'm used to it, I suppose. Over the years, I have gotten quite a few laughs about the Old Mermaids. But they were laughing with me." She was stalling. She smiled. David frowned. "All right. That night I had the dream, I remember George coming over. I think we argued. But then I don't remember much. You and I had dinner? I'm sorry, but I think I may have blacked out. I've heard of that happening, but I didn't know if it ever happened to me. The next morning I was embarrassed because I had had too much to drink. I-I didn't make a pass at you or anything, did I? I was very sad back then, and you were—you were very kind. And, okay, you were—you are—an attractive man. I hope I didn't do anything to embarrass you. That's all."

David sighed. "No, you did not do anything to embarrass me or yourself."

"Oh good. That is a relief! So you staying away from here didn't have anything to do with me? How could it? The whole world does not revolve around me! It revolves around Theresa, let her tell you."

116

"Did I hear my name being taken in vain?" Theresa stood outside the kitchen door.

"Come on in," David said.

Theresa opened the door and stepped into the kitchen. Maria came in after her. They both looked drawn, tired.

"You want some tea or coffee?" Myla asked.

David went to the stove and got the kettle.

"Where's Lily?" Maria asked.

"She's in the back, down the hall in the room next to the bathroom," Myla said.

Maria left the kitchen. Theresa sat at the table.

"That was rough," Theresa said. She rubbed her face. "A lot of people have died near the border recently. So we looked at photos of dead people. We didn't find him, which I guess is a good thing."

"What now?" Myla asked.

"I don't know what else to do," Theresa said. "I've already telephoned every jail and cop shop in the Southwest looking for him. Doesn't mean he isn't in a jail somewhere. Doesn't mean Homeland Security doesn't have him someplace. But I can't find him. Unfortunately there is another option. I mentioned it to Maria in passing, and I'm not sure it sunk in. There are quite a few Juan Does."

"That's not funny," Myla said.

"I know it's not," Theresa said. "I'm sorry. I'm tired. I kept hearing that today: We've got a lot of Juan Does. That's what some of the guys call unidentified dead migrants. Anyway, there is an organization in Texas that is storing DNA of unidentified migrants who were found dead in the desert or who died in car accidents near the border. Since Lily is a blood relative of Juan, they could compare her DNA with the dead men to see if anything matches. I gotta tell you though, Maria's getting pretty depressed about this whole situation."

"It's probably hard for her to be in that big house by herself all day with a five year old," David said. He brought the steaming kettle over to the table along with two new cups and poured water all around.

Myla looked up at him.

"What big house?" Theresa asked.

David sat with the women.

"The Wentworth house," he said.

Myla and Theresa sat silently. Myla didn't know what to say.

"We don't know what you mean," Theresa said.

Myla shook her head.

"Lily told me where she was staying," David said. "She didn't know the name, but I recognized what house she was talking about—especially since Ernesto kept trying to get her to change the subject. It was kind of funny, plus that whole thing about Cathy and Stefan."

"What about Cathy and Stefan?" Theresa asked.

"I'll tell you later," Myla said. "David, I found Maria and Lily out in the desert, near the border. They could have frozen to death or died of hypothermia."

"You don't need to explain anything to me," David said. "I'm just suggesting it might be difficult living in that big house alone and not being able to do anything besides clean. Lily said they've been doing a lot of cleaning. Lily says the woman who owns the house must be afraid of dirt if she needs it cleaned every day. If she's that afraid of dirt, Lily wanted to know, why does she live where there is so much of it."

Myla smiled. "I only suggested she should keep the house looking good while they were there," she said.

"They can stay here," David said. "This house has three bedrooms. Lily and Maria can stay in Mom and Dad's room. Ernesto and Stefan can stay in my room. For some odd reason that room has always had bunk beds. I'll sleep in Susan's room."

"Ernesto?" Myla said.

David looked at her.

"Uh, I'll go check on Maria and Lily," Theresa said.

"How'd you figure it out?" Myla asked after Theresa left the room. "I mean besides Lily. No one's figured it out before."

"You've done this before?" David asked.

Myla nodded.

"Wow."

"Usually I don't bring anyone here unless all the owners are gone," Myla said. "Once or twice someone has been in one of the houses when another owner showed up, and we just took them somewhere else."

"But you didn't do that when I showed up?"

Myla shook her head. "No. A lot of things have been happening. I guess. I wasn't being very careful." She looked at him. "And even though it has been many years, I think of you as a friend. It didn't worry me that you were here."

"It should," he said. "The other homeowners could put you in jail for this."

"But these big beautiful houses sit empty for months and months," Myla said. "And people needed help. They needed temporary homes. They always do work. And the owners said I could hire workers. I did. In exchange for room and board. The owners provided the room; the Church of the Old Mermaids provided the board."

"At what risk to them and to yourself, not to mention the private property of the homeowners?" David asked.

"All of life is a risk," Myla said. "I risked very little. The people coming here risked everything, including their lives. They just want to feed their families. I wanted to help, and this was how I chose to do it. You might not agree with what I did, but there it is. I haven't done as much as I would have liked, but I've done something." Myla leaned back in her chair. "What are you going to do now?"

"Me? I'm not going to do anything," David said. "I'll call Mom and let her know I'm having a few guests over."

Maria and Theresa came into the room.

"Lily was sleeping so soundly that we left her," Theresa said. "What's with the orange rope on the bed?"

"We found it in the wash," Myla said. "She likes being tied to people. She said if she had had a rope she wouldn't have been separated from Maria."

"She got very scared when she fell in the river," Maria said. "It was my fault. I should have held more tightly to her hand."

"What river was that?" Theresa said. "I kept meaning to ask you that. I thought you crossed near Nogales."

"I don't know where he took us," Maria said. "But he said the arroyo was usually dry."

"There's been some strange flash flooding this winter," Myla said. "Lily said she was separated from you in the desert."

"No, I never left her side," Maria said. "Except for a moment, just before you found us, but she was sleeping then. She must have dreamed it."

"Here's some tea," Myla said to Maria. "And there are leftovers. We could make you lunch."

Maria shook her head. "We ate."

"Maria, if it's all right with you," Myla said, "you and Lily will stay in this house with David, Ernesto, and Stefan. And I'll be close by. You can come and go as you please and you won't have to worry about anyone seeing you."

"But I'm illegal," Maria said in Spanish.

"That's still true," Myla said, "but David is the owner of this

120

house, and he says you can stay here. Would that be all right?"

Maria said, "If you think that would be best. I am very tired."

"Do we need to go to the other house and get your things?" David asked.

Maria nodded toward the small backpack she had dropped by the door. "That is what we have," she said.

"I'll show you which room," David said. "You can have the master bedroom." The two of them left the kitchen together.

"Now what about Cathy and Stefan," Theresa said.

"I guess you haven't checked your phone messages yet?" Myla said. Theresa shook her head. "Well, Cathy's drunk. She trashed the room. You have to take her tonight. I want Stefan to go with his mother, but if she's going back to her stepdad he doesn't want to go. He says the stepdad beats him too."

"I didn't know that," Theresa said. "I thought Cathy was clean and sober. I thought she was really serious this time."

"*This* time? She's done this before? You kept that little tidbit to yourself."

"I'm sorry," Theresa said. "I should have told you. I will take her with me tonight, but I think this is the end for me, Myla. I'll finish with Maria and Lily, of course. I'll contact the organization in Texas and find out how to get Lily's DNA to them. But after that I'm out. I'm sorry, Myla. I don't want to disappoint you, but it's more stress than I can do right now. Don't you ever worry? I mean what if we were caught? I didn't used to think about that. I don't want to go to jail."

"No one is going to put you in jail!" Myla said.

"You haven't been paying attention," Theresa said. "They arrested that couple for transporting migrants to a hospital."

"I do pay attention," Myla said. "It is difficult. I appreciate everything you've done. Now you need to take care of your daughter and husband. I understand."

The two women reached across the table, held hands, and looked at one another.

"What are you going to do?" Theresa asked.

"I don't know," Myla said. "I'll see what happens."

"I'll go get Cathy," Theresa said. "She didn't want to go to the women's shelter before. Maybe now she will."

"I'll walk over with you," Myla said. "I want to make certain Stefan is all right."

They left the house together. The day had turned to afternoon. Everything was still. Dry. They walked down the drive.

"Did I tell you Luisa started school?" Theresa said. "And she's mentioned the Old Mermaid cards a couple of times. I think she likes being here."

"Bring her to the Church of the Old Mermaids on Saturday," Myla said.

"You think she could sit still for that?" Theresa said. "She'd probably keep interrupting you."

"I probably need interrupting," Myla said.

At the Ford house, Myla took out her keys and unlocked the door. Cathy and Stefan sat at the dining room table. Cathy's face was puffy, her eyes red. She ran her fingers through her greasy hair. Stefan looked at Myla hopefully. She walked down the hallway to the back bedrooms. Both rooms were clean. The smell of cigarettes was gone. She'd check the bathroom later.

Myla went into the dining room.

"Have you stolen anything from here?" Myla asked Cathy.

"No! Of course not! I just got drunk. I'm sorry!"

"I'm sorry too," Myla said. "We were trying to help you get a new start. But Theresa is going to take you with her now."

"I won't drink again," Cathy said. "I promise."

"It's best," Myla said.

Stefan looked at his hands.

Myla sighed. "David Crow said that Stefan can stay with him—with us—for a while—if you think that would be best for him."

"No! He stays with me," Cathy said. "My baby goes where I go."

"I'm not a baby, Mom," Stefan said. "You're going to go back to that jerk and I don't want him hitting me."

"I've never seen him hit you!" Cathy said.

"That's because you're too damn drunk!"

"I didn't mean what I said," Cathy said, looking at Myla. "I won't tell anyone you're smuggling illegal aliens. Really."

"We are not smuggling illegal aliens!" Theresa said. "Good grief, Cathy. We offered you a place to stay. We offered a couple other people a place to stay. We're not smuggling anything or anybody."

"Well, I won't tell," Cathy said. "Whatever you're doing."

"I called the owner of the house," Myla said. "I told her what happened."

Theresa looked at her. "You did?"

Myla nodded. She'd tell her the whole conversation later. Right now, she knew Cathy was threatening her by saying she wouldn't report her. In essence, she was saying she would tell if Myla did not let her stay.

"I won't contact social services about Stefan getting hit by his stepdad," Myla said. "Not yet. If I find out he is in danger again, I will not hesitate to call the police."

"I wouldn't put my son in danger," Cathy said. "Never."

"For now, you can both come home with me," Theresa said. "Stefan, Luisa would love to see you. You can decorate some more Old Mermaid cards if you like. And on Saturday we'll come here for dinner."

"Does that work for you, Cathy?" Myla asked.

"Sure," Cathy said. "Sure. That's what I wanted all along, but

Theresa said she was too crowded at her place."

Myla and Theresa glanced at each other.

"Stefan, are you all right with that?" Myla asked.

He shrugged. "As long as she doesn't go back with him."

"My son does what I tell him to do," Cathy said. "Don't ya, honey?" She reached for him; he moved away.

"All right, all right," Cathy said. "He can stay here while I'm with Theresa. We'll take him back with us on Saturday. Maybe I'll have a place by then. And a job. Come on. Let's get outta here."

They carried Cathy's bags to Theresa's car. Stefan put his clothes in his backpack and watched as his mother got into the car.

"Call me every night," Cathy said.

"I will," Stefan said.

She waved as they drove away.

"Love you!" Cathy called out the window.

Stefan and Myla stepped away from the dust. Then he and Myla walked to David's house.

"Hello," Myla called as they came in through the kitchen door. "We're home."

David sat in the living room reading.

"Thanks for letting me stay, Mr. Crow," Stefan said. "I'll be good."

"I'm not sure what being good means," David said. "But you're welcome here."

"These are the ground rules," Myla said. "No smoking, no drinking, no drugs, no bringing anyone here. And you do what David says. Keep your room clean—you'll be sharing it with Ernesto. And help around the house. All right?"

Stefan nodded.

"Your room is the one with the bunk beds," David said. "Maria and Lily are in the opposite room. They're taking a nap."

"I'll be quiet," Stefan said. "I should take the top bunk, right?"

"That's very considerate," Myla said.

Stefan hurried away. Myla sat on the couch with David.

"This is very kind of you," Myla said. "Really. Very generous."

"I talked with Mom," David said. "She thinks it's a kick. She said, and I quote, 'It's about time you got a little revolution in your soul.'"

Myla laughed. "I think painting the mermaid in the pool was a revolutionary act, don't you?"

"It was an act of love," David said. "I suppose that is the greatest revolutionary act there is."

"An act of love?" Myla said. "Because art is an act of love?"

David laughed. "You and I need to sit down and have a long talk."

"We're sitting," Myla said. "Can't we talk now?"

"I need to prepare myself," David said. "And I'd prefer it if we were alone."

"You are being very mysterious," Myla said.

"It's the Old Mermaid way," he said.

Stefan came into the room. "Should I go get Ernesto from the other house?" he asked.

"Why don't we both go," Myla said. "We'll walk through the wash and I'll show you where the Old Mermaids once had an art studio."

Later, after Lily and Maria awakened, they all went for a walk in the wash—except for Ernesto. He stayed behind to sit in the spa. Lily wanted to be tied to Maria as they walked, but she said no. At first Lily protested, but then she skipped up to Stefan and asked to be tied to him. He consented, and the two children walked a bit ahead of the adults. Maria hung back. Myla and David glanced at one another, and then he slowed so that he could walk with Maria. Myla listened to his halting Spanish. Maria answered in English. Like her daughter, Maria's English was improving every day. Myla walked between these couples as the sun went down and turned everything sunset gold. Mourning doves fluttered away as they walked past the mesquite and palo verde that crowded the trail. The doves startled Lily at first. Then she started clapping each time the doves flew off their perches.

"Help us find treasure," Lily said after a while, looking back at Myla.

The children slowed until she caught up with them.

"Well, Lily my Lily, I suppose each treasure hunt is different for each person," Myla said. "I ask the wash and the Old Mermaids to show me what is here for me on this day. Often I find things as I walk. At this time of year when it's been dry for a long time, the pickings are slim. So sometimes I just stop. I don't know where or when. I stop when it moves me, and I close my eyes and breathe. When I open my eyes and look around, I almost always see something I hadn't seen before."

Lily did not say anything at first. She kept walking with Stefan in tow. Then she said in Spanish, "Now!" She stopped and closed her eyes. Stefan and Myla did the same. Myla breathed deeply. Then she opened her eyes and looked around. The children did the same. Just out of the wash she noticed something metallic looking. Lily spotted it too. She ran over to it—with Stefan—and picked it up. It looked like the grate from a barbecue, only the slats were thinner.

"That's wonderful," Myla said.

"What did the Old Mermaids use this for?" Stefan asked. "Their cookouts?"

"That's a good question," Myla said, "and I'm sure an answer

126

will come to me later."

They started walking again. The sky began turning pink as the sun fell. The last rays highlighted the thorns on a cholla. Lily stopped to gaze at the gold and green spectacle. Thousands of needles suddenly became golden.

"They look connected," Stefan said. "Almost like a spider web."

"Now!" Lily said, and she closed her eyes. Myla laughed and did the same. She breathed deeply. She opened her eyes and looked around. Beneath a palo verde, the sun highlighted something green and yellow. The three of them walked closer to the tree. It was an arrow, stuck deep in the ground. To get to it, they would have to somehow move the cholla limbs and palo verde branches: a prickly and sticky proposition. Myla looked at the grate in Lily's hand.

"I think I just remembered what this is for," Myla said. "Could you give that to Stefan, Lily?" Lily handed the grate to the boy. "Now use that to hold back the prickly stuff while I lean it to get the arrow."

Stefan did as he was asked. The grate worked perfectly. Myla bent over, reached in, and pulled out a gold arrow with plastic green and yellow feathers. She stepped away from the trees and cactus, and the three of them looked at the arrow. The point was blunted where it had hit the ground.

"Look," Stefan said. "It says 'gold stalker.'"

"Yes, but the words all run together," Myla said. "It could be golds talker."

"What would that mean?" Stefan asked.

Myla laughed. "I'm not sure, but I think this is the arrow which almost hit Sister Lyra Musica Mermaid."

"I don't remember her," Stefan said.

Maria and David caught up with them.

"We found an arrow," Lily said.

"I see that," David said. "What do the Old Mermaids have to say about it?"

"I'll tell you as we walk back to the house," Myla said as she turned around. "Sister Lyra Musica Mermaid spent a great deal of time in the wash, along with Sister Laughs A Lot Mermaid and the others, but Sister Lyra Musica Mermaid had a particular affinity to it, you might say. She was a very sensitive mermaid. When she was younger, she knew the Old Sea was drying up long before anyone else did. She was a very happy mermaid when she was younger. But she had a difficult time adjusting to life after the ocean dried up. Grand Mother Yemaya Mermaid counseled her. She explained that the world is always changing, and it works best if she can accept that change. Sister Lyra Musica Mermaid missed the Old Sea, and she thought they should have been able to do something to stop it from drying up."

"Could the Old Mermaids have prevented the sea from drying up?" Stefan asked.

"The Old Mermaids were very capable," Myla said. "And they had many abilities, just as you have many abilities. And you Lily, And Maria. David. Myself. But no, they did not cause the sea to dry up, and they could not stop it from drying up. Sister Lyra Musica Mermaid enjoyed creating the house and the Old Mermaid Sanctuary with the other Old Mermaids. She liked being here, even though it was so different from the Old Sea. But she did not adjust as well as the others. She was often afraid. She worried about spiders and rattlesnakes and mountain lions. She worried that someone was going to come and hurt the Old Mermaids."

"Why would someone hurt the Old Mermaids?" Lily asked.

"Bad people are everywhere, Lily," Maria said.

"The unexpected is a part of our lives," Myla said, "and it was a part of the lives of the Old Mermaids. But the unexpected made

Sister Lyra Musica Mermaid afraid and sick. To make matters even worse, a neighbor began hunting in the area. He couldn't see very well and he was old, but he was hungry and poor and he needed something to eat. He didn't like feeling old and sick, and hunting made him feel stronger. Only he kept mistaking the Old Mermaids for deer or mountain lions or javelinas. Sometimes the Old Mermaids would be walking in the wash and an arrow would whiz over their heads or land beside them. They'd know it was Mr. Hunter. Fortunately he was a lousy shot, but Sister Lyra Musica Mermaid became so afraid that she didn't even walk the wash for comfort any more."

"Couldn't the other Old Mermaids help her?" Stefan asked.

"They tried," Myla said. "Sister Sophia Mermaid shared with her the wisdom traditions from all over the planet while Grand Mother Yemaya Mermaid gave her lots of hugs. This comforted Sister Lyra Musica Mermaid for a while. Sister Sheila Na Giggles Mermaid and Sister Laughs A Lot told her many jokes — and Sister Ruby Rosarita Mermaid cooked her many special meals. Sister Bridget Mermaid wrote her poetry and consulted with Sister Faye Mermaid on which herbs would make her feel better. Sister DeeDee Lightful Mermaid encouraged her to change her diet and to never eat fish again. Sister Bea Wilder Mermaid told her she needed to get over it. Sissy Maggie Mermaid suggested she fall in love. Sister Ursula Divine Mermaid took her out into the wilds of the desert for a vision quest. She got cold, hungry, and afraid. The Old Man of the Mountains came by and asked her what she was doing. When she told him, he said, 'You lost your soul.' He looked around. 'It's not here. Go home.'

"And so Sister Lyra Musica Mermaid returned to the Old Mermaid Sanctuary," Myla said. "It is sad to say this but by this time some of the Old Mermaids were frustrated with Sister Lyra Musica Mermaid. She used to be fun. She used to be strong. Sister Lyra

Musica Mermaid became more and more isolated. Mother Star Stupendous Mermaid tried to reassure her. She encouraged her to go back into the wash. 'Listen to the wind. Listen to the rocks. Listen to the birds. You will find your soul. It isn't lost. But you are. You'll find your way back to one another.'

"So Sister Lyra Musica Mermaid began walking the wash again even though she was afraid of Mr. Hunter. One afternoon as she was listening she heard a kind of dry whoosh. And then phet! There in the sand very close to her was this arrow. She pulled it out of the sand and marched up the rise over there and banged on Mr. Hunter's door. When he opened it, she said, 'Do you recognize this?' He shook his head quite vigorously. Sister Lyra Musica Mermaid said, 'Take a good look at me. And take a good look at my sister mermaids. We are not your prey. If you're so hungry that you have to try to shoot mermaids, you are in serious trouble.' Mr. Hunter sputtered and spouted and didn't know what to say. 'Would you like our help?' she asked. 'We have plenty of food and you are welcome to share with us.' He finally said that might be a good thing.

"Sister Lyra Musica Mermaid brought him down to the Old Mermaid Sanctuary and showed him around. Mother Star Stupendous Mermaid and Sister Faye Mermaid negotiated with him to help around the sanctuary in exchange for his meals. He promised never to hunt around his house or the sanctuary again. 'Can I have my arrow back?' he asked. 'You may not,' Sister Lyra Musica Mermaid said. She took the arrow and went back into the wash. As she walked, she noticed that it said 'gold stalker.' Only the letters were all mashed together. She decided she liked 'golds talker' better. She wanted to be a golds talker. She figured a gold talker would be a good talker so a golds talker would be a great talker!"

Stefan and David laughed.

130

"And Sister Lyra Musica Mermaid started talking. She began telling stories about the Old Mermaids. And she painted mermaids too. She put mermaids everywhere. At first she painted mermaids in the sea. But then she began painting Old Mermaids in the desert. On the mountains. In the valleys. Everywhere. Sometimes the Old Mermaids had tails. Sometimes they had legs. Sissy Maggie Mermaid helped her. They built an art and writing studio. Right up there. Mr. Hunter helped." Myla stopped and pointed. "The Old Mermaids could go up there to be by themselves and write or paint or play music. When they were ready, they'd share whatever they created with the others."

"So she found her soul?" Stefan asked.

"I think she did," Myla said. "She stopped being so afraid. Sometimes she would look at Mr. Hunter and wonder what all the fuss had been about."

"Mr. Hunter was a bad man," Lily said.

"No, I don't think he was," Myla said. "He was just nearsighted."

Lily held her hand up close to her face. "I can see close too."

Myla laughed.

"I'm glad he doesn't try to hit the Old Mermaids with arrows any more," Lily said. "Can I show the arrow to Ernesto?"

Myla nodded.

By this time, they had reached the house. Lily quietly allowed Stefan to untie himself from her. Then she ran into the house.

"Ernesto! Ernesto!"

"Lily! Don't run with that arrow!" Myla called.

Maria said, "I would like to call my parents to see if they have heard anything about Juan. Would that be all right?"

"Sure," David said. "You know where the phone is?"

"Yes, thank you." Maria went into the house.

"Stefan," Myla said, "you've been out of school for over two weeks now."

"That's all right," he said. "I was going to quit anyway."

"No, you are not," Myla said. "We need to get you back into school or at least get you a tutor for the next little while so you can catch up. Theresa was bringing you your school work, right?"

"Yes, but I haven't done much of it," he said.

"Why don't we look at it together?" David said. "Maybe I can help."

"That's good," Myla said. "And I know a boy who is a little older than you are, Stefan. He comes to the Church of the Old Mermaids. I'm sure he would come and help with your school work. Can I call him?"

"Sure," Stefan said.

Myla put her arm across Stefan's shoulders. "That was so enthusiastic."

Stefan smiled.

"You'll thank us later," Myla said.

"I'm just glad to be here," Stefan said. "I'll do whatever you want."

Myla glanced at him. She wasn't sure it was good for him to be so compliant.

They went into the house. When Maria finished with her phone call, she told Myla, "One of the men who went with Juan, Miguel Ortiz, has returned to the village. My father-in-law spoke with him. Miguel said they did cross together, but they got separated when the Border Patrol chased them. Miguel got caught, and he never saw Juan after that so he isn't sure what happened. On the way back home, a man told Miguel that he had seen Juan in Nogales working at one of the tourist shops, probably to get money to cross again. He didn't know if it was true or not. Could you or Theresa go to Nogales and look for him? I have a photograph of him you could take."

132

"Of course," Myla said. "This is good news, Maria. You look so tired. Are you all right?"

"I will be fine once we find Juan," she said.

"You said you missed your mother," Myla said. "Would you feel better if you went back home?"

Maria shook her head. "I need to find Juan. But what if he is dead? Then I may never know."

"I hope he isn't dead," Myla said. "But once we send in Lily's DNA you will have a more definitive answer to that question."

"I am very tired," Maria said. "I think I will go to sleep."

Myla watched her walk away. She wished she could do more to help her.

Myla phoned James and Trevor and arranged for Trevor to come over after school on Thursday and tutor Stefan. She also invited both over for dinner on Saturday.

After Myla got off the phone, Lily came and sat with her in the living room. David and Stefan sat at the kitchen table going over his school work.

"Mama is sleeping," Lily said. "Could you tie me to her now?"

"You'll be sleeping in the same bed," Myla said. "You'll be together. If I tie you, you might get tangled."

"But they keep going away," Lily said.

"Who, Lily my Lily?"

"Papa," she said. "Momma."

"Momma is just in the other room," Myla said. She put her arms around Lily and pulled her up onto her lap. Lily curled up snugly against her. "And at night I'll be right next door, and David, Ernesto, and Stefan are all here. When you wake up, everyone will still be here. I promise. You have your dreamcatcher?"

"Yes," Lily said. "It catches all my bad dreams."

"That's right," Myla said.

"And the Old Mermaids watch over me all night and day,"

Lily said.

"Come on, sweetheart. Why don't you help me with dinner."

Lily nodded and slid off Myla's lap. Soon everyone except Maria had congregated in the kitchen. Ernesto and Stefan peeled and chopped apples, bananas, and pears. Lily ripped up spinach and lettuce leaves. Myla and David cut up vegetables for steaming while the quinoa cooked.

"Did you have mermaids where you come from?" Stefan asked Ernesto.

"I don't remember mermaids when I was a boy," Ernesto said. "But when I traveled up the coast looking for work one summer, I heard stories about *la sirenas*. Especially when I went out fishing. The captain of one boat, The Dolphin, warned me that when we went past this certain pile of rocks off shore I should put something in my ears, so I would not hear. When I asked him why, he said the mermaids would try to lure us away from our wives and family with their siren songs. I did not have a wife or family then so I said I would not mind. I had seen pictures of *la sirenas* and—" He glanced at Lily. "—and they were very beautiful. Maybe I would marry one. So I left my ears open. The captain was not happy with me. He said if I jumped overboard and tried to swim to the mermaids, he would be angry. I said I was willing to take that risk. We went by the rocks the captain had warned me about, and I did begin to hear something. I could not understand the words. As we got closer, the sound grew louder, and I could see shapes on the rocks. My heart started racing. What if I was about to meet my truest love?"

"What happened?" Stefan asked.

Ernesto shrugged. "We got closer and I could see the shapes were only walruses. I laughed at the other men and the captain. They felt foolish, I think, and they told me that this time it was only walruses, but in the past they had heard *la sirenas*. I called

134

them many names as the boat went away from the rocks. I looked back once. And as I did so, I saw an arm and then another arm, as though someone had just awakened and was stretching. The body these arms belonged to unfolded itself and sat up, right there among the walruses. It was a woman. She was very beautiful. She had long dark hair that fell down over her front and back. I was very far away, but I was certain she had green eyes. Green like the sea, only it was as though her eyes were tiny green lights— lighthouse beacons. They seemed to go on and off, on and off. She looked at me and waved. I could not move! I could not cry out or wave. I could only look."

"Did you see her tail?" Stefan asked.

"I could not see a tail or legs," Ernesto said, "because the walruses blocked my view. Finally I was able to move and I raised my hand and waved. She smiled and picked up a ukulele and began playing it. I could hear the music. I turned and looked at my *compañeros*, but none of them had noticed. The boat moved away quickly and I could no longer see her. I never told the others because I did not want them to make fun of me. I thought of her for a long time."

"Do you think she was really a mermaid?" Stefan asked.

Ernesto said, "This is what I decided: It is a very old world. And the sea is the oldest of all. Who knows what is true about such things and what is false. I will tell you this, though. I do not think she was trying to get me to jump into the sea or to take me away from anything or anyone. I do not think her being on the rocks had much to do with us. She found herself a beautiful spot amongst friends and she was satisfied with that."

Lily clapped. "I like your mermaid! Do you think she was from here, Myla?"

"I think there are Old Mermaid Sanctuaries everywhere," Myla said. "Ernesto, you should come to the Church of the Old Mermaids with me and tell more stories."

"My English is not so good," he said. "Although it has gotten better, I will admit. But that is the only mermaid story I know."

"Maybe you will remember more," Myla said.

"What is a siren song?" Lily asked.

"That's one of those things that's gotten mixed up in the legends," Myla said. "They tell stories of horrible songs mermaids sing to make men jump in the water. That's silly. Every Old Mermaid—and every person—has her own siren song. It's something she starts creating when she's small. It's a combination of sound and poetry—it expresses her true self. Before the Old Sea dried up, the Old Mermaids would sit on rocks near shore and sing their songs. They are amazing creations, these songs. Completely truthful. Everyone has a siren song—it's not always a song, per se. It's whatever you do that you love completely, or that you think is really you. Something fluid, beautiful, all yours—and something that contributes to the community in some way. The Old Mermaids loved sitting together and singing their siren songs."

"I like that," Stefan said. "Maybe I'll try and figure out my siren song."

"Me too," Lily said. Lily began to hum. Stefan hummed along with her. Soon everyone in the kitchen was humming or laughing.

When dinner was ready, Myla went into the bedroom to awaken Maria. At first, she didn't move. Myla sat on the bed.

"Maria," she said, gently touching her shoulder. "It's time for dinner."

Maria finally opened her eyes. She slowly sat up.

"Are you not feeling well?" Myla asked. She put her arm across Maria's shoulders.

"I am not ill," Maria said. "I just can't seem to get enough sleep."

"May I ask you something?"

Maria nodded.

"How did you think you were going to find Juan when you got here?"

"I don't know," Maria said. "I thought I would be with people like me and I would ask them. I didn't think it would be like this. I didn't think the *guia* would leave us out in the desert. Will you go to Nogales tomorrow?"

"Yes, I'll go," Myla said.

After dinner, Myla tucked Lily into bed next to her mother. She convinced Lily to take off the orange rope for the night by promising "on the shiny colorful scales of the Old Mermaids' tails" that her mother would not leave her in the night.

"Will you tell me a story about the Old Mermaids?" Lily whispered.

"All right," she said. "What would you like to hear? I could tell you the story of how they solved the problem of Grand Mother Yemaya Mermaid snoring."

"Momma snores," Lily said.

"No!" Maria said.

"Yes," Lily said. "Sometimes it sounds like a very strange animal."

Myla laughed.

"Then you can imagine what Grand Mother Yemaya Mermaid sounded like when she snored. She slept alone, Grand Mother Yemaya Mermaid did, but nearly all the Old Mermaids could hear her snores, except for Sister Magdelene Mermaid who could sleep through a tidal wave. Truth to tell, Grand Mother Yemaya Mermaid had trouble sleeping after they left the Old Sea, at least in the beginning, so the others were reluctant to wake her and tell her she was snoring. They tried to figure out a way to stop the noise without disturbing Grand Mother Yemaya Mermaid.

"They shut her door and put something against the door, but they could still hear it. They tried shutting the window, but that only made her snore louder. One night the snores got so bad that one by one the Old Mermaids tiptoed into Grand Mother Yemaya Mermaid's room to try and figure out what to do. Sister Sophia Mermaid whispered that the problem was that Grand Mother Yemaya Mermaid was sleeping on her back. That was probably why her snores were raising the roof. Sister Ursula Divine Mermaid suggested tickling her with a feather. One of the Old Mermaids found a feather left by Rocky the Crow, and Sister Ursula Divine tickled Grand Mother Yemaya Mermaid's face with it. Didn't do any good.

"Sister Ruby Rosarita Mermaid thought the smell of something cooking might cause her to roll over, so she went to the kitchen and put on a pot of stew. Still Grand Mother Yemaya Mermaid snored. Mother Star Stupendous Mermaid suggested they go back to their respective beds and put a pillow over their ears. Sister Sheila Na Giggles Mermaid said she'd heard putting someone's fingers in ice water might help. Sister DeeDee Lightful Mermaid confessed she had tried that once with Sister Bea Wilder Mermaid and it hadn't made her turn over but it had produced other interesting results. Not funny, Sister Bea Wilder Mermaid reminded her.

"Sister Laughs A Lot Mermaid suggested Sister Bridget Mermaid whisper a sea chanty, which she did. 'Three times round the house her snores did go; three times round as she slept; three times round the house her snores did go; and three times round we wept.' Sister Lyra Musica Mermaid said, 'How's that going to make her turn over?' Sister Bridget Mermaid shrugged. She didn't do well on no sleep. They urged Sister Faye Mermaid to sing an effective chant. She sang, 'My bonnie lies over the ocean, my bonnie lies over the sea. So bring back, bring back, bring back my bonnie to me.' 'Wait,' Sissy Maggie Mermaid said, 'I think that's a song about a dead woman, isn't it?' 'So?' Sister Sophia Mermaid said. 'Death is part of life.' 'Granted,' Sissy Maggie Mermaid said, 'but how does that help get Grand Mother Yemaya Mermaid to turn over?' Just then Grand Mother Yemaya Mermaid hiccuped snored and snorted, and the Old Mermaids got very quiet so they wouldn't wake her. 'That gives me an idea,' Sister Lyra Musica Mermaid said. She hurried out of the room and the house. She stood on the lip of the wash and asked the moon and the Old Sea to give up their dead. Then she leaned over and saw what looked like an eye in the sand in the dark and she pulled it out of the dirt. You know what it was?"

"No," Lily whispered, her eyes closed, her voice sleepy.

"It was a sea shell," Myla said. "A small one but the kind you can put to your ear and hear the Old Sea still flowing, still roaring. She put it to her ear and listened to the Old Sea for a moment. Then she went to the house and into Grand Mother Yemaya's room where the other Old Mermaids still gathered. She put the sea shell near Grand Mother Yemaya's ear and then moved it away a bit. In her sleep, Grand Mother Yemaya Mermaid turned to follow the Old Sea shell, until she was on her side. The snoring immediately ceased. And you know what else? As Grand Mother Yemaya Mermaid listened to the sea in her sleep, the other Old Mermaids saw her tails in the dark, beautiful and luminous, like they had been when the Old Mermaids lived in the Old Sea. They wept and laughed at the beauty of it. All very quietly. The next morning, Grand Mother Yemaya Mermaid said she had had a wonderful sleep and glorious dreams of the Old Sea. Sister Lyra Musica Mermaid and Sister Sheila Na Giggles Mermaid hung the sea shell from the ceiling, right over the bed, so that Grand Mother Yemaya Mermaid could hear the Old Sea every night from then on."

Myla listened to the child and mother breathing together in sleep.

"Sweet dreams," she whispered.

She went into the living room and made certain the lock on the door to the patio and the pool was turned. It was higher than Lily could reach, even if she dragged a chair over and stood on it.

Stefan and David sat at the kitchen table going over Stefan's homework. She kissed the top of Stefan's head.

"Get some sleep," she said. "It's been a big day for you. You have a lot to think about."

"Can I keep the arrow for a while?" Stefan asked.

"Of course," Myla said.

"It'll remind me—it'll remind me not to be afraid," he said. He looked up at her.

"I'll walk you to the barn," David said.

"Sure," Myla said. "There might be some ol' coyote out there waiting to sing me a song."

"You never know," David said.

"Good night," Myla said to Stefan.

David and Myla stepped off the porch and into the darkness. Myla stopped for a moment to let her eyes adjust before she kept walking.

"You want some company going to Nogales tomorrow?" David asked.

"Sure. That would be great," Myla said. "I don't know if I'll find out anything. Theresa usually does this sort of thing, but she's leaving the Old Mermaid Sanctuary."

"Did she tell you that today?" he asked. "I hope it wasn't because I found out."

140

"A lot of things happened today," Myla said. "It has been a very eventful day. I had this quiet uncomplicated life until last Saturday. Then everything changed. I don't blame you, however."

"Me? Why would you blame me?"

"Because that's the day you got to town," Myla said.

David laughed. "I don't think you've been living an uncomplicated life."

Myla shrugged. "It felt uncomplicated. Now it's as if everything is unraveling, as they say. One thing the Old Mermaids have taught me is that things change. I appreciate you letting Stefan stay here by the way, although I think we're postponing the inevitable. He needs to go back with his mother." They stopped at the door to her apartment. "And now, I'm very tired, David Thomas Crow, and I am going to bed. We'll leave about eight a.m. Okay? Good night." She hugged him. He kissed her cheek as they let each other go.

"Sweet dreams," he said. "I'll pack us a lunch."

Myla did not fall asleep right away. This was unusual. She had not had trouble sleeping since she first moved to the Old Mermaid Sanctuary. She had had the occasional sleepless night, of course. She did not ordinarily fuss over details of the day, yet that was exactly what was happening this night. She kept wondering if Cathy would return to the sanctuary with her abusive husband. And now that Theresa was quitting, should Myla go on with the Old Mermaid Sanctuary without her? What about Lily and Maria? And David. How could someone she had not seen in a decade seem so familiar to her?

Then there was the mermaid tile—and this niggling feeling that she had misinterpreted her dream all those years ago. Dream, vision, whatever it was she experienced the night after a particularly serious drunk. A night she barely remembered—except for the dream—and maybe an argument with George. She also had a vague memory of making love with George before the argument. Was that before or after she had dinner with David? Not that anything that happened before the dream really mattered. What was important to her was the dream. Whenever she recounted the dream out loud, she knew it did not sound spectacular. Dreams were like that. What was horrific or wonderful to one person seemed silly or ordinary to another. But after she dreamed of the Old Mermaids in the wash, her life changed. It had already changed the moment she caught her husband with George's wife. After the dream, it changed again, this time for the better. After the dream, she had a purpose. A mission.

No, it was more than that. She sat up in bed. The Old Mermaids in her dream wanted her to join them—to be a part of them and the great Old Sea and all that meant. After she dreamed of the Old Mermaids and found the bottle in the wash, she understood that she was not alone in this world—she was loved, she was wanted just the way she was, and more was happening in the world than she could ever know. That had been a wonderful gift. She smiled. It was still a wonderful gift.

So what if she had forgotten about the mermaid tile in her old house? She still had the dream. She still had the stories. She had the Old Mermaids. Her ex-husband could not take that from her. No one could.

She lay down again and closed her eyes. This time she fell to sleep.

Seven

Sing, dance, create. If you have to choose one, do
all three at once.   *Sister Bridget Mermaid*

Myla dreamed a grizzly bear was stalking her. Once she got away
from the bear, a mountain lion and a jaguar came after her, one
on each side. She kept climbing higher and higher to get away
from them. When she could go no further, she looked down and
saw water. She either had to jump or let the cats get her. She
decided to jump. She pushed away from the mountain and fell.
On either side of her, the cats fell too. She awakened before she
hit water.

It was dawn. She cooked and ate oatmeal; then she walked the
wash, not in search of treasure but to look over the properties.
She went inside each house. Everything appeared to be as it
should. The Ford house was a bit cold since she'd left the windows open all night to air it out, but otherwise it looked as deserted and empty as it had before Stefan and Cathy arrived. When

she returned to the Crow house, David, Stefan, Ernesto, and Lily were eating breakfast. Tortillas and eggs. As always, Lily ran into Myla's arms and let her give her a wet kiss on the cheek. Myla sat at the table with them while they ate.

When it was time for Myla and David to leave for Nogales, Myla instructed Ernesto and Stefan on how to care for Lily.

"Until her mother awakens, you need to keep an eye on her," Myla said. "If you're not out at the pool, those doors need to stay locked so she can't go by herself. You understand this, right, Lily?" Lily nodded. "And no roughhousing, Stefan. She's too young."

"Myla," Stefan said, "I've baby-sat before."

"I'm not a baby," Lily said.

"And her mother is in the bedroom," Stefan said.

"I am going to sit in the spa," Ernesto said. "She can sit beside me and tell me stories. But you can't come into the spa, *niña*. It's too hot for you."

"Trevor might show up to tutor you before I get home," Myla said. "He's a friend of mine, Stefan. I've known him for a long time."

"I promise I'll be nice to him," Stefan said.

"I wasn't worried about whether you'd be nice to him or not," Myla said. "We'll see you later."

"Don't burn the house down," David said.

Myla rolled her eyes. "Don't give them any ideas."

Myla drove her and David out of the Old Mermaid Sanctuary and onto Speedway. They hit construction a couple of miles out. David and Myla sat quietly, listening to the radio: zydeco. Beau Jacques. Myla put the car into park and danced inside the car, putting her hands up, moving her body. David laughed and did the same. They opened the windows and zydeco music spilled out into the warm blue day. Myla imagined the entire road suddenly filled with people dancing and singing. No one moved, however, at least not that she could tell. Everyone remained inside their cars, their windows up.

"Paved paradise," Myla murmured, "and put up a parking lot."

Finally traffic cleared. They stopped at a photocopy place to make an extra copy of Juan's photograph. Then they drove out of town and headed south. The desert rolled by. Haze covered distant mountains.

"It needs to rain," Myla said. "Then it will clear all of this out."

David nodded. "It would help if we had some mass transportation out here."

"People love their cars," Myla said. "They don't care so much about their lungs."

David laughed. "She says as she drives."

"So David," Myla said. "What are you going to do now?"

"I don't know yet," he said. "I'm taking a break."

"A break? That sounds like a good idea," she said. "Maybe I'll take a break, too."

"From the Old Mermaids?"

"Maybe," she said. "With Theresa leaving, I need to think about the Church of the Old Mermaids. I didn't start bringing people to the houses right away, you know. I should show you the binder. I take photos and write things down about each visitor, so that I can show the owners one day."

"Just before they haul you off to jail?" David asked.

"I suppose," Myla said. "It seems impossible that people can go to jail for helping other people."

"Some people view illegal immigrants as criminals," David said. "And what you're doing is definitely illegal."

Myla was silent.

"I don't think they're criminals, and I don't think you're a criminal," David said. "But I am worried about you."

"You don't see me for ten years and now you're worried about me?" Myla laughed. "That is funny, David."

"I didn't worry about you before because I didn't know what you were doing," David said.

"What about you?" Myla asked. "What have you been doing for the last decade?"

"I told you I was working in Chicago," he said.

"What about your life, though?" she asked. "Have you fallen in love? Do you have a girl?"

"I did have a girlfriend," he said. "Although it seems a bit strange at my age to have a girlfriend."

"You had a lover then," Myla said.

"That sounds even more peculiar," he said. "As though a relationship can be defined by one aspect of it. But yes, we lived together for a few years, but she left me. She said I wasn't available to her."

"What did that mean?" Myla asked.

"She said I wasn't all there," David said.

Myla laughed.

"No, not like that," David said. "I was physically there, but I wasn't emotionally present."

"Many men are like that," Myla said. "It's a cultural thing. You're raised to stand on your own. If you show up, you figure that's enough. I don't mean you, I mean men."

"I don't like being put in a slot with other men like that," David said. "We don't all act the same, you know."

"Yes, I know David."

"I was unhappy at work. I know that sounds like an excuse. But I didn't have a lot to say to her at the end of the day. I think I was afraid I'd wake up one day and she'd be gone. And then one day she was."

"I'm sorry it didn't work out," Myla said. "Were you going to

146

marry?"

"We talked about it," David said. "I wanted to leave my job, and she wanted to buy a house. I wanted to get back to my art. She didn't even know I painted. It wasn't her fault. I didn't tell her. She might have thought it was great. I don't know. She wanted so many things. I couldn't give her everything she needed."

"No one can give another person everything they need," Myla said. "That just does not happen. And why should it?"

"Didn't you think your husband would make you happy?"

"No," Myla said. "I was glad he loved me. It is a relaxing thing to be loved. And I felt relaxed. When he didn't love me, I wasn't relaxed. In the beginning. Now I feel better. At least most of the time."

"Did you fall in love again?"

"No," she said. "What can a man do for me that I can't do for myself?"

David laughed. "Do you want me to answer that?"

"You mean sex?" Myla made a noise. "It is nice, sex. But it's not everything. And all the other stuff that comes along with it. My ex-husband was a control freak. He wanted everything done his way. He made a pretense of talking to me about things, but then he'd keep talking and talking until I got exhausted and I had to agree with him to get him to stop! I don't want that again."

"Not everyone is like that," David said.

"I know," Myla said. "Do you want to get back to your art? Now your house is full. When will you get the time?"

"I like a full house," he said. "I don't need to be by myself to do art. I've been having fun with everyone around. I feel more relaxed. And the kids seem to be relaxing too. They really liked working on the Old Mermaid cards."

"The same thing happens when I tell stories. I notice people kind of settle down or something. Not like they're sedated or anything like that—it's like what I said about being loved. They relax. We need art and stories and ceremony, and we don't have it. Not really."

"Art does a body good," David said. "All the studies say so."

Myla laughed. "Maybe you'll start your own art school for kids. It could be organic art—creating art from found materials. Turning trash into art. I like that idea."

"You create stories from found material," David said. "We could combine our talents. Call it the Old Mermaid School of Telling Tales and Finding Art. OMSOTTAFA. Sounds like a mantra. Remember we used to talk about starting a school together."

"Just a fairy tale, though, isn't it?"

"Who knows," David said.

An hour later, Myla drove the car into a dirt parking lot across from the Burger King in Nogales, Arizona. She paid a man with Mayan features wearing a fluorescent orange vest four dollars. She touched her own face. Were her ancestors Mayan? Her mother was Anglo, her father Mexican American. Perhaps she was distantly related to the man in the orange vest. But then she believed she was related to everyone and everything, including the trees, animals, stones, and the Moon and Stars. She was grateful to whichever ancestor had gifted her with that particular attitude.

The Mayan man told her they could cut through the parking lot to get to the entrance to Mexico. Myla thanked him, and she and David left the lot and went across a paved parking lot, past a Mexican bus, and down to the street. Myla had been here many times, so she confidently led David across the street and down the concrete stairs. On the left hand side of them, people leaving Mexico crowded the screened walkway. She and David walked under a sign that read "To Mexico." Hardly anyone walked with them into Mexico.

"Have you been here before?" Myla asked.

"No," David said.

"Really? Gail never comes here either. She hates it."

"Why?"

"She says there's too many foreigners," Myla said.

David laughed. "And she's your friend?"

"She means there are too many Americans."

"Oh, I figured she was being an ugly American," he said.

"She's certainly capable of that," Myla said. "I've been here with her a couple of times. She could bargain the tail off a mermaid. She likes negotiations."

They walked by a row of offices, a pair of restrooms, and a line of people, all of which paralleled the border wall behind the building. They stepped off the walk onto the streets of Nogales, Mexico. Most of Myla's friends hated *la frontera* towns. Too many drugs, prostitutes, poverty. She agreed all that was true, yet she was fascinated by the border. It was alarming and tantalizing that life could be so different on either side of an arbitrary line. An artificial line. A political line. On one side of the line was Burger King and Taco Bell. On one side of the line nothing seemed possible. On the other side everything seemed possible. And the possibilities changed. Switched. Here it was possible to dream of a better life. There reality set in. Here reality set in. There mermaids were a memory. Here you could hear their songs. Here everything was different. There everything was the same. Now...switch.

Thresholds. That was what it was. *La frontera* was a threshold. Like the wash. A betwixt and between place. Magic existed. Even though the magic was sometimes cruel and arbitrary.

So many souls crossed that line looking for the promised land. The promised land was in your heart, Myla wanted to say, but she realized only a person who had enough to eat had the freedom to make such a statement.

Now she and David stood in the street. To their right, a twelve foot fence went up the hill and beyond. Someone had spray-painted words in huge block letters: FRONTERAS: CICATRICES EN LA TIERRA. BORDERS: SCARS IN THE EARTH. Below the barbed wire, two white crosses hung from the fence.

"If we get separated we'll meet at the church up there," Myla said, pointing down the street. "Do you see it?"

David nodded. They began walking. Men lined both sides of the streets.

"Pharmacy?" one of them called as Myla and David walked by.

Myla shook her head. Others called out too. She scanned their faces, looking for Juan.

They walked by a curio shop. "Come in, this way. This way. We'll give you a good price."

Myla ducked into the shop.

"No customers today," the man said. "No money, no tacos. I've got a wife and two kids. You want to buy something? Name it."

"Have you seen this man?" Myla asked in Spanish. She pulled out the photo of Juan and showed it to the man. "He's not in trouble. His wife and daughter are worried about him."

"No, no," the man said. "What about a purse? You need a new purse. I'll give you a good price."

"No, *gracias*," she said.

Myla walked through the crowded store. Curios hung from the ceiling and were packed into every part of the building. She was surrounded by so much stuff that she could not see it all. Blankets. Talavera dishes. Catrina dolls. Purses. Jackets. Her eyes slid over it all. She was looking for a man. One particular man. She walked to the back of the store which opened into more and more shops.

150

"You like the talavera?" one of the men asked in English. "I can give you a good price. *Patrone!* How much can I sell this for? *Patrone!*"

Myla smiled and shook her head. He was not the man. Her fingers touched the talavera plates.

"Beautiful, aren't they?" the man said. "I'll give you a good price."

"They are beautiful," Myla said in Spanish. Even if they were painted by numbers—and she didn't know how they were painted—each plate had been handled by a human being. That human being had painted this green, that purple, the other yellow. Had their working conditions been safe? Were they allowed to delight in their artistry? Did they take breaks to dance?

"You have no customers today?" Myla said. "It's slow this time of year."

"Yes, no one is coming," he said. "And as they say, no money, no honey."

Myla laughed. She had heard that one before.

"I'm looking for someone," she said.

"I can be that someone," the man said.

Myla smiled. He was teasing her, but she appreciated his good nature. He was having fun.

Myla held up the photograph. "He's not in trouble. He crossed the border about three months ago and has been missing since. His wife and daughter are looking for him. That's them with him."

The man shook his head. "It is sad. So many die now. Many more get across, of course, so maybe it is worth the trip. I tried when I was younger. I didn't like it. You?"

"I was born there," Myla said. "So were my parents and grandparents. Some of my ancestors were Mexican. They just happened to be on the north side when the line was drawn."

"You've checked with *la migra*?" the man asked.

"Of course," Myla said, "but what do they know and what would they tell us?"

"Even if you found the *guia* who took him over, you would learn nothing," he said. "To the coyotes, they aren't wetbacks; they're greenbacks. Once the coyote gets the money from the *pollos*, they forget their faces. Your friend has probably made a new life for himself. Or else he's dead."

Myla nodded. She glanced behind her. David was gone. At some point, they had gotten separated. She continued through the store and out into the alleyway. Men and women cajoled her to come inside and buy something. She went into nearly every store and showed Juan's photograph. She passed several Mayan women huddled by the curb, surrounded by children, selling gum. On one street corner a man stood beside a donkey and a cart, waiting for a fare. The donkey wore a sombrero around his neck. Across the street another donkey flicked his tail sleepily. Nearby an old woman sat by her food cart, rolling white tortillas. Myla kept walking. So many people called out to her.

"No money, no tacos." "I've got to eat. I got children to feed." "I'll make a good price for you." "What do you need? Name it, just name it."

Myla started to feel a bit dizzy. She stepped into a nearly empty bakery. She breathed deeply as she closed the door behind her. Had she been in the desert so long that she could no longer handle crowds? Only it was not that crowded. The people on the streets were brown. Just like her. Only different. What if it had been the other way around and the north side of the line had become the "wrong" place to be economically—what if she had to cross the desert to feed her family?

She shook herself. Why had she come here? What chance did she have of finding Juan in a few hours? Why would anyone tell her anything? She knew how it all worked—human smuggling.

She knew the process: step one, step two. She had seen photographs of the inside of a stash house — a *clavo*. She had heard the stories of what happened when something went wrong, when people wandered the desert without water or got lost or were abandoned. A few of those times she had been there to save one of those people. What would have happened if she had not started wandering the desert? What if she had not dreamed of the Old Mermaids? Would Grace and Roberto have died? What about Lily and Maria?

She picked up tongs and a round tin tray from a shelf next to the door and went to the window and put two *bolillos* onto the tray. She took the tray to the counter. A woman with blue eyelids and rusty-colored lips dropped the rolls into a paper sack and handed it to her. Myla gave her an American dollar. The woman returned change. Not a word passed between them. Myla smiled. The woman looked away from her.

Myla went back outside. She walked down the block to the church. The doors were open. Men sat on the steps. She waited on the steps for a few minutes before David appeared. He shook his head. She handed him a *bolillo*. They stood together on the steps eating and watching men on a scaffold across the street.

"No one recognized the photograph," Myla said, "and I didn't see him."

"I didn't either," David said. "But there are more shops."

"What's it like for you being here?" Myla asked. "An Anglo man in a brown world instead of the other way around."

"I'm always in the minority," David said. "I'm a good man in a bad world looking for love in all the wrong places."

Myla laughed. "Very funny, David Thomas Crow. Back into the breach. Meet you here after we finish."

David reached for her hand and squeezed it, then they separated. Myla took a breath and stepped onto the sidewalk again.

This time she was able to ignore the calls from the merchants and beggars: It all became a kind of white noise, like radio commercials. At one point she saw a man with a mermaid on his T-shirt, so she followed him, hoping he would lead her to Juan. But he didn't. No one did.

Sometime later, she met David at the church. They decided they had gone to most of the tourist shops in town. Even if they hadn't, it seemed impossible that they would actually find Juan.

Myla and David returned to the border entrance and stood in line. An older blond border guard questioned a man from Cuba who had no identification. Myla tugged on David's sleeve and they moved to the next line, where a dark young guard cheerfully called out names of those wishing to enter the United States.

"You are a citizen from what country?" he asked when Myla got to him.

"The United States," she said, handing him her driver's license.

"Myla! Thank you, Myla!" he said. "Have a good day. And you sir, are a citizen of what country?"

"The United States," David said.

"David! Of David and Goliath fame!" the guard said. "Have a good day!"

Myla and David laughed quietly and hurried out of the tunnel and into the bright blue day.

"Let's go into the desert and have lunch," Myla said. "I'll show you where I found Lily and Maria."

They left Nogales—this time David drove—and headed up Highway 19 until they got to the signs for Arivica. Then they turned off the highway. The road wound through the mesquite-dotted hillsides for a long while. As they went through the tiny town of Arivica, a white Border Patrol pickup and van passed them. A white Border Patrol car with a green stripe travelled by them in the opposite direction.

"They're everywhere," Myla said. "On the way back to Tucson we'll have to go through a checkpoint, you know."

"But we're in the United States," David said.

"Doesn't seem to matter," she said.

"How did you get Maria and Lily through?"

"I returned to Tucson another way," she said. "Wasn't that difficult."

Myla parked at a trailhead near a group of cottonwoods. David and Myla got out of the car and stretched. It was a dry, quiet day. David took the small cooler from the trunk and followed Myla into the woods. They walked above the dry wash. Myla smiled and waved to the cottonwoods.

"How have you been?" she called to the trees. "I love these old trees."

"I heard jaguars were coming back into the United States somewhere near this area," David said.

Myla nodded. "They like washes, too. Wouldn't it be something if they do come back and stay? Actually thrive. So far they think there is only one jaguar, maybe two of them. It is an amazing thing—a valiant effort I heard someone say—a valiant effort by the jaguars to return to this part of the world. Jaguars don't do well with barriers across their territory. Many animals will not cross artificial barriers, so a wall on the border isn't good for them. I dreamed of a jaguar last night, come to think of it. A jaguar and a mountain lion were after me."

"What does that mean?"

"I see dreams as gifts," Myla said. "Like moving art pieces. Literally moving, I mean. You don't always know what a painting means, but you can still enjoy it or dislike it. I'm not sure if I liked this dream or not. As for meaning: I'm not sure what it meant."

Myla led them down the trail and into the wash. She stopped at a downed tree. "This is a good place," she said. "It's shady. Look at the footprints in the sand. All sorts of creatures have been going to and fro here."

They sat on the log together. David unpacked two small glass dishes filled with cold quinoa, peas, and wild salmon. He gave one dish to Myla and opened the other one. Myla handed him a fork and napkin. They ate quietly for a while. A woodpecker hammered a nearby tree.

"I found Lily and Maria not far from here," Maria said. "I don't think they had an easy crossing."

"I don't really understand how it all works," David said. "I've heard of coyotes, but I don't know much beyond that."

"I don't like the term coyote when it's used to describe a human smuggler because they are often not very respectable. Why denigrate a coyote? They're pretty amazing animals. So I don't use that term. Maria probably went to an *enganchador*—a recruiter—maybe even someone local to start the process. She would have had to pay him. Then he probably sold her and Lily to an *encaminador*; he's the one who took them to a stash house. A *clavo*, they call it. They're locked inside this place with dozens of other people. They're not very nice places, not very sanitary, to say the least. The *encargado*—the guy in charge of the stash house—is paid to keep them locked up and to keep any other gangs from stealing the *pollos*—yes, they call them chickens.

"A *guia*, or guide, takes them to *el otro lado*, the other side. Once across, they sometimes have to stay in another stash house, although I don't think Lily and Maria did. The *guia* takes them to the *chofer*—that's usually a couple of guys with a van. But to get to the *chofer* is often the most dangerous part these days. The migrants usually have to walk in the desert for a long time. The *chofer* takes them to the *repartidor*, who takes them to a place where they can get somewhere else—like an airport, bus station.

156

In between all that, of course, the migrants can die, the women can be raped. They can also get stolen by other gangs. Maria and Lily never got as far as the *chofer*. The people we find in the desert rarely get that far."

"That's more complicated than I thought," David said.

"In the nineties, it was decided to step up patrols around the border towns," Myla said. "So what happened is that most people began crossing away from the towns, in the country. The rationale for all this beefed up security was that drugs were coming across the border—terrorism became the reason later. It turns out that only eight percent of the drugs come across the Mexican border. Now these ranches and small towns are inundated with migrants and some drug traffickers. This has lots of implications obviously, including harm to the land from all the foot traffic and trash left behind. This impacts the quality of life for the ranchers and inhabitants of the small towns. And the migrants aren't prepared for the desert, so they die. The U.S. needs to come up with a sane border policy. I don't think much about the politics of it all because I have no control over that. I just want to help the people. They always seem so lost—probably because when I find them they actually are lost."

"Sounds like quite a business," David said.

Myla remembered what the man in Nogales had called the migrants: greenbacks.

"And that's only one way of crossing," she said. "The ways change all the time. Oops. I forgot the water in the car. I'll go get it."

Myla slipped off the log and hurried up the trail out of the arroyo. A white pickup was now parked next to their car. Maybe the Border Patrol wanted to lunch in the woods too. Myla unlocked the trunk of her car and reached in and took out two water bottles.

"May I see your papers?" a man's voice asked in Spanish.

Myla turned around. "You startled me," she said in English. A man in a brown uniform stood a few feet from the car, his legs slightly apart.

"May I see your papers?" he repeated in English.

She squinted at him. She wanted to say, "Show some respect. Take off those sunglasses." Instead she said, "What papers? I'm an American citizen. Since when are we supposed to have papers? I'm out here having a picnic with a friend of mine and you're asking me for some nonexistent papers. This reminds me of those movies of Nazi Germany I used to watch when I was a child. The Nazis were always asking the Jews for their papers. Oh wait, and me without my brown star! Or cross. Or whatever it is I should be wearing to show you that I understand that you see me as an outsider."

The Border Patrol officer took off his sunglasses.

"I work for Immigration and—"

"And you can do whatever the hell you want," Myla said. "I know that. You don't need probable cause. You don't need anything. You think I've got brown skin so I have to prove I belong here. My people have been here longer than your people."

"Actually, ma'am," the man said, "I'm Mexican and Indian. So my people are your people."

"Then you should be ashamed of yourself," Myla said.

She knew she should stop talking. This was not really something she did. She prodded, she told stories, she cajoled. She didn't yell.

Until now.

"We've had a lot of illegals through here," the man said. "It's not safe for a woman such as yourself."

"Not safe? What? Are they going to mug me for my job!"

The man stepped back from her. She knew she was fortunate

158

he was not an angry young man.

"And I'm just doing my job," he said.

Myla shut the trunk and started to walk away. "*Vaquero*," she murmured.

"You sound like *mi madre*," he said. "She calls me a cowboy too. She wants me to quit."

Myla stopped and turned around. "She's probably worried about you."

"When I didn't have a job she was worried," the man said. "I can't seem to please her."

"What is your name?" Myla said.

"Ruben Morales," he said.

"I am Myla Alvarez," she said. She held out her hand, and he shook it. "How do you do?"

"I do all right," he said. "It's a nice day and I'm out of doors."

"Harassing old ladies," Myla said.

"Hardly old," he said. "My mother is older than you and she says she wears her oldness proudly. That's what she calls it. Her Oldness. Like Her Highness. She's very funny."

"She sounds like a good woman," Myla said. "But why are you so worried about pleasing her? It would please her if you are safe and happy."

"With a job," he said. "She wanted me to be a dentist."

Myla laughed. "Why'd you ask me for my papers?"

"I meant to ask you for your ID," the man said. "I guess it was a slip of the tongue. I don't really like being compared with the Nazis, by the way."

"I apologize for that," Myla said. "Doesn't it worry you that you have such broad powers? Within a hundred miles of the border you can stop anyone without any real justification."

"I couldn't come into your house," he said. "I could call the local police and have them come into your house, but I couldn't do that."

"How comforting," Myla said.

"When I saw you, I thought of my mother," he said. "I haven't seen her in a few weeks."

"A hello would have been nicer," she said.

"You're right," he said.

Myla smiled.

He didn't seem to want to leave. "Sometimes we actually help people," he said. "I know we send them back to Mexico, but when I was working the Devil's Highway, especially in the summer, we'd often find people who were almost dead—who would have died if we hadn't been there."

"So why'd you arrest those people for trying to transport the men they'd found in the desert to a hospital? I don't mean you personally."

"We do what they tell us to do," he said. "Homeland Security."

Myla made a noise.

"We don't always find them in time," Ruben said. "Once I carried out a seven year old girl. She was so tiny. And warm. Her head lay against my chest. I could almost imagine that she was asleep and I was carrying her to her bed. I didn't know if she'd been dead five minutes, five hours, or five days. And I wanted to know. I had dreams for a long time about her. Everywhere I went in my dreams I'd find her right around the corner and she'd die seconds before I found her. I kept wondering if I could have saved her if I'd left sooner that day or if I'd made my partner drive faster. If only something had been different. Sometimes I feel like she's haunting me." He shook his head. "I wasn't angry with her. I don't get angry much at the migrants. I get angry at the coyotes, the *guias*, who bring them into the desert. I get angry at the whole screwed up system."

"Let me tell you something," Myla said, "but you have to promise not to tell anyone else, especially the Border Patrol." She smiled. "I was here one afternoon, down in that wash, and I heard a child crying. I walked the wash until I saw a little girl, her hair in two ponytails. Her eyes were closed and her face was stained with tears. She looked so afraid. I said to her in Spanish, 'Well look what has washed up on my shores.' I don't think she understood, but she held out her arms to me, and I embraced her. From that second on, I knew I would lay down my life for her; it was as though I had given birth to her—or she to me. I gave her water and a sandwich, and then her mother returned and I gave her the same. If I hadn't been there, they might have died. I was glad I was there that day. And even though you did not find that little girl before she died, it was good you were there because you carried her away from the place where she died. You carried her with respect and tenderness. Maybe she isn't haunting you. Maybe she is reminding you that everyone you meet deserves to be treated with dignity. And even if you don't think they deserve it, you deserve it. You deserve to go to sleep each night knowing you did the best you could. At least, that is what I think."

"We never found her mother or father or whoever was responsible for her. That night I lit a candle and said a prayer for her."

They stood in silence for a bit. This was what Myla loved about the desert almost more than anything: the silence.

"May she rest in peace," Myla said. "And may you live in peace, Ruben Morales."

"What happened to the little girl you found?" Ruben asked.

"That is a story for a different day," Myla said. She looked at his face and into his eyes. She wondered if she could trust him. "Well, since you asked and we are friends now, I'll show you their photograph."

She pulled the picture from her pocket and held it out to him. "That's Maria and the little girl is Lily. The man holding her is

Juan Martinez. He's been missing for three months. They've been everywhere looking for him, even the morgue. Have you seen him?"

Ruben Morales took the photograph and looked at it carefully. He shook his head.

"I don't think I've seen him," he said. "But I could have. He could still be out in the desert. I don't think we find even half the bodies. But he could be alive and just hasn't been able to get in touch. Maybe he got involved in drugs or maybe he found another woman. It happens."

"I know," Myla said. "But I know his daughter, and it's difficult to imagine him deserting her. Or his wife. Keep the photograph. In case you see him. My friend and I are having lunch in the wash. Would you like to join us? He's legal."

Ruben smiled. "I need to get back to work and find someone who wants to mug me for my job."

"Give my regards to your mother," Myla said.

"What would you like me to do in case I find this Juan Martinez?" he asked. "Send him to you, Myla Alvarez?"

She stared at him. Was he his mother's son?

"If you find him on your time off," she said, "you could send him to me. Every Saturday I'm on Fourth Avenue at the Church of the Old Mermaids in Tucson."

He started to laugh. "You're kidding? Talk about your small world. My mother keeps telling me I should visit the Church of the Old Mermaids. She says that the woman who runs it will have just the thing I need. She must have been talking about you. She went once not long after my father died. She picked up a piece of broken mirror. You told her the story of one of the Old Mermaids who was feeling lost and lonely—she missed the Old Sea. I forget the name of the mermaid. My mother knows."

"Sister Ursula Divine Mermaid," Myla said.

162

"You remember?"

Myla nodded. "What was the rest of the story?"

"The Old Mermaid found a piece of mirror in the wash," he said. "And she was certain it was a mirror they had had when they were still in the sea, when they were still mermaids. She wanted to find all the pieces. She became obsessed with it. If she found all the pieces, she thought everything would be all right again. She wanted her old life back—even though none of the other Old Mermaids would have guessed she was having any trouble with her new life. To everyone else she seemed absolutely comfortable in the new world. Mom said that wild animals were drawn to this Old Mermaid, and she never seemed afraid.

"Anyway—what'd you say her name was? Ursula Divine? She couldn't find any more pieces of the mirror. She kept that one piece on her dresser. In the morning, she'd glance at it to see how she looked. To comb her hair, things like that. It kept falling over because it was a fragment and wasn't shaped like a mirror. Plus she kept cutting herself on it. So she went out to the wash and found some pieces of wood and built a kind of frame around the glass, just until she found the other pieces. Eventually, she hung the framed piece on the wall. Every day she looked at herself. After a while, she forgot that the piece of mirror wasn't a whole mirror—she didn't actually forget, I suppose. She realized it was a mirror on its own, and she began to recognize herself in the mirror. She stopped looking for the lost pieces, and she went on with her life. You told this all to my mother. She brought the broken piece of mirror home and framed it, just like the Old Mermaid had in the story."

"Rosa Morales," Myla said.

Ruben shook his head. "You remember her. Coming to the Church of the Old Mermaids and talking to you meant a lot to her. She looks into that mirror every day. It still hurts, she told

163

me, but she realized she still has a life."

"I'm so glad," Myla said.

"I hope you find Juan Martinez," he said. He reached for her hand and shook it, then held it for a moment.

"I hope so too," Myla said. "Now you be careful out there. Don't forget to say hello to your mother."

"I won't," he said. "She'll get such a kick out of this."

Myla watched Ruben get into his truck and drive away. Then she hurried down the path and into the wash where David waited.

"I was starting to worry," David said. Myla tossed him a water bottle.

"I met up with the Border Patrol," Myla said. "He thought I was illegal. He actually asked for my papers. I was so mad. Then I thought, what would the Old Mermaids do and I got calmer. We had a conversation. It turned out his mother had been to the Church of the Old Mermaids! One of those great small world stories. I told him about Juan."

"You think that's safe?" he asked.

"My judgment about people has been fairly reliable," Myla said. "Up until recently. I thought it was worth the risk. What if he had seen Juan? Wouldn't that have been something? But it was enough that we talked, and I got to hear someone tell me one of my stories."

"I'm glad," David said.

"Do you want me to show you where I found Lily and Maria? It's nearby."

"Okay."

They left the cooler and walked away from the downed tree and followed the curves of the wash. Myla stopped near an old gnarled cottonwood, its roots partially exposed and reaching across the wash.

"Lily was over here," Myla said, pointing to the tree. "She was crying. Then I saw Maria up there out of the wash. You can see all these footprints here. Probably from migrants. I don't think they're prints from hikers. And this old plastic water jug, that's telltale."

"But this isn't far from a road and a town," David said.

"That's true," Myla said. "But Maria didn't know that. Plus she was here illegally. She didn't want anyone to find them." Myla stood in the sun. She closed her eyes and breathed deeply. When she opened her eyes again, she said, "I think something happened out here that scared Lily and is troubling Maria."

David looked around. "This would be a frightening place to be all night."

"Yes." She sighed. "I guess we should finish lunch, then go tell Maria we could not find her husband."

They returned to the fallen tree. David pulled the food from the cooler again.

"Myla," David said, after he took a drink of water, "remember I told you I wanted to talk to you about some things."

"Uh-huh," she said.

"Well, I think it's time," he said. He cleared his throat. He glanced at her, then down at his sandwich. He looked up again. "When I first met you all those years ago, I really liked you. We were friends right away. Even though you were having trouble, you were still articulate and passionate. I loved you very much."

"I was glad we were friends then too," Myla said.

"No, Myla. I fell in love with you."

Myla looked at him. "What are you talking about? You never told me this."

"Actually I did," David said. "Remember the night of your dream? You and I had dinner that night, before your dream. It was after George left. I told you that I loved you then."

"But I don't remember," Myla said.

"I know," David said. "I realized the next morning that you and George must have been drinking before I came over. I didn't know it that night. I couldn't tell you were drunk. You seemed a little tipsy, but that wasn't anything new. And we drank some wine too. I told you I loved you and that I wanted to stay in Tucson with you."

"What did I say?" Myla asked.

"You kissed me," David said. "And you cried. You talked about feeling homeless. You said at your old house there'd been a big tub and you liked to soak in it. It reminded you of one you'd had when you were a girl—one that you'd spent hours in. Your mother had told you the desert used to be a sea, you said, so you pretended you were a mermaid. You'd pretend to swim all the way to California where your father lived because you knew he lived by the sea. You even talked about the mermaid tile in your old house. How you touched it nearly every day, and it felt like a blessing each time."

"All of that was true," Myla said.

"I was so happy that night," David said. "I'd finally told you how I felt. After I left you, I started painting the mermaid in the empty pool. That night, I mean. I was almost finished when you came out to the pool. You didn't say a word. You looked at the mermaid, you looked at me standing there with a jar of water in one hand and a paint brush in the other, paint all over me, and then you turned around and walked away—like you were sleepwalking. When I finished, I went to your apartment and looked in on you. You were sleeping. In the morning, you told me about the dream—and that's all you seemed to remember. You didn't remember me being there or me telling you that I loved you. Later I showed you the mermaid. By that time, you were talking about treasures in the wash, the Old Mermaids, and your new mission in life."

"You were standing near the pool with a bottle in one hand?" Myla asked. Like the mermaid was holding a bottle in her dream?

"Yes."

Myla closed her eyes. "I had that dream because I saw you in the pool painting the mermaid."

"You probably had that dream because you needed to have that dream," David said. "You said dreams are gifts. There's no reason to question that now."

"And you're telling me that you loved me and I forgot about it so you left," Myla said. "Is that right?"

"That about sums it up," he said.

"Why didn't you try to tell me again?" Myla asked. "You weren't very persistent."

"You were going through a divorce," David said. "You made it pretty clear you weren't interested in me. The age difference bothered you. You kept telling me that you weren't your husband, whatever that meant."

"The woman he left me for was much younger than he was," Myla said.

"I knew that," David said.

They were silent. A distant bird sang.

"There's more," David said.

"More?"

"I'm so sorry, Myla," David said. "I had no idea you were drunk that night or it would not have happened."

"What?"

"That night," David said, "we made love."

Myla heard a roar in her ears. She couldn't quite concentrate. What was he saying? What had he said?

"That's why I didn't pursue it—you," David said. "I was ashamed. I thought you'd believe I'd taken advantage of you."

What would the Old Mermaids do?

Myla wanted to scream. She put her hands on her cheeks. They were burning up. Or were her hands burning up? She couldn't tell which. She felt odd. Not quite herself.

"I thought you said I didn't do anything to embarrass myself," Myla said.

"You didn't," David said. "Myla—" He reached for her hand, but she pulled it away.

"It was beautiful, lovely," David said. "Very tender. And then a little wild."

"And then? It happened more than once?" She put her hands over her eyes. "You should have told me. You should have said, by the way, Myla, you were drunk on your ass, but we did the wild thing half the night."

"I know I should have told you," David said. "I came back to tell you."

"After ten years? Why? To clear your conscience? So you can leave again?"

"No, Myla. I came back because I still love you."

"That is ridiculous! You don't know me. Ten years have gone by. Ten years, David. Who knows what would have happened if you had told me then."

"You seemed so happy without knowing."

"I was happy because of the mermaid dream," Myla said. "I was happy because I felt loved again. But it wasn't the Old Mermaids who loved me. It was you! My entire life for the last ten years had been based on a falsehood!"

"What falsehood?" David said. "You had a dream and you were inspired by it."

"I want to go home," she said. She got up and walked away. She mumbled as she hurried to the car. "But where is home? I stayed in that tiny little shit room for ten years because I thought that piece of land was home. I thought that's where the Old Mer-

168

maids wanted me."

They got into the car together, and David drove the car back onto the main road.

"If I'd known all this," Myla said, "maybe I would have become a teacher. Or something different. My ex-husband wanted the store, so I did the store. I was so compliant. I wanted to do what he wanted to do. So I helped build up that stupid store. I made all the contacts. He could barely speak a word of Spanish. And he hated crossing the border. I used to joke that he had only married me because I spoke Spanish. Maybe it wasn't such a joke. He said he liked Mexican women. I told him I was an American woman. We were dating then. He said Mexican women were more respectful to their husbands. I slugged him, and he laughed. He said he was kidding. But I don't think he was. I think he believed that stupid stereotype. I was compliant. I was. I was."

She looked out the window.

"I can't imagine you were ever compliant," David said.

"You don't know anything about me," Myla said. "I did what he wanted because I didn't care enough not to. Or least I didn't think I did. He made decisions for me, and so did you. I expected that of him, but I didn't expect it of you."

She was not going to cry. She was not going to cry.

"The Old Mermaids were mine," Myla said.

"They still are," David said.

Myla shook her head. "I was in an alcohol induced haze and I saw you and dressed you up in mermaid drag for my dream." Tears flowed down her cheeks. She turned her head, so David could not see her face. "Why are you telling me this now? I was fine not knowing."

"I-I thought you should know," David said. "I couldn't forget you, and I didn't think it was honest to come here and pretend nothing happened. I wasn't sure what to do. I thought about trying to woo you again."

"Woo me? Hah!" Myla angrily wiped her tears away. "First, no one uses the word any more. Second, you never wooed me. You had sex with a drunk. Isn't that so special!"

"It was special," David said. His voice suddenly had an edge to it. "It wasn't like that."

"Then you should have told me!"

"I know, I know," David said. "I wish I had."

"Tell me it was at least safe sex?"

"Yes, it was," he said.

David pulled the car over to the side of the road. Cholla limbs brushed Myla's door.

"I didn't know you were drunk," David said. "I loved you. You wanted to make love with me. At least I thought you did. And you were not compliant. Jesus, Myla. I knew you might be angry and disappointed, but I didn't think it would cause you to reassess your entire life."

"If you loved me so much," Myla asked, "why didn't you stay?"

"Myla, I'll say it as many times as you need to hear it. I didn't stay because I didn't think you loved me. I was ashamed I had made love to you when you were drunk."

"Why didn't you think I loved you?" Myla said. "That shows how little you knew me. I can count on my right hand how many people I have made love with in my entire lifetime and I would still have fingers left over. It's not something I do on a whim."

"The morning after I made love with the woman I loved," David said, "she didn't want anything to do with me. *You* didn't wanted anything to do with me. I was young. I was embarrassed. I was hurt. I was stupid. Please, please, forgive me."

Myla shook her head. "I don't want to talk to you right now," she said. "I don't want to be in this car with you."

"I'll get out then," he said. "I'll hitch a ride back."

"Don't be stupid," Myla said. "Oh wait, too late."

David looked at her. She turned away.

"Just drive," she said.

Eight

A good bean is hard to find. Everything else is easy.   *Sister Ruby Rosarita Mermaid*

Myla hoped no one would see them drive up to the Crow house, but Lily, Stefan, James, and Trevor were sitting on the front porch. They all waved. Lily came running toward them as soon as the car stopped, her arms outstretched. Myla got out of the car and bent to embrace her. Lily kissed her on the cheek. Myla kissed her back. "Oh, Lily my Lily, it is so nice to see you."

James walked up to them.

"Hello, James," Myla said. "I'm glad to see you." It wasn't a lie. She always enjoyed seeing James and Trevor.

"I'm James Goodman," James said, holding his hand out to David. "I was dropping Trevor off to study with Stefan. Ernesto mentioned you wanted to pull up a few cholla trees. He's out around back. I've had some experience with that if you need help. Between the three of us we might be able to handle a few cholla."

"That would be great," David said. He glanced at Myla. She looked down at Lily.

"I'll go change," David said. "I'll be right out."

"So what have you been doing all day?" Myla asked Lily.

"Stefan is teaching me my letters in English," Lily said. "I already know them in Spanish."

"That's great," Myla said.

She held Lily's hand as they walked up the steps to the porch. "Hello, Trevor. Stefan. I won't hug or kiss either of you so that I don't embarrass you in front of one another."

"No, I want my kiss," Trevor said. "I've never had a weekday kiss from you."

"Me, too," Stefan said. "I'll get jealous otherwise."

She gave each boy a hug and a kiss on the cheek. "You going inside to study?"

"We were just about to," Stefan said. "Maria is sleeping. I didn't want to wake her."

"Has she been sleeping all day?"

"No," Stefan said. "She went in not too long ago."

"Can I watch them study?" Lily asked.

"Is it all right with you boys?" Myla asked.

"Sure," Trevor said. Stefan nodded.

"Don't ask them too many questions or interrupt too much," Myla said. "Maybe when they're finished, they'll help you with your letters again."

Myla followed the children inside. Then she went to Maria's door and knocked. When she got no response, she opened the door. Maria sat up on the bed and turned to face her.

"Did you find out anything about Juan?" she asked.

"No, I'm sorry," Myla said. "That doesn't mean he isn't there. It means we didn't see him."

"Thank you," Maria said. "I didn't think you would find him.

174

If he could, he would have phoned someone in the village. Or he would have written. I'm sure of it. He must be dead."

"I'm sorry," Myla said again. "Theresa was going to find out how to do the DNA tests. We could send that in next week."

Maria nodded. "Yes, okay. Then we would know. I better get up now. I sleep and sleep and I'm still tired. Maybe I will make dinner for everyone."

"That would probably do you some good," Myla said. "Or take a walk. You need to get some fresh air, some exercise. There's a park down the road a couple of miles. David could take you. There are lots of trails."

"Couldn't they find me there?"

"I've never seen the Border Patrol at that park," Myla said. "I've never seen them in this neighborhood."

She was not going to tell her about her encounter with the Border Patrol earlier.

"I need to take care of a few things," Myla said. She felt tired, too, and she wanted to be alone. "I'll see you later. Lily is in the kitchen with the boys."

Myla left Maria, walked by the children, and went outside and over to her apartment. She lay on her bed. Maybe Maria had the right idea. She reached over and turned off the phone. Then she closed her eyes.

She almost came awake when someone knocked on her door, but she murmured, "Go away," and drifted back to sleep. She came fully awake when someone turned on the light.

George.

"We had a date, woman," he said. "I called and called."

"A date?" she said.

"Dinner and a movie," he said. "I told you I'd be here if I didn't hear from you."

Myla moaned. She had forgotten to call him.

"George," Myla said. "I'm not in the mood."

"Luckily I am not a sensitive man," George said, "or I might have my feelings hurt here. You said we should go on a date. So here I am." He sat on the bed. "What's wrong with you? Why are you sleeping in the middle of the day?"

"It's not the middle of the day," Myla said. She squinted. "What time is it?"

"Six o'clock," he said.

"Little early for a date isn't it?"

"I've got to work in the morning," he said.

Myla laughed.

"All right," she said. "Dinner but no movie. We have gone to dinner before, you know."

"It's usually not before," George said. "It's usually after. We get the munchies."

"You old romantic you," Myla said. She glanced at the phone. She did not want to see David, and she did not want to pretend to be happy around everyone else, but they needed to know where she was going. She picked up the phone and pressed in the Crow number. David answered.

"I'm going out," Myla said. "Is everyone all right?"

"Trevor and James had dinner with us," David said. "They were disappointed you weren't here. Maria made it. They've left, and we're cleaning up."

"Tell Lily good night for me," she said. "I'll see her in the morning."

"All right," he said.

Myla set the phone down.

"You don't say good-bye?" George asked. "It's good to know you're rude to someone besides me. So that David guy is still here. Has he made a pass at you yet?"

"Shut up, George," Myla said. "Take me to eat."

176

"That's my girl."

They drove to Maya Quetzal. The small restaurant was packed, and only one waitress—someone new—hurried from table to table.

"Two?" she asked Myla.

"Yes," Myla said. "You all by yourself? Don't rush for us."

"A table will probably open up in ten minutes."

She and George sat on the green wooden chairs near the door, under the mural of a Guatemalan village in the mountains. George picked up a wrinkled *Tucson Weekly*, pulled out half the sheets, and gave the rest to Myla. They sat side by side reading until a table opened.

George ordered chicken enchiladas and a beer. Myla got beans, rice, vegetable tacquitos, and limonada.

"Why did you call Richard?" Myla asked. They shared a small bowl of fried corn chips.

"You seemed upset about the mermaid tile," he said. "So I wanted to get it for you. And why are you saying his name? I haven't heard you say that name for a decade."

"Because it's stupid not to say it," Myla said. "We've been acting like two year olds. I'm not going out to the house on the anniversary next year. I don't want to know anything about their lives. Let's concentrate on us. I don't mean us us. I mean us as individual human beings. We can't be defined by what happened to us ten years ago."

"You sound like you're trying to convince yourself," he said.

"I am," Myla said. "A lot of things happened this week."

"Besides you breaking into your ex-husband's house?"

"Beside me breaking into my old house," Myla said. "And let's get back to that. What were you thinking phoning him? He could have called the police on me."

"I knew he wouldn't," George said.

"How, George? How could you know that?"

"Because I told him if he did I'd hunt him down," George said. He put a chip in his mouth and bit down on it. "I guess he called you, eh?"

"Yes. Said you and I should get lives," Myla said.

George laughed. "Look who's talking. Is he going to give you the tile?"

"No," Myla said. "He's going to deliver the old oak dresser though." She thought about telling him about Cathy trashing the Ford bedroom, Stefan staying at David's, and Theresa quitting the Old Mermaid Sanctuary, but she decided to keep quiet. George did not know anything about her work at the sanctuary. She had no idea how he would react. Well, maybe she had some idea. He'd probably shrug and say it wasn't any of his business. But they never discussed books or politics or immigration reform. For all she knew, he could be one of the minutemen up at the border waving around a rifle and guzzling beer.

The waitress brought their dinners.

"George," Myla said. "We don't know much about each other, do you realize that?"

"I know enough," he said. "You can't lie about much when you're naked."

"Sure you can," Myla said. "I lie to you all the time when we're naked."

"About what?"

"About what a great lover you are," Myla said. "The beans and rice are especially tasty tonight. You want some?"

"No, that's women folk food," he said. "I gotta eat me some dead things. And I know you weren't lying about me being a great lover. Your satisfied smiles were a dead giveaway."

Myla laughed. She did enjoy George's sense of humor.

"I've been thinking about some things since Sunday," George

178

said. "I like your company. You like mine, for the most part. I think it would be nice if we saw each other more. You've been to my place. It's not so bad. You could come live with me."

"How would I take care of the Old Mermaid Sanctuary if I lived with you?" she asked.

"I don't know," he said. "I could come live with you, but I'm guessing our affection for one another might whither being in such close proximity all the time."

"You got that right," Myla said. She started to say, "Gee, George, this is so sudden," but given they had been sleeping together for ten years, it was not exactly an impulsive move.

"But we've never been serious that way with one another," Myla said.

"I know," he said. "We've both dated other people while we saw one another, and that was just fine. But something happened this week that made me see things differently."

"What did you do, George?"

"Just hear me out," he said. "After we went to the house Sunday, I started thinking about that mermaid tile and how upset you were. I wanted to get it back for you. I called old asshole you know who and he said no. Over his dead body I wish he'd said just so I could say that could be arranged, but he had the voice he gets where he tries to talk like a college professor. Like he knows more than anyone."

"He does that to other people?" Myla asked. "I thought he reserved that voice for me."

"Well, on Tuesday I waited until he was gone and the new missus was at home, alone," he said, "and I knocked on the door. She actually invited me inside, Myla, like we were old friends. We talked for a bit. She asked me what I'd been up to. I said not much. I asked her how she liked her lousy life. She said fine. Then one thing led to another, Myla, and I was in your old bed with her. She was naked. I was almost naked."

Myla put up her hand. "George! Spare me the details! You had sex with your ex-wife?"

He sat back in his chair and grinned. "In your old bed. I was doing to her what he was doing to her when we found them together. It was sweet revenge. I even heard the front door open and close and I thought for sure he was home and was going to catch us. Wouldn't that have been great? But then I heard the girl's voice. I kicked the door shut, so she wouldn't see. No kid needs to see something like that. A few seconds later, we finished up and I stayed in the bathroom until she told the kid to go next door and play."

"I cannot believe you," Myla said.

"I'm not lying," he said. "You know better than that. She started crying after the girl left. I was getting dressed and she sat on the bed naked crying. She begged me not to tell her husband. 'Don't tell my husband,' she said it just like that. Like I hadn't been friends with him for years, like I hadn't been her husband for years. I said, 'I'm your husband.' And then I realized I wasn't. I mean I really felt it for the first time. I was thinking about you the whole time I was with her."

"Yuck, George."

"I mean I would have rather been with you," he said. "I told her I wouldn't tell her husband. But I said I wanted the mermaid tile. I told her I'd done all of this for you, to get that tile. She called me a few names. Then I left."

"And so from this you decided we should move in together?"

"That's about it," he said. "What do you think?"

"I think that was a mean thing to do to her," Myla said.

"It wasn't planned," he said, "and she enjoyed herself."

"George."

He shrugged.

"What if Bethany had seen you two?" Myla asked. "The sight of you naked could have scarred her for life."

"I don't care," George said. "Really. I don't care about them. I'm ready to move on."

Myla shook her head. "I don't know what to say, George. I don't know if I should slap you or slug you."

"Will you think about it?" he asked.

"I'll think about it," Myla said, "but it's hard for me to imagine us living together."

"You don't seem to have a problem having sex with me," George said.

"That's different," Myla said. "Sex is easy compared with living with someone every day."

George leaned forward and said quietly, "I do love you, Myla. You know that."

"I love you, too," Myla said. "We love each other like friends."

"Isn't that great?" George said.

"Yes, it is," Myla said. "Can I talk to you about something? Mostly so I can get the image out of my mind of you and Nadine in my old bed together."

"Sure," he said.

"Do you remember the night I had the dream about the mermaids?"

"Yeah, I remember," he said, "because you stopped drinking with me after that."

"What happened that night?"

"Man, Myla," he said, "that was a long time ago. I came over to your place. You and I had a bit to drink. You'd been drinking before I got there I seem to remember. I was in the mood for a little romp in the hay, so to speak. You weren't, which was fine. That David guy brought over dinner and I left. The next day you stopped drinking."

"Did I ever have sex with you when I was really drunk?" Myla asked. "And then not remember it the next day?"

"I don't know," George said. "It's not like I'd call you up the next day and say, hey, baby, do you remember us doing it or were you too plastered? But I will say, Myla, you held your liquor good."

"Apparently not," she said.

George started laughing.

"What?"

"Let me guess," George said. "You got drunk and had sex with that boy, didn't you? All those years ago. And he never told you. I knew he was hot for you. And apparently you were for him."

"He wasn't a boy," Myla said. "And lower your voice. I remembered making love that night. Sort of. It was quite wonderful. But I thought it was you."

"Naturally," George said. "Since it was so wonderful."

"Shut up, George," she said.

"So are you two going to pick up where you left off?"

"You mean with me as a drunk and him as—as sleeping with a drunk? I don't think so."

He looked at her. "This has really upset you. Just like the mermaid tile? Well, I can't go to David Crow and demand your virtue back."

"George," she said.

"Come on," he said. "I'll take you home and pleasure you and you'll forget all about that boy."

"Could you say that a bit louder?" Myla said. "I don't think the guy in the next room quite got it."

"Hey, the body is a beautiful thing," he said. He slapped his belly. "Even this one."

"Yes, it is," Myla said. "Take me home."

George and Myla went to her apartment. She wanted to take

her clothes off and make wild and passionate love to George. Or she wanted to want to. But she didn't.

"Don't take it personally," Myla said as she sent George on his way. "Remember how satisfied your ex-wife was only a couple of days ago."

George kissed her lightly on the lips.

"I fear you've grown tired of me," George said quietly.

"I may stop having sex with you one day, George," she said. "But I won't tire of you. You are a good friend. You're welcome to come to dinner on Saturday, as always."

"Maybe I'll show up," George said. "Check out my competition."

"There's no competition," Myla said. "Now go home. Thanks for dinner."

She stood on the porch and watched George drive away, her hands on her hips. She breathed deeply and gazed at the Crow house as the dust settled. The light over the sink was on in the kitchen. She wondered how David was doing now that he had spilled his secret to her. Butterflies tickled her stomach. A particular breed of butterflies. She recognized the sensation. She had had it years before, when David used to visit her or walk in the wash with her. She had ignored it then. She had not wanted to appear foolish. She had not wanted to be a woman desperate for a man—and she had not been desperate.

She sighed. She wished she could remember making love with David. She had always thought her drinking had harmed no one— how could it? She had been careful. She had stayed to herself on this land. Who could it have harmed? Besides herself, of course.

Ah well. That was then. This was now. Now. Now. What was she going to do now?

She stared at the house. The butterflies started to settle in her stomach. Good.

Time to go to bed.

In the morning, Myla walked the wash by herself. The quail clucked and fussed on either side of her, wandering the floor of the desert beneath the palo verde, mesquite, and cacti, like feathery nuns traveling a maze. The great horned owl moaned from the palm. Song birds chattered and flew from here to there. Morning shadowed the Rincons. Later in the day sunlight would bleach the mountains with its gaze and all the shadows would shrink to miniature, waiting for the moon to call them out again. Myla's feet slipped in the sand as she walked. She longed for moonlight. The sunlight felt too harsh. Too enlightening. You couldn't hide anything in the desert. Trash. Bones. Failure. It was all still on the surface. Waiting for you to come by and pick it up. *Hey you, there. This is your failure. You can't just leave it here.* Yet people dumped things in the desert all the time, and whatever they left behind didn't seem to come back and haunt them.

Myla had been dumped in the desert. Her husband had left her in the desert. Well, he had deserted her while they lived in a desert town. Her being in the desert had been coincidental to the desertion. Her father had left her and her mother in the desert. Went to live by the ocean. But that was coincidental, too, wasn't it? She could have been left on a mountain top. In a valley. By the ocean. Everyone got left, one way or another.

David had left her, and she hadn't even known it. How might her life had been different? She shook her head. She did not want to think about her and David. Not yet. It felt too fresh.

Every wound she had ever had suddenly felt fresh. Her body ached all over. It was as if she had been transported back in time to the day her husband told her he didn't love her. She had felt so nauseated then. Breathless. Small. It had been too overwhelming. For a long while. The night she moved into her studio apart-

184

ment in the barn, she had poured herself a glass of wine. After she gulped it down, she poured another. Then another. And another. Until she didn't feel anything. Except nausea — so she had stepped outside, walked into the desert, and thrown up.

There, she remembered thinking, it's all gone now.

But the next morning she hurt all over again. She walked the wash feeling...just feeling. And she felt sick. So she drank more wine. Until at the end of the day she went outside, walked into the desert, and threw up.

She wasn't sure how long she had followed this routine. Maybe until David came to visit his parents. He had been kind and interesting. She liked being near him. The ache, nausea, and her desire for him had gotten all mixed up. So she drank and threw up.

Then she had the Old Mermaid dream, and the ache, nausea, and desire had disappeared.

Had the Old Mermaids saved her or stopped her?

Myla looked at her feet. She felt a pinch of vertigo. She closed her eyes and breathed deeply. She felt the ground beneath her feet, the air on her face, the songs of the birds in her ears. She opened her eyes and saw an odd shape under a creosote bush growing just out of the wash. She walked toward the bush. Tiny fuzzy white balls hung from the stems amidst the small dark green leaves, reminding Myla of miniature Christmas tree ornaments. She leaned over and breathed in the smell of Arizona rain: creosote. The pungent aroma made her eyes water. She looked at the ground to see what had caught her eye. It was a shovel. It looked as though it had been in this same place, under this bush, partially covered in sand, for years. She bent over and lifted up the shovel by the sawed off wooden handle. The flat metal blade was mostly whitish gray mixed with rust.

How had she missed this shovel in the dirt after all these years?

"Thank you, creosote," she said.

She took the shovel back to the barn and placed it near her door.

Then she went to the Crow house and knocked on the kitchen door.

David opened it. "You don't need to knock," he said. "You are always welcome here."

She didn't look at him as she stepped into the house.

"Myla!" Lily called. She jumped down from her chair at the kitchen table—the orange rope hanging from her waist—and ran into Myla's arms. Myla started laughing. How had she ever survived without this little girl's embraces? She looked up at David as the girl kissed her on the cheek. He was smiling.

"Good morning, everyone," Myla said. Lily pulled her toward the table. "What's everyone doing today?" She sat at the table between Ernesto and Lily.

"We're going to do some work on the house and the property," Stefan said. "Manly stuff." He smiled.

"And girlie stuff," David said. "Lily wants to tag along."

"Nothing dangerous?" Myla said.

David shook his head. "We're going to take turns being tied to her. Right, Lily?"

Lily nodded.

"Maria, is there something you want to do today?" Myla asked. "I could take you into town. If David would lend me the car."

"Theresa called and she's taking me into town to talk to another group that helps migrants," Maria said in Spanish. "You can come, if you like. She tried calling you she said."

"Maybe I'll take the car and go shopping then," Myla said. "May I use the car?" She looked at David.

"It's more your car than it is mine," David said. "You don't need to ask my permission."

"No, it doesn't belong to me," Myla said.

"But it's part of the agreement you have with the families," David said. "It's part of your payment."

"My payment? What do you know about my arrangement with the families? I use that car as little as possible. I try to use everything as little as possible. No footprints! No sign that I was ever here—that any of us were ever here. Just ghosts, drifting from house to house, cleaning up messes, then moving on."

Myla stopped. Everyone was looking at her.

"Are you and Crow mad at one another?" Lily asked after a moment of silence.

"His name is David," Maria reminded Lily in Spanish.

"It's a lover's quarrel," Ernesto said.

"What is that?" Lily asked.

Myla glanced at David. He shrugged as if to say, "I didn't say anything."

"I am just a little...*gruñón*," Myla said.

Maria said, "It's hard to imagine you ever get grumpy."

"Everyone gets cranky once in a while," Myla said.

"You should kiss and make up," Stefan said. He looked at her slyly. She smiled—in spite of her best efforts not to.

"I'm willing," David said.

"In your dreams," Myla said.

"That's a start," he said.

"Is Crow your son?" Lily asked Myla.

"No," Myla said. "Ernesto is."

"And I'm her husband," Stefan said.

"I remember," Lily said. "Crow is your father."

"America is a very strange place," Maria said.

"You got that right," Myla said.

Myla spent the day indoors. She took down the binder and looked at the photographs of everyone who had stayed at the Old Mermaid Sanctuary. Then she cleaned the apartment. She was glad to be alone, but she felt lonely—an unusual sensation for her. Unusual and uncomfortable. She started to phone George more than once, but she never completed the call.

Near dinner time she sat on the edge of her bed trying to decide if she wanted to eat dinner with the others at the Crow house. Maybe she could skip dinner again. But she wanted to see Lily. And Ernesto. Stefan. Maria. David. The Old Mermaid in the pool. How could everything in her life have changed so drastically in such a short time?

Someone knocked on the door.

"Myla?" David called.

She got up and opened the door. When she saw David, she started to cry, silently. The tears fell down her cheeks. She hoped in the semidarkness David would not notice.

"Are you all right?" David asked.

She nodded. Then she shook her head.

"Can I come in?"

"No," she said.

"Please let me help."

She shook her head. "I was young ten years ago," Myla said. "We had possibility then."

"We have possibility now," he said.

"I wanted a family," she said. She was still whispering. She could hear herself speaking, barely, but it was as if someone else were talking: telling truths she had not known a moment before. "You're a young man. You must want a family."

"You have a family," he said. "Right here. You've created one. And that's all the family I need."

"That's what my old husband said. But he left me and got another family."

"I'm not your ex-husband," David said. "I tried to tell you that ten years ago."

"You didn't try hard enough," she said. "And now I don't believe you. Now I'm an old woman who walks the bottom of a dried up sea. It's very metaphoric, don't you think? I'm the Old Sea hag of a nonexistent sea." She could not stop the words from spilling out of her. She felt unpleasantly giddy. "It was all pretend, you know. Every bit of it."

"Myla, I—have you been drinking?"

"Why? Would you like to come in and have sex with a drunk again?"

David stepped back from the door. He looked wobbly, as though she had punched him.

"Maybe you're right," David said. "Maybe I don't know you. The Myla I knew was never cruel. Never."

He turned and walked away. Myla shut the door and stood next to it for a bit.

Then she opened a can of beans and poured them into a saucepan and heated them. When they were ready, she sat on the bed eating the beans from the pan. She heard the coyotes howling the sun down, but she did not go outside to listen. She set the pan on the night table, turned off the light, and went to sleep.

She awakened to the sound of someone pounding on her door. She got up and pulled the door open. Stefan stood on her threshold in pajamas and bare feet.

"Lily is calling for you," he said.

Myla grabbed a sweatshirt and pulled it over her pajama top, put on her slippers, and followed Stefan over to the house. She glanced up at the moon and wondered what time it was. She heard Lily's cries as soon as she stepped into the house. The light over the kitchen sink seemed to pulse each time she screamed. Myla hurried toward the sound. David stood outside Maria and Lily's room. Maria sat on the chair in a corner, her shoulders hunched, her eyes red from crying.

"Lily," Myla said quietly as she walked into the room. Lily sobbed and held out her arms to her. Myla sat on the bed and pulled the girl onto her lap.

"She left me," Lily said in Spanish. "She's going to leave me again. She won't tie herself to me. We'll be carried away."

Myla rocked her. "Lily my Lily, you can't be tied to each other as you sleep. You might get tangled and hurt yourself."

Lily sobbed.

Myla looked at Maria. Tears streamed down her face.

"I did leave her," Maria said, "but only for a few minutes. She was sleeping. I thought she'd be safe. I went to look for the others. She was so tired and I couldn't carry her. I came right back. You saw me. I would never hurt her."

"She says my daddy is never coming back," Lily said.

"I talked with those people and showed Juan's photograph around," Maria said. "No one has seen him. I thought I should tell her he might not be coming back."

"Lily," Myla said. "Your mother is here. She is not going to desert you. I'm here. I won't leave you."

"She doesn't like me," Maria said. "She never has."

Lily was crying so loudly that Myla was not certain she had heard Maria correctly. She glanced at David who still stood in the doorway.

"Lily loves you, Maria," Myla said. "She's afraid she's going to lose her mother as well as her father. She needs some reassurance."

"I've tried," Maria said. She pulled a tissue from the pocket of her jeans and blew her nose.

"Lily, Lily darling," Myla said. "Listen to me. Everything is going to be all right. You are safe."

"Will you stay here?" Lily asked.

"I'll stay in the house," Myla said. "If you call me, I'll come, but you need to sleep with your mother. Come on. Can you get under the covers again?"

Lily wiped her face with her sleeve, then slipped under the covers. Myla looked at Maria.

"Do you need some pajamas? That can't be comfortable sleeping in your jeans," she said. "*La Migra* isn't going to come and take you from here, Maria. Maybe if you were in pajamas or out of your jeans, it wouldn't look like you were about to get up and leave Lily."

"I don't have any pajamas," she said.

"My mom probably has some in her dresser," David said. He disappeared from the door and returned a moment later with a folded pair of pajamas. Myla took them from him.

"I'll be right out," she said to him.

She closed the door.

"Maria," she said gently, "I know you've had a terrible time. Your husband has disappeared. You're young. You're in a new country. But Lily needs you."

Maria looked at her daughter.

"I don't think I can help her," she said.

"Being with her is help enough," Myla said. She held out the folded pajamas to her. "And I'm here if you need anything."

Maria took off her shirt and jeans and lay them carefully on the chair. Then she put on the pajamas. She got into bed with her daughter.

Myla pulled the sheet and blanket up to their chins. They both looked like children. She kissed first Lily, then Maria.

"I love you both," Myla said. "It'll be all right. Now close your eyes, both of you."

She switched off the light. It was a stupid lie; everything might not be all right. But for this moment, everything was all right.

They were safe.

"I'll leave the door open a bit," she said. "You can call me if you need anything."

"Can you tell us a story?" Lily asked. "About the Old Mermaids."

Myla sat on the edge of the bed. Lily and Maria both turned toward her in the dark.

"Let me tell you about Tulip," Myla said. "She was a girl just about your age who lived near the Old Mermaids but didn't know it for a long time. She had trouble sleeping some nights. She had had some scary things happen in her life."

"Like what?" Lily asked.

"Well, her daddy was gone for a long time," Myla said, "and her mother was often sad because of this. Tulip thought she was pretty much alone in the world until she walked down the wash one day and found Sister Laughs A Lot Mermaid in the wash looking around in the dirt for treasure."

"Like you," Lily said.

"Yep," Myla said. "Sister Laughs a Lot Mermaid took Tulip back to the Old Mermaid Sanctuary and Sister Ruby Rosarita Mermaid gave her some lunch. Tulip talked all through the meal of beans, rice, and vegetables. The Old Mermaids immediately loved the little girl, and she became a frequent visitor to the Old Mermaid Sanctuary. Her mother Poppy visited too. As time went on, Poppy was not as sad. She was an excellent seamstress, and she showed the Old Mermaids how to sew.

"The Old Mermaids were not used to clothing from their days in the Old Sea, and they hadn't quite grasped the concept yet. But Poppy showed them how they could dress themselves like they would paint a painting—use the cloth like paint. Grand Mother Yemaya Mermaid already had her own style. Same with Mother Star Stupendous Mermaid. And Sissy Maggie Mermaid

192

had been making clothes her art for a while. But Sister Lyra Musica Mermaid, Sister Ursula Divine Mermaid, Sister Bea Wilder Mermaid, and Sister DeeDee Lightful Mermaid didn't mind some helpful hints. The desert could be rather prickly—as could some of the neighbors who were startled on more than one occasion by the singular (or duo) Old Mermaid walking the wash with nothing more than the memory of a tail to cover her.

"Anyway, Tulip and Poppy began spending more time with the Old Mermaids. One day, Poppy told Sister Laughs a Lot Mermaid that Tulip had nightmares and was afraid to go to sleep at night. Sister Laughs a Lot Mermaid told Grand Mother Yemaya Mermaid and Mother Star Stupendous Mermaid. Grand Mother Yemaya Mermaid said, 'Hasn't Tulip been gifted yet?' Poppy told them she had never heard of being Gifted. The Old Mermaids were shocked. 'This explains a great deal,' said Sister Sophia Mermaid. The others nodded. It did explain a lot.

"'In the Old Sea,' Mother Star Stupendous Mermaid explained, 'every young Old Mermaid has a ceremony, and her mermothers bestow on her various gifts. That's being Gifted.' 'That sounds lovely,' Poppy said. 'Something like that might help Tulip very much.' The Old Mermaids volunteered to be mermothers for Tulip. 'And for you,' Sister Faye Mermaid said. 'Mother and daughter will be Gifted the same!' Sister Faye Mermaid and Sister Bridget Mermaid organized the ceremony. Sister Ruby Rosarita Mermaid and Sister Lyra Musica Mermaid prepared the feast. Poppy and Sissy Maggie Mermaid made beautiful clothes for Poppy and Tulip—they looked like colorful flashy mermaid tails!"

Lily laughed. Maria was part of the darkness now, and Myla couldn't tell if she was awake or not.

"Tulip and Poppy sat out by the pool," Myla said, "in chairs just like the ones we have on the patio. It was around dusk. Twilight. When the veil between worlds is supposed to be thinnest.

First Sister Bridget Mermaid put a seashell necklace around
Tulip's neck and Sister Faye Mermaid did the same for Poppy.
Then they sang a couple of sea chanties. One by one the Old
Mermaids came and stood before Tulip and her mother. Sister
DeeDee Lightful Mermaid said, 'I gift you with joy!' She kissed
the top of Poppy's head, then the top of Tulip's head. Sister Bea
Wilder Mermaid came next. 'I gift you with ecstatic dance,' she
said and whirled around. 'I gift you with laughter,' Sister Laughs
A Lot Mermaid said. Then she rubbed her tummy and laughed.
She kissed the mother and daughter on the cheek.

"'I gift you with enough to eat,' Sister Ruby Rosarito Mermaid
said. She placed a piece of cake in their laps. 'I gift you with
guts!' Sister Sheila Na Giggles Mermaid said. And she shook
their hands. 'I gift you with this reminder: you are a part of Nature,' Sister Ursula Divine Mermaid said. She gave them each a
walking stick made from sycamore branches she had found up
on the mountain. Sister Bridget Mermaid said, 'I gift you with
poetry and music.'

"'I gift you with healing and magic,' Sister Faye Mermaid said.
She turned her closed hands up and opened them. A humming-
bird flew off of each palm. I heard tell they glowed, those birds,
like lightning bugs. They flew up close to Tulip and Poppy, and
then flew away. 'I gift you with stories,' Sister Lyra Musica Mermaid said. She kissed first the mother and then the daughter on
the forehead. 'I gift you with wisdom,' Sister Sophia Mermaid
said. 'I gift you with the stars, the earth, the moon, and the sun,'
Mother Star Stupendous Mermaid said. Then Grand Mother
Yemaya Mermaid stood before them. Poppy and Tulip got off
the chairs and held hands while they awaited Grand Mother
Yemaya Mermaid's gift. Grand Mother smiled and said, 'I gift
you with the mysteries of the Old Sea.'" They all cheered and
laughed and recited more poetry—then they went and ate the

wonderful feast."

"Did Tulip have nightmares afterward?" Lily asked.

"I don't think so. If she did, she probably wasn't as afraid. She had the gifts of thirteen Old Mermaids! How could she go wrong? Tulip said she didn't feel different after being Gifted, only more herself, and Grand Mother Yemaya Mermaid said that was because she had always had the gifts. That was the mystery of the Old Sea. At least one of them. And guess what?"

"What?" Lily asked.

"Now that you've heard this story, you and your mom have been gifted, too," Myla said. "Just like Tulip and Poppy."

"We'll feast later?" Lily asked.

"Yep. Now go to sleep, my dears!"

She tiptoed out of the room and into the hall. David was waiting for her.

"You can sleep in my room," he whispered.

"No, I'll sleep on the couch," she said.

"Then I'll stay out here with you," he said.

"David, you're getting on my last nerve," she said.

He took her hand and led her into his room—his sister's old room—across the hall from Maria and Lily.

"This is a lot more comfortable than the couch," he said.

"Does that mean you'll have a lousy night's sleep out on the couch?" she asked.

"Yes, but don't worry about that," he said.

"I wasn't worried," she said. "I was using that as an incentive to sleep here."

David smiled. "Whatever works for you."

"Good night, David," Myla said. "Don't let the Old Mermaids bite."

Nine

You ask me to tell you about love? Showing is so
much better.   *Sister Magdelene Mermaid*

In the morning, Lily seemed to have forgotten her night terrors.
Stefan made oatmeal for everyone. David cut up fruit. Ernesto
asked if he could please have some meat. Myla laughed. Lily tied
herself to Stefan while they ate breakfast.

"Can I come with you to the Church of the Old Mermaids this
morning?" Stefan asked.

"Me too!" Lily said.

"Sure," Myla said, "as long as Maria doesn't mind."

"Is it safe for her?" Maria asked.

"Yes," Myla said. "No one will bother her there."

Maria nodded.

"You wanna come, David?" Stefan asked.

"No," Myla said at the same time David said, "Sure."

Stefan looked at Myla, then David. "Better get your stories

straight."

"Actually, I'll hang out here with Ernesto and Maria," David said.

A car came up the drive.

"There's Gail," Myla said. "Let's get going."

Myla, Lily, and Stefan went outside. Myla introduced Gail to the children, they put Myla's boxes in the car, and then they were off.

"What's with the orange rope?" Gail asked. "They brother and sister?"

"It's a long story," Myla told her.

Gail dropped them off on Fourth Avenue. Lily let Stefan untie himself from her. Then they helped Myla set up the church in front of the bookstore. Lily ran her fingers over the mermaid on the cigar box. Myla put the newly-found shovel next to the table. Pietra brought her out a chair, and Myla introduced her to the children.

"Well, you've got helpers today," Pietra said. "That's great. I'll get you a couple more chairs. Stefan, you want to help me?"

Stefan followed Pietra into the store. A few minutes later he rolled out two more office chairs.

He whispered to Myla, "There are a lot of girls in that store."

Myla laughed. "Well, feel free to go to the bookstore any time. It'll be good for your mind."

He grinned. "Thanks, Myla."

James and Trevor arrived. Stefan decided to stick around outside the store once Trevor unfolded his chair. Trevor gave Stefan some blank pages from his notebook, "In case you want to sketch anything." Lily tied herself to James for a bit, then to Trevor.

"How are you this morning?" James asked Myla.

"I'm fine," Myla said. She wasn't sure that was quite true, but she was not going to burden him with stories of her newly sordid past. No, that wasn't right. How could her past be "newly" sordid? How could she tell him or anyone that the Old Mermaids had been born out of an alcohol-induced debauch?

She touched each of the items on the table. Her fingers lingered on the arrow. Stefan had donated it, said he didn't need it any longer. Then she touched the marble. The "Who?" T-shirt. Two bottles. The shovel handle.

She looked up. Theresa and Luisa stood on the other side of the table.

"Good morning," Theresa said.

"Hello," Myla said. "Hello, Luisa."

"Luisa wanted to come to church today," Theresa said.

"Good," Myla said. "The more the merrier." Myla smiled. Normally a visit from someone like Luisa would cause an Old Mermaid story to bubble to the surface and spill over Myla's lips. But nothing bubbled, gurgled, or babbled.

"Hey, Luisa," Stefan said.

"Hey, Stefan."

Lily quickly untied herself from Trevor and ran to Luisa, her arms outstretched. Luisa hugged her and let Lily tie the orange rope around her hand without a word or question. Lily led her to the boys, and Trevor introduced himself.

"Can Luisa go home with you?" Theresa asked. "I've got some things to do, and then I'll come by for dinner."

"Sure," Myla said.

"You okay?" Theresa asked.

"Sure," Myla said. That appeared to be her word this morning: sure. Although she was not sure of anything any more, was she? That couldn't be true. She couldn't be unsure of everything.

"Okay, I'll see you later then." Theresa waved, blew a kiss to her daughter, then left.

A woman Myla did not know came up to the table and picked

up the broken marble.

"What's this?" the woman asked.

Myla looked at the marble. She started to say, "It's a broken marble." But she stopped herself. She stared at the glass in the woman's fingers.

"I think one of the Old Mermaids lost her marbles," Myla said.

The woman looked at her and then at the marble again.

"You're selling this?" She set the marble down. "I'd have to have lost all my marbles to buy something like this." She walked away.

Myla moved the marble back into place on the table.

A man came forward and touched one of the glass bottles. He had been here before, but Myla couldn't remember his name. Samuel?

"Good morning, Myla," he said.

"Hello," she said. She watched him look at the bottle. She knew he was waiting for her to say something.

But nothing was coming to her.

"What did the Old Mermaids use this bottle for?" he asked.

Myla looked at the bottle, then at the man.

"Vinegar," Myla said. "I think they used that bottle for vinegar."

"Hmmm," he said. "Not quite what I needed."

He looked around a bit, then said good-bye.

Myla's throat felt dry.

"Trevor," she asked. "Could you get me something to drink? I forgot my water."

He nodded and got out of his chair. Luisa, Lily, and Stefan followed him to Maya Quetzal. James moved his chair closer to Myla.

"Is everything all right?" he asked her.

"Fine," she said. "I guess I haven't been sleeping well."

200

A woman stopped at the table. She picked up the arrow.

"This is new," the woman said. "Have you ever found anything like this in the wash?"

"I don't think I have," Myla said. She knew normally she would say, "Everything I find in the wash is unique and wonderful, particularly this piece because..." But she couldn't get her lips to move.

"Did the Old Mermaids actually use this?"

Myla pressed her tongue against her teeth. She was not going to say, "Lady, it was manufactured about a year ago. Have you seen any mermaids anywhere in the last year or so?"

Trevor set a glass of limonada in front of her.

Myla stared at the drink.

"Myla," the woman said. "What did the Old Mermaids use this for?"

Myla felt a pinch of panic. Had the Old Mermaids deserted her too?

"That is the arrow that almost killed Sister Lyra Musica Mermaid," Stefan said.

Myla looked up. Stefan stood beside her.

"Sister Lyra Musica Mermaid was having a tough time living in the desert after the Old Sea dried up," Stefan said. "She was afraid of many things in this new world. She was really afraid of Mr. Hunter, the old man who lived up the hill and seemed to be hunting mermaids. In truth, he was nearsighted and thought he was shooting at deer or mountain lions. All the Old Mermaids tried to help Sister Lyra Musica Mermaid, but she was still afraid. She didn't feel well a lot of the time. Is that right, Myla? She missed her old life. She'd had a good life, and she couldn't get used to this new life. Grand Mother Yemaya Mermaid encouraged her to go outside and walk the wash even though she was afraid. She did it and Mr. Hunter shot an arrow and it barely missed her. That scared her, but it pissed her off, too. She grabbed the arrow and went to Mr. Hunter and told him to look at her and see that she was not a lion or a deer. She was an Old Mermaid so quit trying to shoot her, and if he was really that hungry, she'd take him to the Old Mermaid Sanctuary and feed him. So she did. Mr. Hunter started working there, and Sister Lyra Musica Mermaid stopped being so afraid and kind of got used to her new life. I'm Stefan, and I'm a novice at the Church of the Old Mermaids."

Several people clapped.

The woman said, "That is just what I need. I'm afraid of too many things."

"I kept that with me for a while," Stefan said, "and I stopped being so afraid."

"Are you sure you want to let go of it?" the woman asked.

Stefan nodded. "That's the Old Mermaid way."

The woman slipped dollar bills into the cigar box.

"Thank you, Stefan," Myla said after the woman had gone.

A teenage girl and her mother stepped up to the table. The girl picked up the T-shirt.

"What does this mean?" she asked. "'Who?'"

"It's a question," Myla said. They waited for her to say something else, but she had nothing. No words. No stories. She wanted to tell the girl to go away.

"Isn't that the T-shirt the other Old Mermaids made for Sister Magdelene Mermaid?" Trevor asked. He and Myla glanced at one another.

"They called her Sissy Maggie Mermaid," Trevor said, "and she was often getting into trouble. Not big trouble because that was not the Old Mermaid way except when necessary, by all means. But Sissy Maggie Mermaid would start an art project, not finish it, then go on to something else. And she was always falling in love."

"In love?" the teenage girl said. "With mermen?"

"No," Trevor said, "this was after the Old Sea had dried up. She fell in love with the guy who made the kitchen tiles. She fell in love with the woman she saw walking with the coyotes in the wash. She loved intensely, but it faded, so I suppose you could say she became infatuated easily and intensely, although she would claim she loved and stayed in love—she just moved on to the next being who needed her love. Anyway, she did other things too. She'd begin painting a beautiful mural and then she'd lose interest. When the other Old Mermaids asked her about her unfinished work or the man down the road who was crying over their ended love affair, Sissy Maggie Mermaid always said, 'Who didn't finish that mural? Who made that poor man cry?' Sister Sophia Mermaid said, 'You sound like that owl in the palm tree. Who? Who? Who? The who is you, little miss Sissy Maggie.'

"For her birthday one year, they made that T-shirt for her. I can't be sure, of course, but I believe that's the one. They made that after the Old Sea had been dried up for a long time. And when they gave it to her, they reminded her of when she first came out of the Old Sea and she fell in love with the moon. In the sea, the Old Mermaids didn't really see the moon, so the first time Sissy Maggie Mermaid saw the moon, she loved it instantly. She didn't know if the moon was a he or a she and she didn't care. She loved that it came out mostly after dark. She loved that it seemed to follow her as she walked in the wash. She really mooned over the moon. The other Old Mermaids thought she was a bit looney—sorry about all the puns—but then they were all a bit off-balanced when the Old Sea first dried up.

"Every night, Sissy Maggie would try to get the moon to come down to her and it wouldn't. And then it went away. She cried and cried. Sister Sophia Mermaid and Sister Bridget Mermaid explained to her that the moon was a rock in the sky and it was never coming down to her—and if it ever did, the whole planet would be in trouble. She listened carefully to all this and said, 'But rocks have feelings too.' Fortunately soon after she became enamored with the man who made the tiles, and as time went on, the other Old Mermaids teased her about falling in love with a rock. She'd say, 'Yes, but oh what a pretty rock!'"

The girl holding the T-shirt smiled. "I like Sissy Maggie Mermaid."

"I think that T-shirt would look nice on you," Trevor said. "By the way, I'm Trevor and I'm a novice too. But I'm a little more experienced than he is."

Stefan punched him lightly in the shoulder.

Luisa came and stood by Myla. She said to the girl. "I've known some boys that are as dumb as rocks. But cute." The girls laughed. The mother smiled.

The girl pulled out a few dollar bills and put them in the mermaid cigar box. Then the daughter and mother walked away.

Lily came up to Myla and said, "You can tie yourself to me if that will make you feel better."

"Don't you worry about me, sugar," Myla said. "Why don't you go with the big kids into the book store? See if there's a book you like. Maybe they'll read to you. Stefan?"

"Sure," he said. He reached for Lily's hand. "Was it all right that we did that? Tell the stories."

"It was fine," Myla said. "I appreciate it."

The four children giggled and talked as they went into Antigone Books.

"I'm thinking I should pack up early and go home," Myla said to James. "If I need to do that, can you take us home?"

"Absolutely," James said. "Is there anything I can do?"

"I don't know," Myla said. "I think I've lost the Old Mermaids. I don't seem to have any more stories."

204

"You're just having an off day," James said. "We all have those."

James got up and walked around the table.

"This shovel is quite a find," he said, picking it up. "If I'd lost this, I would be missing it."

"I found it under a creosote bush," Myla said. "It looked like it had been there for years. I was really surprised I hadn't seen it before. I love creosote. I hate that they call that wood preservative that stinks to high heaven creosote. Everyone thinks it's the same thing. I like creosote because it is so suited for the desert."

James nodded. "You mean it's not something someone brought here from somewhere else? It fits here."

"Yes. Things that are in the desert should be things that belong in the desert," Myla said. "I think that's why Sister Lyra Musica Mermaid felt so awful after the sea dried up. She didn't think mermaids belonged in the desert. Maybe she was right. Who knows?"

"Actually, mermaids in a desert clime seem to make more sense than being in the seas around Ireland or Great Britain," James said, "given that they're often depicted half-naked."

Myla smiled. "True."

"That's a nice shovel," Bob said. Bob of Bob and Dolores. Last week he had bought the Mariner's ticket.

"Hello you two," Myla said. "I'm afraid the Old Mermaids aren't talking to me this morning."

"We were looking at this shovel," James said. "Myla found it under an old creosote bush in the wash at the Old Mermaid Sanctuary."

Myla nodded. "The creosote can tolerate drought better than almost any plant in North American. Isn't that amazing? And even though they're so slender—that's not really the right word, but you know what I mean—even though they're so slender they act as nurse logs. I've seen pack rats burrow around creosote and snakes slip-sliding under them, using them for shelter. Creosote can live for a long time. They found one in the Mojave desert that is more than 11,000 years old." She heard herself reciting these facts about the creosote and couldn't stop herself. It wasn't a story, but it was something. Maybe it would eventually turn into a story.

"The Tohono O'odham believe creosote was the first plant created. Of course, I don't think Sister Lyra Musica Mermaid knew any of this as she stood at the edge of the wash, next to the creosote bush, leaning against the shovel." Ah, there it was. A story. Maybe.

"I can't remember why she had the shovel. I don't think she remembered why she had the shovel. It was strangely muggy that day, so she couldn't concentrate very well. She was drawn to the wash, as she often was, remembering the days in the Old Sea. It had been raining in the mountains that day. She could see the storm clouds. She watched them turn from black to that grayish color after they've dumped all their water. Then quite unexpectedly, water began running by her in the wash. This was when they were relatively new to the Old Mermaid Sanctuary and she had never seen the wash anything but dry. She was so excited when she first saw the water. She thought the sea had come back. The water moved faster and faster and got deeper and deeper. Sister Lyra Musica Mermaid started to step into the flow when she suddenly remembered she did not have her sea legs any longer—or her sea tail, as it were. She wasn't sure she could go back to the sea without drowning. In fact, she was certain she would drown. She had a moment of absolute grief. Here before her was what she believed was the answer to all her desires: the Old Sea. But she'd been away so long. She had changed. Her body had changed. She suddenly knew she could not go back. She fell to her knees and sobbed. Then she realized the water would soon overflow the banks of the wash and flood the Old Mermaid Sanctuary. All of their hard work creating the house and art studio and shed and everything would be ruined.

"So she started shoveling sand onto the berm to make it higher. Maybe she could keep the water away from the house at least. She wasn't thinking very clearly, obviously. She was one person shoveling dirt much slower than the new river was eating it away. After a few minutes—or seconds, time was strange then—she looked down and realized she had dug herself into a hole. The water would breach the berm any second, fill up the hole, and she would probably drown."

Myla paused. A small crowd had gathered. Her vision was blurred by tears. What was happening to her? Was she crying? Other people sometimes cried when she told her stories, but she never did.

"So what happened?" someone asked when she didn't continue.

Myla closed her eyes. What did happen? What would happen? *Don't desert me now.*

"The water roared over the berm," Myla said. "It knocked Sister Lyra Musica Mermaid over. Yet she clung to that shovel. The one James is holding. At least I think that is the same one. It was heavy. The shovel. Partially made from metal. But she didn't let go. The water swirled all around her. She was once again reunited with the sea."

Myla stopped again.

"Is that the end?" someone asked.

"She didn't die," Trevor said. "She couldn't have. Because you said this was near the beginning and I've heard stories about her after." He opened his journal and began flipping through.

"Yes, she's the one Mr. Hunter almost hit with the arrow," Stefan said. "Wasn't the arrow after this?"

Myla looked at the people gathered around her. Lily watched her.

"Did she die?"

Myla reached out and touched Lily's face.

Did the Old Mermaid die? Was that what was going to happen?

"Well," Myla said, "the other Old Mermaids heard the roar of the water and they ran down to the wash and saw the end of the shovel poking up in the roiling water. They got a piece of rope—maybe it was rope from the same roll where they got the orange rope that Lily is wearing—and they tied themselves to a mesquite tree, because the mesquite roots are so deep. They formed a human line until they could reach Sister Lyra Musica Mermaid. And they did reach her. They pulled her out of the flood and lay her on the dirt. She was still for a moment, quiet, and then she coughed and came to her senses. She was so happy to be alive. They all were. Sister Lyra Musica Mermaid suffered no long term effects from her ride in the wash, but she did realize finally and forever that she could never go back to the sea."

"Does that mean she wasn't a mermaid any more?" someone asked. Who?

"Yes," Myla said. "I guess that meant she wasn't a mermaid any longer."

Which meant none of them were mermaids.

Which meant no need for an Old Mermaid Sanctuary.

Which meant no Church of the Old Mermaids.

Didn't it?

Myla stood. "I think that's all for today." Maybe forever.

The small crowd began to disperse.

James set the shovel down.

"It's not what you need?" Myla asked.

He shook his head. "Not today. You might want to hold onto

it."

"It won't do me much good," Myla said.

"It saved Sister Lyra Musica Mermaid," James said.

I made her up, she wanted to say. *I made it all up.*

Gail's car pulled up to the curve. She got out and came over to them.

"Hey, what's going on? I came back early so I could hear some stories," Gail said.

"It's done," Myla said.

Gail frowned. "What do you mean?"

"Would you all mind going with James?" Myla asked the children. "You were coming for dinner tonight, right, James?"

James nodded.

"You could just come over now," she said.

"That's fine with me," James said.

"I want to talk to Gail. Lily and Luisa, you okay going with the guys?"

"Sure," Luisa said. "As long as they're not going to kidnap us or anything."

Lily looked up at her.

"Oops. Sorry. No, it'll be fine. I'll go with."

Lily held the orange rope out to Luisa, and she took it.

They all helped put away the Church of the Old Mermaids and pack the boxes and table into Gail's car. Then James and the children drove away. Myla got into the car with Gail, and they headed down Speedway toward the Crow house.

"What's going on, Myla?" Gail asked.

"I think the Old Mermaids are gone," Myla said.

"What do you mean gone? You made them up. Don't you have control over that?"

"That's what I mean," Myla said. "I think maybe I did just make them up."

Gail gripped the steering wheel. "I don't mean to be dense, Myla, but I don't understand."

"You never understood the Old Mermaids," Myla said.

"Oh, so this is about me and how obtuse I am?"

"No!" Myla said. "This is about me. Can't you just listen?"

Gail was silent.

"I told you about the mermaid tile," Myla said. "Well, there's more. It turns out that David Thomas Crow and I had a relationship."

Gail glanced over at her and then back at the road. "What do you mean 'it turns out.' Wouldn't you know if you had a relationship with him?"

"We were friends," Myla said. "We had that kind of relationship. But one night I got drunk and he told me he loved me and we had sex. I didn't remember the next morning and he never told me, until a couple of days ago."

"You got so drunk you had sex and didn't remember it? Geez, Myla. I didn't know you had it in ya."

"Not funny," Myla said.

"So what's the big tragedy?" Gail said. "You didn't catch anything did you?"

"No!" Myla said. "He told me that after we had sex he went and painted the mermaid in the pool. He said I came out and found him there. He was holding a bottle."

"So what?"

"Don't you remember the dream?" Myla said. "In the dream the mermaid was holding out a bottle to me."

Gail started to laugh. "You mean you dressed David Crow in women's clothes—or a mermaid's tail—and mistook him for a mermaid?"

"It's not funny!" Myla said.

"It most certainly is," Gail said. "First you're upset about the mermaid tile and now you think the mermaid in your dream was David."

"I didn't say that," Myla said. "Not exactly. It's just that I thought the mermaids were mine, damn it. The Church of the Old Mermaids was my siren song! Now I don't know what it is. I thought the freaking universe chose me to tell the Old Mermaid stories and help save a few people in the process."

"What's a siren song? What do you mean save a few people?"

"I use the money from the Church of the Old Mermaids to help migrants who cross the border and get lost in the desert," Myla said.

"What?"

"That's right," Myla said. "I'm been aiding and abetting illegal aliens. I've got my own stash houses, right out there at the Old Mermaid Sanctuary. Houses, actually. Call *la migra*. Make fun of me. Lecture me about whatever you want to lecture me about."

"I can only say again: what?"

"You heard me."

"Jesus H. Christ."

"Yeah, well."

Gail started laughing again. "You old subversive, you. Why didn't you tell me?"

"I thought you'd turn me in."

"What a bitch you must take me for," Gail said.

"Okay. I didn't really think you would turn me in," Myla said. "It was just something I did, and I didn't want to involve you."

"Does Theresa know?"

"No, no, it's been all me."

"She's been helping you, hasn't she?"

"Okay, maybe a little."

"She's not so bad," Gail said. "We had fun going out to the

movies. We made fun of Luisa the whole time."

"I bet Luisa appreciated that," Myla said.

"Does this have anything to do with why you closed the church early today?" Gail asked.

"I didn't have any stories," Myla said. "Trevor and Stefan had to step in and help me. When I finally had a story I almost drowned one of the Old Mermaids."

"You were going to kill one of them?"

"I wasn't personally going to kill a mermaid," Myla said. "But one of them was going to drown."

"Dying is part of life," Gail said. "Even for mermaids, I would imagine. What did happen to the Old Mermaids, anyway? I mean why did they leave the Old Mermaid Sanctuary?"

"That's a story for another day," Myla said.

"That's what you always say," Gail said.

"I know, but aren't you listening? I don't have any stories today."

"Except the one where you almost drowned some poor little mermaid."

"She wasn't little. Don't ever say little mermaid around me. Even if some of them were little, they were not any of them the little mermaid."

"All right! For someone who has decided the Old Mermaids are not real and that you made them all up after all, you are awfully touchy about them."

"Do you ever wonder why we're friends?" Myla asked.

"Because my husband is a sonofabitch and I need an excuse to get out of the house every Saturday."

"And I'm just what you needed," Myla said.

"Yep."

"I wonder what I need now?"

"Why not try another roll in the hay with David Crow?" Gail

said. "This time do it when you're sober. Might be fun."

"You're not helping," Myla said.

"You know, you did get over your divorce pretty fast."

"You were just complaining last week that I wasn't getting over it, that I was hanging onto the memories of a man who wasn't worth it."

"Okay, but besides stalking Richard once a year," Gail said, "and a month or more of drunkenness ten years ago, I don't remember you actually dealing with how you felt about it all."

"I felt terrible," Myla said. "Once you know that, you move on."

"I agree with you there," Gail said. "You know I'm not one of these touchy feely types who wants to analyze everything. I think most therapists are quacks. Come on. Look at the word therapist: the rapist."

"Your point, Gail?"

"I just mean you went from seeing your husband having sex with your next door neighbor straight to the Crow place, practically, you indulged in a bit of wanton drunkenness, and then you were on to the Church of the Old Mermaids. And then apparently you began saving people in the desert. What about your own private life?"

"That was my own private life," Myla said. "*Is* my own private life."

"That's my point," Gail said. "What about love? What about family? What about community? You used to be involved in things. You were one of the *los Tucsonenses*. You used to have lots of friends. You disappeared."

"I didn't disappear," Myla said. "I'm right here. And I am involved in a community. It's just a private community."

"I'm assuming you don't see the migrants you rescue from the desert once they leave the sanctuary, right?" Gail said. "I think it's great you've been helping people, but they aren't your friends. I'm just wondering about the rest of your life. You can't actually call what you have with George a relationship."

"George wants me to move in with him," Myla said.

"What? When did this happen?"

"Yesterday, day before," she said. "I've lost track."

"Sounds like you've had quite the week," Gail said.

"And you don't know even half of it," Myla said. "I talked to Richard. I told him I wanted my old dresser. And the mermaid tile. He said he'd send the dresser but not the tile, so George went over there to get the tile and he had sex with his ex-wife."

"You're saying Richard's name again," Gail said. "I guess that's something. George had sex with your ex-husband's wife? You've got to tell Richard about it, Myla. What great revenge."

"I don't want revenge," Myla said. "I don't want anything from him. I just want to be free of him. All these...feelings—or whatever they are—have been coming back this week and I don't like it."

"I love you, Myla," Gail said. "You know that. And I've always understood you're an all or nothing kind of person. You were all in your marriage and all in your business because that's what your husband required. And when it was over, it was over. You couldn't have anything to do with anything that had to do with him. I was lucky you and I stayed friends. Once you moved to the Crow house and you had the dream, everything was about the Church of the Old Mermaids, just like before it was all about Richard and the business. It's great to be so dedicated to one thing, but in real life, most things don't stand up to that kind of dedication."

"What do you mean?" Myla asked.

"I think you expect things to be perfect," Gail said.

"I do not," Myla said. "Look at my life. It's far from perfect."

"It's perfect in it's imperfection," Gail said.

"Richard was imperfect and I allowed for that."

"No, you didn't," Gail said. "You didn't see what a controlling imperfect freak he was until his imperfection was spread naked on the bed before you. It never occurred to you that he was imperfect before that."

"I don't expect my friends to be anyone but who they are," Myla said. "I'm not a perfectionist."

"I know that," Gail said. "I just mean that you sometimes see perfection where there isn't any."

Myla looked out the window. "I feel so sad," Myla said. "I don't know what to do about it."

"Oh sweetheart," Gail said. "You don't have to do anything about it. Just feel it. Dance under the moon and howl. Cry. Walk the wash."

"You sound so wise," Myla asked. "How did that happen?"

"It started in my ass and just spread," Gail said.

Myla laughed. "You remind me of Sister Sophia Mermaid," she said. "Or she reminds me of you."

"Actually, several years ago when I was sad about my marriage, you gave me the same advice I just gave you. Things don't always turn out all right, you said, but they always turn out."

"One way or the other," Myla said. "Are you coming for dinner tonight?"

"I might."

Myla looked over at her friend.

"Are you feeling sorry for me?" Myla asked.

"No, I thought it might be fun," Gail said.

"Right. And hell just froze over."

Gail helped Myla put the boxes back in her apartment, and then she left. James waited for Myla by his car. The children sat on the front porch with David and Maria.

"Trevor wants to hang out here until dinner," James said, "if that's all right. I have some work to do at home, but I'll come back later."

Myla nodded. "Thanks, James."

James hugged her. "Three teenagers are a lot to take," he said. "You sure?"

"Teenagers got nothing on adults," Myla said. "It'll be fine."

James waved to the children, said good-bye to Myla, then got in his car and drove away.

"Let's show Trevor the Old Mermaid cards we were working on," Luisa said to Stefan.

"I put everything out on the kitchen table," David said, "just like last week."

The children hurried into the house. Myla smiled. Funny how children always seemed to be running. Always in a hurry. Maria got up and followed them inside.

"I ended the Church of the Old Mermaids early today," Myla said.

"Everything all right?" David asked.

"Fine."

"We've been working on dinner," he said. "We got some recipes from my mom's cookbooks. We roasted chiles and made tomato sauce to put on blue cornmeal tortilla pizza. We chopped up some veggies too. We also made pumpkin pudding, which I need to take out of the oven soon. Plus we have a salad of fresh greens and black bean soup."

"I didn't think we were gone long enough for you to do all that," she said. She couldn't think of what else to say.

"I soaked the beans yesterday," he said, "and started cooking this morning. Maria and Ernesto helped. It seemed to cheer Maria. And Ernesto said his wife never let him cook. When he gets home,

216

he said, he's going to surprise her by making dinner one day."

"He's talking about going home?"

"He is," David said. "Either that or going to Washington or Oregon. He got a hold of a friend of his who said he thought he could get him work on an organic farm, so he wouldn't be exposed to pesticides again. But that's seasonal. He's talking about trying to get work on a trawler again, in Mexico. Might see another mermaid, he said."

They were silent for a moment. Then Myla said, "I'm shutting down the Old Mermaid Sanctuary. I see now that it was wrong to lie to the owners. I know how betrayed they would feel." She looked at David. "I'll call and tell them all."

"They might have you arrested."

"Then I'll be arrested."

"You can't be that sanguine about it," he said.

Myla walked down the steps and went across the drive toward her apartment. David followed.

"I don't want to be arrested," Myla said, "but that seems the least of it. I'll tell them. Then I'll leave here, one way or another."

"When did you decide this?" David asked.

"Just now," she said. "Just as I said it."

He gently touched her arm to get her to stop. "Why?"

"Because it all feels wrong now," Myla said. "Everything feels different."

"Different isn't always bad," David said.

"All of it feels—" She stopped.

"What? What does it feel like?"

"Like I have no control over any of it," she said. Just like when my husband left, she didn't say. Or she left her husband. Whichever.

She kept walking until she turned the corner of the barn and saw her old oak dresser sitting in the dirt near her porch.

"I forgot to tell you," David said. "This was delivered soon after you left this morning."

She ran her finger through the dust on the dresser top.

"I didn't know where you wanted it," he said.

"Who brought it?" she asked.

"Some guys in a truck," he said. "I had to sign for it."

The dresser looked smaller than she remembered and utterly out of place here, standing in the sand between her apartment and the corrals. She opened the top left drawer. Empty. She continued opening the drawers on the left side from top to bottom. All empty. Then she went up the right side, opening one after another. Empty. Empty. Empty. She opened the top right hand drawer. Inside it a mermaid tile lay in pieces.

Myla stared at the mermaid.

David came and stood next to her.

"Is that the mermaid tile from your old house?" he asked.

Myla slowly closed the drawer. "I think so," she said.

She started to walk away. David reached for her hand.

"Myla, come into the house," he said. "Help the kids with the Old Mermaid cards. They could use your guidance."

Myla laughed unhappily.

"I doubt I could give them any guidance," she said.

"Don't be alone now," he said.

"You don't know anything about me," she said.

"I know," he said, "but come into the house anyway."

She hesitated, then nodded and went with David to the house. She left her hand in his for a moment and then she pulled it away.

Myla watched as the four children worked on new Old Mermaid cards. The kitchen smelled of cilantro, corn, and tomato sauce: like an Italian and Mexican restaurant. Maria took the pumpkin pudding out of the oven. David went over to her, and they conferred about whether the pudding was done or not.

"It's a beautiful blue day," Myla said. "Why are you all in here? You want to make some art? Let's go outside!"

The children followed Myla outside. She led them through the dusty barn to the door at the furthest end of it. She opened it. Inside the ten by ten room were cacti skeletons, branches, feathers, bones, and other less organic odds and ends she had found in the wash but had not taken with her to the Church of the Old Mermaids.

"Wow," Luisa said as she walked into the room. "Are these the skeletons of the Old Mermaids?"

"That would explain what happened to them," Trevor said. "Where'd this all come from?"

"The wash," Myla said. "I've been collecting it for the last ten years. You can use it all."

"Not a lot of color," Luisa said.

"That's what happens when things die," Myla said.

"They've got moon beauty," Stefan said. "Remember that story Maria told about her grandmother."

"That's right," Luisa said. "Moon beautiful."

"We can use the stuff David gave us, too," Stefan said, "if we want some other colors"

"Are you ever going to tell us where the Old Mermaids went?" Trevor asked.

Myla said, "I don't know."

"You don't know if you'll tell us or you don't know what happened to them?" Luisa asked.

"I know where the Old Mermaids are," Lily said.

"Sure you do," Luisa said. "Are you going to show us?"

Lily swayed back and forth and smiled.

"Well, go ahead and make whatever art you want," Myla said.

"It all belongs to the wash, however. So, I'll ask you not to take any of it from the Old Mermaid Sanctuary."

"What were you saving it for?" Luisa asked.

"I was saving it for you," Myla said. "Take care you watch out for Lily. Don't let her get that rope tangled up in anything."

Myla started to leave the barn.

"Aren't you going to stay with us?" Stefan asked.

"I just remembered some other things you can use," she said.

She hurried to her apartment, picked up two Church of the Old Mermaids boxes, and carried them out to the barn. Then she went back to her apartment and got the other boxes.

"You can use any of the things in these boxes," Myla said.

"But these belong to the church," Trevor said. "You won't have anything else to sell."

Myla shrugged. "Then maybe that will be the end of the Church of the Old Mermaids. Wait. There's one more thing."

She walked out to where the dresser was, pulled out the top right drawer, and carried it over to the boxes. She opened the top box, then turned the drawer upside down and let the pieces of the mermaid fall into the box.

"There you are," Myla said. She handed Trevor the drawer. "You can use the dresser if you like, too. Have fun now."

Myla waved and walked away. She went back inside her apartment, closed the door, and went to sleep.

Ten

Laugh or weep. We swim in your tears.
Grand Mother Yemaya Mermaid

"Goddamnit woman, open the door!" George pounded on the door for the third time.

Myla sighed, got up off the bed, and opened the door.

"What?" she said

"What are you doing? Are you sleeping in the middle of the day again? I called you several times."

"I was reading," she said.

"With your eyes closed I guess."

"Yeah, well."

"I'm here for the Saturday night dinner," he said.

"Now?" she said.

"Yep," he said. "It's Saturday. It's dark. Time for dinner."

"I guess hell hath froze over," Gail said, coming up behind George. "I'm here. Theresa is right behind me. She brought that

Cathy person. And her husband."

"She brought Cathy's husband?" Myla said.

"No. Theresa brought her own husband. His name is Raygun or something."

"It's Del Rey," Myla said.

"Are we eating in here?" George asked. "I wanted to take a looksee at my competition in the house."

"His competition?" Gail said. "What's he talking about?"

"I don't know," Myla said. She grabbed a sweater from her bed and put it on. Then she left the apartment with George and Gail right behind her. "Maybe George thinks I have the hots for Ernesto."

"Who's Ernesto?" they both asked.

Then George said, "Myla knows what I'm talking about."

"She told me you asked her to move in with her," Gail said as they walked toward the house. "You think she'll do it?"

"She said she didn't think so," George said, "but I'm still hopeful."

"Don't talk about me like I'm not here," Myla said.

In front of them, Theresa and Cathy were walking up the steps to the kitchen; both carried dishes. Del Rey unrolled himself from his car. At least that was what it looked like. He was so tall and lean.

"Del Rey," Myla said. "As I live and breathe, as you would say."

"Hello, darlin'," he said. Myla and Del Rey embraced.

"You smell nice," Myla said. "What is that?"

"Just Texan charm," he said.

"It's about time you turned up here," Myla said. "This may be our last Saturday night."

"On Earth?" he asked, putting his arm across her shoulders. "Then it is a good thing we came."

"Our last Saturday night dinner," Myla said. "You promise to ignore anything illegal that might be going on here, right? You being a cop and everything."

"As long as you've got the crack house locked up tight," he said. "I won't notice a thing."

"Yep," Myla said as they all went inside. "How you doing tonight, Cathy?"

"I'm fine," Cathy said. "Clean and sober. Where's my boy?"

"I'm right here, Mom," Stefan said as he came into the kitchen. He hugged his mother. "Man, you smell like cigarettes."

"One addiction at a time, sweetheart," she said.

"Don't worry, son," Del Rey said. "I don't let her smoke in our house and I leave photos of dead people under her pillow."

"Now that's just creepy," Gail said.

George made a point of shaking David's hand and not letting go straight away when Myla introduced them to one another. David looked him in the eyes, and they stared at each other. Myla rolled her eyes.

"Are we eating inside or out?" Myla asked. She felt better in the company of all these people—even if some of them, i.e., George and David, were acting childishly. James gave her a hug.

"You feeling better?" he asked.

"I think so," Myla said.

"How many chairs do we need?" David asked.

"Thirteen," Luisa said. "Just like the Old Mermaids. We'll each be one of the Old Mermaids tonight. Dibs on Sissy Maggie."

"I wanted to be Sissy Maggie," Stefan said. "She's an artist."

"There are other artists," Luisa said. "I want Sissy Maggie Mermaid because she's a lover, not a fighter."

"Oh lord," Theresa said. "Which one of the Old Mermaids stayed a virgin her whole life and never dated?"

"None of them," Luisa said. She looked at the boys and the

223

three of them said together, "It's not the Old Mermaid way."

"I will be Sister Sheila Na Giggles Mermaid," Ernesto said.

They all looked at him.

"Why Sheila?" Theresa asked.

"I know why," Myla said.

Ernesto grinned.

"Sister Sheila Na Giggles Mermaid tells her fair share of off-color jokes," Trevor said. "I've noticed you like those jokes too. Is that why?"

Everyone laughed.

"We can figure out what mermaids we are later," Theresa said. "I'm hungry."

"Now that—" Stefan began and Luisa and Trevor joined in to finish "—is the Old Mermaid way."

"And that," Gail said, "is going to get annoying."

"*Get* annoying?" Cathy said.

"We're going to have to put up a couple of card tables if we want to eat outside," David said.

"Let's get busy," Myla said.

A few minutes later they dropped two oilcloths over one patio table and two card tables. Then they brought out plates, glasses, and flatware, followed by the food.

They all sat around the table. A cool breeze fluttered the dry leaves that hung down below the tree's green leaves, like the skirt on a hula dancer. The light in the pool glowed eerily.

Everyone looked at Myla expectantly.

"It's not my house," Myla said. "David?"

"But isn't it tradition that you give the blessing at the Saturday dinners? I'm a newcomer."

"We're all newcomers," Myla said. "We can take turns."

"Well then," David said. "I thank Maria for being the co-cook and everyone else who brought food. I thank the land for growing our food and sustaining us. And I am grateful for all of you being here. It's been a strange tumultuous week and I've felt totally defeated and lost and absolutely exhilarated at the same time. Thank you for allowing me to be a part of it."

"It's your house, friend," Cathy said. "We're glad you've opened it to us."

"Can we eat?" Luisa asked. "I'm starving."

"Dig in," Myla said.

They ate in silence for a few minutes. Myla looked around the table. Lily grinned at her as she chewed her salad. Maria stared into space while she ate. Cathy glanced over at Stefan. Her face looked better—not as red, calmer, sober. Trevor and Luisa whispered to each other about something. James asked Gail about the dish she brought. Theresa and Del Rey held hands under the table. Ernesto ate with gusto. He had gotten so much better since he first arrived at the Old Mermaid Sanctuary.

"Did you see the mermaid in the pool?" Theresa asked Del Rey.

"I did," he said. "I'm not sure I understand the Old Mermaids, but it sounds interesting. I seem to remember mermaids were pretty naked."

"Pretty naked," Myla asked, "or pretty and naked?"

"Del Rey," Theresa said.

"I'm just trying to understand," he said. "And if mermaids are beautiful and naked, then what about Old Mermaids? Are they still lookers?"

Theresa and Gail moaned.

"What does that even mean?" Myla asked.

"What *does* it mean?" Gail asked. "What is your definition of a looker?"

"My wife," Del Rey said.

"I'm sure all the mermaids don't look like Theresa," Gail said.

"He's trying to get you all riled up," Theresa said. "That's what he does."

"That's a good skill for a police officer to have, eh?" Myla said.

"I understand irony, Miss Myla," Del Rey said. "But don't you think an old mermaid would be gray and wrinkly? Not very attractive."

"Who says gray and wrinkly isn't beautiful?" Luisa said. "Maria said where she comes from that's called moon beauty."

"We're all the same when the lights are out," Cathy said.

"You men back me up here," Del Rey said. "Gray and wrinkled ain't beautiful."

"I'm not backing you up," James said. "You're digging the hole yourself and you can stand in it by yourself. Besides I don't agree with you."

"Didn't we have this conversation last Saturday?" Theresa asked.

"You mean you talk about this kind of stuff every Saturday?" Gail said. "How fun. I think."

"This just proves how much better women are than men," Luisa said. "Look at you, Del Rey. You're as skinny as a toothbrush, with a pot belly hanging over your belt and not enough hair to cover a turnip let alone your big ol' head, and you've got a babe like my mother on your arm. You see beautiful women with men that look like turds all the time. We're not as shallow as you all are. We understand beauty is more than skin deep."

"Is this my boy-crazy daughter talking?" Theresa said.

"I'm not boy-crazy," Luisa said.

"I think she's right," David said. "Generally speaking women are more open-minded about who they'll love. Appearance doesn't matter as much."

"Appearance matters," Gail said. "We're just more eclectic in

226

our tastes."

"You're all fooling yourselves," Del Rey said. "Women want someone tall, dark, and handsome, too, but they're more willing to settle. They can close their eyes and pretend. Men aren't as good at pretending."

"You're saying men have no imagination?" Myla said.

"I'm saying Theresa closes her eyes a lot," Del Rey said.

Everyone laughed.

"Gross," Luisa said.

"You Americans are too particular," Ernesto said. "You want everything clean and perfect. Like in an operating room. You want your people like that too. We like things with more color and aroma down south."

"What about Brazil?" Trevor asked. "Don't a lot of people have plastic surgery?"

"Something in the water there," Ernesto said.

"If you like it so much down south as you say," Cathy said, "why do so many of you come up here? Isn't this the life you want?"

"I want to feed my family," Ernesto said. "I wish I could do it in my own country." He started speaking in Spanish and Theresa translated. "There is a difference between wanting to feed your family, wanting clean water and good medical care, and wanting everything to look the same and be the same. I like the smells and sounds and feel of my village. We have not always taken care of the land like we should and our leaders are often corrupt and our economy is not so good, so we come here to the land of plenty." He said, "Land of plenty" in English. "Many people have been kind to me here and I am grateful. But I miss my home. I can't explain it. It's just my home. And the people there have more color."

"I don't know what he means by that," Cathy said.

"It means we don't have much soul here," Stefan said. "We're a bunch of vampires."

"I was only talking about differences," Ernesto said.

"You criticize us, but you'd bring your family here in a heartbeat," Cathy said.

Ernesto nodded. "This is true. I wish I could make a living in my village, but I cannot."

"Why do you sound angry with him?" Del Rey said. "What's wrong with him trying to feed his family? That's what we're all trying to do. People all over the world are trying to do what comes fairly easily to many of us."

"I just think people should obey the law," Cathy said. "They should come here legally. That's all."

"How many times have you gone out drinking and driving?" Stefan asked.

"That's different," Cathy said.

"How's that different?" Stefan asked. "Ernesto didn't kill anyone by coming here."

"I didn't either!" Cathy said. "I was sick."

"You could have killed someone," Stefan said. "Ernesto is trying to save his family. He's trying to get a better life. He's trying to feed his family."

"I don't think most of us in this country understand real poverty," Trevor said.

"I've been very poor in my day," Cathy said. "I've had tough times."

"It's apples and oranges," James said.

"I feel like you're all ganging up on me," Cathy said.

"We're having a discussion," David said. "If you give an opinion, you should be willing to defend it."

"It is a sign of respect that we are having this discussion with you," Myla said. "All good conversation is the search for the truth. If any of us knew exactly what the answer was, we'd say it and then the conversation would be over."

David said, "I'll go put the pizzas in now. Anyone want to come help me decide on toppings?"

The three teenagers, and Lily, Maria, Del Rey, George, and Myla followed David into the kitchen. George pulled Myla aside.

"Can I talk to you?" he asked quietly.

Myla started to ask him what about, but instead she went to the kitchen door and stepped out onto the porch with him.

"What is it?" she asked.

"Have you decided?" George asked.

"About what? About moving in with you?"

He nodded. "I can't stop thinking about it," he said. "About you and me being together. We haven't been together for a while and I miss it."

"George, why the hurry? What's going on? This isn't like you."

"I've realized how much I care about you," he said. "I've been stupid and inconsiderate not to want to do this earlier."

"What do you mean?" Myla said. "I haven't been sitting around waiting for you to invite me to move in with you. I have no desire to live with you. You can be pretty untidy, George. You pick your teeth. You're a slob. When's the last time you cleaned that bathroom? All those little eccentricities are fine in a friend but not in someone you live with day in and day out."

"We're great in bed together," George said.

"George, having sex is not the end all be all thing," Myla said.

"But you've always been satisfied, haven't you?"

"Yes, George. Listen. You and I are great friends. We have fun in bed. Sex is sex. It's a release. It's fun. It's intimate. And it doesn't take a rocket scientist to do it. Insert A into B or rub B against A or—"

"I get the idea," George said. He moved away from her.

"He sent the dresser," Myla said. She reached for George's arm and pulled him toward her. "And the tile."

George smiled slightly. "I got you the tile?"

"You did," Myla said. She didn't need to tell him it was broken. "And I can't tell how much I appreciate that. I know your heart is in the right place."

He took her hand and pressed it against his chest. "It's right here, Myla. Beatin' for you."

She wanted to laugh, but she kissed his cheek instead.

"You're such an old romantic, George."

"Give me a break," he said. "I'm trying. I'm trying to tell you what I'm feeling."

"I think you're feeling all of this because you saw David," Myla said. "And you're feeling like your territory is being threatened. So you've got to go piss around in the corners."

"Naw," George said. "I've always known you weren't mine." He was silent for a moment. "But you might be right. I remember from back then that you two had a way of being together. It was as though you'd been a couple for a long time. And tonight, I see the way you look at each other. Just like an old married couple. You seem to know what the other is thinking."

"Actually we're not getting along so well," Myla said.

"Still mad about him having sex with you when you were drunk?"

"I'm mad at him for not telling me," Myla said. "My life could have been so different."

"Has your life been bad?"

"No," Myla said. "Not at all. I just don't know if what I've been doing has been real."

"I don't understand," George said.

"I know," Myla said. "Let's go back in. They'll think we're out here having sex or something."

230

"I was hoping," George said. "Maybe this David character will put his tail between his legs and run away again."

"George," Myla said. "Don't be small."

"You know I'm not, baby."

"Oh good grief." She slapped his arm, then pushed him toward the door.

"That's another thing," Myla said. "Why do men think a big penis is something women want? As the song says, it ain't the meat it's the motion."

"That would be a good topic for discussion for Saturday night dinner," George said.

"Not with men in the room," Myla said. "We don't want to prick the poor phallus god that is so dear to you all."

"Yeah, it's not a good idea to discuss religion at the table."

George and Myla went back into the house. David looked up from the swarm of children putting toppings on the blue corn-meal tortillas that were spread across the counter and smiled at Myla.

"Put something dead on at least one of them," George said.

"It's all dead," Trevor said.

"The boy's got a point," Del Rey said

"Okay," David said, "I think that's enough. I'll put them in the oven."

"You all go finish your dinner," Myla said. "David and I will bring the pizzas out when they're done."

George hesitated, but then Lily tied herself to his wrist and pulled him away. Myla sat at the kitchen table. David sat across from her. The kitchen sighed. Outside the sound of laughter and voices came to them, muffled, cottony.

"The kids showed me what you'd given them," David said. "They're planning an art installation. I'm not supposed to tell you anything about it. Are you really shutting down the Church of the Old Mermaids?"

"I don't know," Myla said. "Something has definitely changed."

"You and George okay?"

Myla laughed. "Why are you asking about George and me? We've been going on before you were here and we went on after you were gone. Did you think you would show up here and declare your love for me and suddenly my whole life would change?"

David pressed his lips together and looked down at the table. Then he looked up and said, "Actually, yes, I think I did see it that way."

"You and George both," she said. "Just like my husband. He thought my entire world revolved around him. And it didn't. It was our life together."

"I'm not your husband," he said.

"You didn't know my husband," she said. "So you can't really say, can you? I was going to spend my life with him." She paused. "I'm glad I didn't. I'm glad I'm not with him. My life went on without him. It went on without you. It would go on without George."

"I understand all of that," David said. "Is it possible that maybe you and I could start again?"

"George says you and I already act like an old married couple," Myla said.

"I felt like I'd known you my whole life from the first time we met," he said. "And I've missed you for ten years."

"George thinks you're going to run away again," Myla said.

"Who cares what George thinks! What about you? I'm not leaving. I promise. Not unless you tell me to."

"No!" Myla said. "You have to make a decision whether you're going to be here or not. What our relationship is or isn't can't make a difference to whether you stay or leave."

"But it does," he said. "It was too difficult for me to stay last time, to see you and George together, to have you so oblivious to me."

"I'm not oblivious to you now," Myla said. "And if George and I still see each other, you're going to have to learn to deal with it."

"If?"

"We should check those pizzas," Myla said. "That oven is tricky."

"You're avoiding my question," David said.

"Isn't that too bad?" Myla said. She smiled.

"All right," David said. "Let's get the pizzas."

Eventually all the pizzas got baked. The group ate them happily.

"I've never had blue corn before," Luisa said.

"Yes, you have," Theresa said. "You used to eat it when you were younger."

"I don't remember," Luisa said.

"It's getting chilly," Gail said. "I heard it's supposed to storm in the mountains tonight."

"Can we go work in the barn when we're finished with dinner?" Stefan asked.

"It's dark," Cathy said. "Spiders, scorpions, rattlesnakes."

"Not to mention coyotes, mountain lions, and maniacs," Theresa said, laughing.

"There's light out there," Myla said.

"We want to work on the art project," Trevor said.

"Well, as long as you left your crack pipes at home," Theresa said, "it's okay with me. Del Rey will be out to check on you."

"We could use all the help we can get," Trevor said.

"I wouldn't mind seeing what they're up to," Del Rey said.

"I'm in," James said.

"Help clear the table first," Theresa said, "so us women folk can do the dishes."

"Hell with that," Cathy said. "I want to see what my kid has been up to."

"We've got a dishwasher," David said.

"Would that be you?" Theresa asked.

David smiled. "No, I meant a mechanical dishwasher."

They each grabbed something from the table and carried it inside.

"Can't us grown-ups play cards or something?" George asked.

"Sure," David said. "What do you like?"

"Whaddaya got?" George asked.

"I don't know," David said. "Crazy eights."

"That's a tough man's game," George said.

They put their plates on the countertop.

"I never said I was a tough man," David said.

"We haven't played the Old Mermaids card game yet," Luisa said.

"You wanna see tough?" Del Rey said. "I've got my berreta in the car."

"He's joking," Theresa said. "He likes to playact he's a redneck."

"He's not playacting," Luisa said.

"Sure I am," Del Rey said. "If I wasn't, you'd be out on your ass by now."

"Del Rey," Theresa said. "She's going to take you seriously."

"Isn't that called passive aggressive behavior?" Luisa said.

"I told you he's joking," Theresa said. "He just goes too far sometimes."

"I am joking, darlin'," Del Rey said. "Now show me this art project you all are doing. I fancied myself an artiste when I was a young man. When I had more hair than could cover a turnip."

"I like bald men," Gail said. "I wish my husband had less hair.

He's like an ape. Bald men should wear it proudly. Or not wear it proudly, whatever. I like a man who shines."

"I'll be back for that card game," George said.

The group filed out the door. Lily tied herself to Del Rey. Ernesto, David, Maria, and Myla stayed behind.

"I'm going to lie down," Maria said. "Unless you need help cleaning up."

"We can get it," David said.

"That man Deal a ray," Ernesto said.

"Del Rey," Myla said.

"He's a police officer?" Ernesto asked. "Is he going to arrest me and send me back?"

Myla shook her head. "No. He doesn't know anything about you or why you're here. Don't worry."

"He was talking about his gun," Ernesto said.

"That's just what some men do around here," David said. "They talk about their guns."

"As long as no one points one at me," Ernesto said in Spanish.

Eleven

She who laughs a lot laughs a lot.

Sister Laughs A Lot Mermaid

David and Myla loaded the dishwasher together. She rinsed; he dropped the plates in. Then David filled the kettle with water. After a while, George, Gail, Cathy, and Theresa returned. They played hearts with David. Myla watched for a while. Then she wandered out toward the barn; James stopped her before she went inside.

"They want to surprise you," he told her.

She nodded and turned and walked in the other direction, away from the light. The moon had risen, and now the sand looked like snow. Everything looked as though it was covered in a layer of snow. She breathed deeply. She liked the moonlight. She understood why Sissy Maggie Mermaid had fallen in love with the moon.

"Myla?"

She stopped and turned around. Stefan came toward her.

"Hello," she said. "Are you having a good time?"

"Yes," he said. "Can I talk to you about something?"

"Of course," she said. They continued walking down the driveway.

"My mom says she's going into therapy," he said. "With my stepdad. They're both going to go to rehab."

"That sounds like a good idea," Myla said.

"She wants me to go home with her tonight," he said, "until they go in. I'm afraid if I go home, they'll never go in."

"That's a reasonable fear," she said. "Maybe David would let you stay here while your mother is in rehab. Or maybe you could rethink foster care. Or go to a relative."

"I don't want to go to a relative," Stefan said. "They're all users, either drugs or alcohol. I don't want to end up that way."

"You're in a terrible predicament," Myla said. "I understand that."

"Del Rey was just talking to me about my stepdad," he said. "He said that Theresa had mentioned to him that my stepdad was hitting me. He said it was his duty to report it. He hadn't yet because he wanted to talk with me, but if I was going back to live with them, he felt like he had to report it."

"Well, you knew that could happen," Myla said. "It's probably for the best."

"Del Rey said my stepdad could be put away for a long time," Stefan said, "and that I would probably have to testify against him."

"Are you afraid he might retaliate?" Myla asked. They stopped at the end of the driveway. The dirt road opened up. The golden sand now looked like snow, too.

"When my mom and stepdad drink," he said, "they fight. And then they start hitting each other." Stefan paused and looked away.

He cleared his throat. "She hits him as much as he hits her."

"But he's a man," Myla said. "He shouldn't be hitting a woman."

"I understand that completely," Stefan said, "but it's not that simple in this case. It's like they're professional wrestlers who are pounding on each other. My mom gives as good as she gets."

"But he hits you," Myla said. "That's inexcusable."

Stefan didn't say anything.

"Unless—have you been fighting with him like your mom does?"

He shook his head and stared at his fingers.

"Your stepdad does hit you, doesn't he?" Myla asked.

Stefan did not say anything for a long time. Then he said, "No. He's never hit me. He doesn't pay any attention to me. He's a jerk. I hate him and I hate my mom. But I don't want him to go to jail for something he didn't really do."

"Stefan, why did you say he hit you?"

"It was the only way I could think of to get you and my mom to let me stay here," he said. "I didn't want to go back to that house with them."

"How do I know you're not lying now," Myla said, "to get out of testifying?"

He shrugged. "I don't know. But I'm not."

"He hasn't threatened you or anything, has he?" Myla asked. "Is that why you're saying this now?"

"No, I haven't seen him," Stefan said. "I haven't been away from here except with you. He hasn't called. Ask David. I'm telling you the truth now."

"You have to tell your mother," Myla said. "If you want, I'll tell Theresa and Del Rey, but your mother has to know."

"I'm sorry I lied to you," Stefan said.

"I'm glad you told the truth now," Myla said, "before it went too far. You need to tell David too."

"Can't I tell everyone at once?"

"Was it easy for you to lie in the first place?" Myla asked.

"No," he said.

"Good," she said, "but making up for it shouldn't be any easier."

"Can you be there when I tell my mother?" he asked.

"It's between you and your mother," Myla said. "You need to tell her now."

"Yes, ma'am," he said.

Myla watched him walk away until he disappeared into the night, only to reappear when he reached the edge of the circle the porch light made in the sand. It had never occurred to her that Stefan would lie. Never. She had gone along with what he said with never a thought that he was making it all up. What did that mean about her judgment?

Myla went back to the house and got Theresa and took her outside. She told her what Stefan had confessed to her.

"That is one screwed up family," Theresa said. "I'm sorry I ever involved you in this."

"Is she really going into rehab?" Myla asked.

"She said she would, Monday morning. Eddie too. Her husband."

"Stefan needs some professional help," Myla said. "To go this far is an indication that all is not well."

"Clearly," Theresa said. "Cathy wants me to take him home with us tonight, but I really don't have the room. She's sleeping on the couch as it is."

They heard raised voices out near Myla's apartment.

"Ah, there's the mother and son team now," Theresa said. "I'll go mediate—and make certain my husband doesn't go for his gun. He's a cop. He's got a badge."

Myla laughed and went into the house. She caught David's

gaze and motioned him over to her. He excused himself from the card game, and he and Myla went into his bedroom.

"Stefan is going to talk to you about this himself," Myla said, "but I wanted to let you know that he's been lying about his stepdad. He says now that his dad has not been hitting him. He says he lied so he could stay here."

"What does that mean?" David asked. "Besides that he's capable of accusing someone of something like that."

"I don't know," Myla said. "He needs to get help. He could accuse any of us of anything. I believed him about his stepdad. I didn't question him."

"I didn't either," he said. "I believed him because you believed him."

"That's dangerous," Myla said. She sat on the edge of the bed. "I don't really know what to do. Wait and see what his mother says, I guess."

They went back into the kitchen. George looked at her. She mouthed the words, "I'll tell you later." Outside she could see Theresa, Del Rey, Cathy, and Stefan talking. Near the barn, Trevor, James, Luisa, and Lily watched. Myla sighed. She walked across the room and went outside. She glanced at the barn. James was herding the children back inside.

"Are you going to accuse me of hitting you next?" Cathy was saying.

"I'd never do that," Stefan said. "I'd never accuse anyone of doing anything. I panicked. I didn't know what to do. I hate living with you and Eddie. My stomach hurts all the time. I want to drink. I want to do drugs. I don't want to end up like you."

"I'm not a liar," Cathy said.

"It was this one thing," Stefan said. His voice cracked as he spoke, and tears ran down his cheeks.

"This puts a lot of people in an awkward position," Theresa

said. "Anyone who took care of you would be afraid you'd falsely accuse them."

"No! I'm not like that!"

"Lucky for you I never told your stepdad what you said," Cathy said. "Otherwise he probably would beat the shit out of you, and rightly so."

Myla stood next to Stefan.

"Excuse me," Myla said. "I don't want to butt in on a family matter, but I think it's clear that Stefan needs some professional help. Maybe next week we could find him some."

"I'm going into rehab," Cathy said.

"Okay. If you want, maybe I could help Stefan find a therapist. I could talk with his social worker, or someone. Have you heard of Al-Anon for teenagers? Maybe that would help."

"I'm not sick," Stefan said.

"But you do need some help," Myla said, "and obviously none of us is doing you much good."

"Staying here is helping me," Stefan said.

"You started lying here," Cathy said.

"I lied because I'm sick of cleaning up your vomit and hiding while you two tear apart the house," Stefan said. "It's just luck one of you hasn't physically hurt me yet. You've hurt me every other way."

"Cathy, why don't you and Stefan go into my apartment and you can talk privately."

Cathy hesitated. Then she folded her arms across her chest and started toward the barn. Stefan followed.

"Interesting Saturday nights you have here," Del Rey said. "False accusations. A little girl who ties herself to strangers with an orange rope. Mermaids. Illegal aliens."

"Who says anything about illegal aliens?" Theresa said.

"I saw some landing in the corral," Del Rey said.

"Those are called horses, dear," Theresa said.

"With antennae?" Del Rey said. "What about dessert? I'm still hungry. Gotta feed this belly."

"James!" Myla called. "Time for pumpkin pudding."

An instant later the children poured out of the barn like bees out of a hive. Lily swung the end of the rope in the air. Soon, they were all in the kitchen, sitting around the table while David scooped the pumpkin pudding into bowls.

Myla walked down the hall and opened the door to the bathroom. Maria was inside.

"Sorry," Myla said. She quickly closed the door.

Then she realized what she had seen. She opened the door again. Maria stood in front of the medicine cabinet with an open bottle of pills in one hand and a palm full of pills in the other. She started to raise the palm of pills to her open mouth. Myla grabbed her hand, and the pills scattered onto the floor.

"Maria, what is going on?" she asked in Spanish.

Maria began to sob. "I want to die," she said.

"Have you already taken some?"

Maria shook her head. Myla picked up the bottle and looked at it. Some kind of pain medication. Way out of date.

Maria began to collapse. Myla put her arm around her waist.

"David!" Myla screamed.

David, George, and Theresa ran to the bathroom door.

"Call 911! She's taken some pills," Myla said. "Theresa, take Lily outside or something. Don't let her see her mother like this."

"No 911! I didn't take any pills!" Maria cried. "You knocked them all out of my hand."

"Let me see her eyes," Theresa said. "Her pupils look fine. Isn't that a sign?"

"I don't know!" Myla said. "Go take Lily outside before she hears us."

"All right," Theresa said.

"Ten pills," David said as he crouched on the floor. "How many were in the bottle?"

"Ten," George said, holding the bottle up.

"Did you take anything else?" Myla asked her.

Maria shook her head. Myla led Maria out of the bathroom and into Maria and Lily's room.

George and David followed.

"I'll take care of it," Myla said, "just make sure Lily is all right."

They left.

"What's wrong with you?" Myla asked. "You've got a daughter out there. What were you thinking?"

"She doesn't need me," Maria said.

"Of course she does," Myla said. "Why were you going to take those pills?"

"Theresa has the kit to take the DNA sample," Maria said. "She was going to take a swab from Lily tonight."

"So? Isn't that what you want? Then you can see if Juan is one of the unidentified dead men."

Maria shook her head. Myla got a tissue from the box on the night table and gave it to her. Maria began weeping quietly.

"It won't make any difference! We'll never know!"

"Why? Do you already know what happened to Juan?"

She shook her head. "No! But getting Lily's DNA won't help."

"Why? I don't understand you."

"Juan is not Lily's father!" She buried her face in the bedspread and wept.

"All right," Myla said. "You could have told us that and we wouldn't have gotten the kit. I don't understand. Maria!"

"I want this over with," Maria said. "I didn't want anyone to find out."

"So what if she's not Juan's child?" Myla said. "That's not a terrible thing. Doesn't he know?"

"Yes, he knows," she said. "But Lily doesn't. No one else knows." She sat up. "I told Juan the father was some boy who was only in town for a little while."

"And that wasn't true?"

Maria shook her head. "No. It was someone who forced himself on me. And he came back to the village a few weeks ago. That's why I had to leave. I knew he would try it again."

"Couldn't you tell the police?" Myla asked. "Or your family? Your father or brothers could protect you."

"I could never tell anyone!" Maria said. "Lily would be ruined forever. No one would ever come near her."

"Because her father is a bad man? I mean by definition he was a bad man because he raped you, but is there something more? Was it a priest? A drug dealer? That wouldn't matter to your family, would it? Couldn't your family settle it with him?"

"No!" Myla said. "Sometimes you Americans are so stupid!"

"Then enlighten me," Myla said. "Why can't your family help you?"

Maria stared at her.

"Because it was someone in your family?"

"He is the patriarch of the family," Maria said. "He's my father's brother. He came back to the house a few weeks ago—he had been away for several years—and he was very interested in Lily. He doesn't have any children of his own. At least none with his wife. She really wants children. She was very interested in Lily too. He got me alone one night and asked if she was his. He even asked me if I could give him a son. I think he may have given Juan the money to come here. Maybe he made certain he would never return. I don't know. I would never give Lily to him. He might do to her what he did to me. But someone else. I would give her to someone else. I would give her to you, Myla. If I was dead, you would take her. You would care for her." She fell back on the bed sobbing.

Myla sat on the edge of the bed and tried to breathe deeply. So many secrets all around her and she hadn't a clue. She had known something was troubling Maria, but she hadn't guessed anything like this.

"Don't you love Lily?" Myla asked.

Maria didn't say anything for a moment.

"I love Juan," she finally said. "And he loves Lily. When I look at her, I try to imagine Juan is her father. But sometimes I see *him* in her eyes, and then I can't stand to be around her."

"Maria," Myla whispered, barely able to say the words out loud. "Did Lily really fall in the river?"

Maria sat up. "What do you mean?"

"Did you let her go? Did you want her to drown?"

"No!" Maria said. "No!"

"But you left her alone in the desert, didn't you? That's why she's been having nightmares. You kept saying she was wrong, but she wasn't."

Maria sobbed in a breath.

"The others ran away," Maria said, "when they thought *la migra* was there. I stayed with Lily, of course. I could have run. I wanted to run. I wanted to keep up with the others, but Lily couldn't run fast enough and I couldn't carry her for long. In the morning, she was sleeping. I went to look around, to see where we were. I came out to a road. I saw cars go by. I knew people were all around. I was sure someone would find her. She would be safe. She would be adopted by a rich American couple. Then I would find Juan and we would be together."

"So you left her there alone in the desert, in that wash?"

Maria nodded. Tears streamed down her face.

246

"I started walking down the road," Maria said. "I felt such relief. I was away from her. I never had to be reminded of what my uncle had done to me. I wouldn't have to be reminded of him. Of the reason I had to leave my home. I felt like singing! And then I thought about scorpions and rattlesnakes and lions. What if they found Lily before some rich family did? So I ran back as fast as I could. I ran until I heard her cries. By the time I got to her, you were already there. I should have left then. But she saw me. She called for me, and you looked my way. I couldn't run then."

"Maybe you came back because she is your daughter and you love her," Myla said. "She is not my daughter, and I love her."

"He did not hurt you," Maria said.

"And she did not hurt you," Myla said.

"See?" Maria said. "That's why I should die. I am not a good person."

Myla sighed. "If everyone who was not a good person killed themselves, the world would be pretty empty. And what does that mean anyway, not a good person? Anyone in your circumstances would be struggling. Please promise me you won't try anything like this again. Next week we'll try to find some help for you."

"Can't you keep Lily?" Maria asked. "She loves you. She trusts you. Then I can go by myself and look for Juan."

"No," Myla said. "I am not taking your child from you. You need to figure this out. She's not a piece of trash you can just throw out."

"But that's what you do," Maria said. "You find trash and make it into gold. Lily is your gold."

"You love that child," Myla said. "I don't care what you believe now. You are lost now. I think when that man hurt you you switched off your feelings. If you can find that switch and turn it back on, you'll discover how much you love that little girl. And if she's not with you, you'll both be lost. Come on. Why don't you get undressed and try to sleep?"

They got off the bed. Maria leaned against Myla, and Myla put her arms around the younger woman.

"I don't mean to be so bad," Maria said.

Myla held her tightly. "You are not bad, child. You're hurt. Come on. Take off your clothes and put on your pajamas."

She gently helped Maria undress and dress again. Maria slid under the covers. Myla pulled the sheet and blanket up to her shoulders. Then she kissed her on the face.

"You're safe here, sweetheart," Myla said. "I'll protect you."

She sat on the bed and held Maria's hand. She didn't care what was happening in her own life. She was not going to let Maria and Lily down. She would take care of them—come hell or high water. She listened for Maria's sleep breathing. Then she returned to the kitchen.

All the adults were there, including Cathy.

"Everything all right?" Theresa asked.

"Not really," Myla said. "Where's Lily?"

"She's out in the barn with the kids," James said.

"Stefan?"

"He's out there, too," Cathy said. "David said he could stay here for a while longer."

George got up from the table first. "I think it's time for me to call it a night," he said. He came over to Myla and kissed her on the cheek. "I'll call you tomorrow, so turn on your goddamn phone."

Myla nodded. "Thanks, George."

"Me, too, sister," Gail said. "Quite a shindig you throw here. You'll have to explain what happened some time."

She kissed Myla and then left.

"Trevor wants to come over tomorrow and work on the art

project," James said as he got up to leave. "Is that all right?"

"Of course," Myla said. "At least it is with me. David?"

"Any time," David said.

"I think Luisa will want to come too," Theresa said. "Which will be great. It'll give Del Rey and me some time alone. Call me tomorrow."

"Thanks for a great night," Del Rey said. "Better than a movie."

Soon everyone was gone except Cathy and David.

"I'm riding with Del Rey and Theresa," Cathy said, "but I wanted to tell you something."

"I'll go get the kids and Ernesto," David said. "Excuse me."

When he was gone, Cathy said, "I appreciate that you got Stefan to tell me what he'd done. That was nice of you. You've been really good to me and Stefan and I appreciate it."

"You're welcome," Myla said. "I hope everything works out for you."

"I hope I stay sober," she said. "I'm trying. When Del Rey and Theresa went to work on Thursday I got really drunk. I mean really drunk. And when I drink, I'm fairly pissed off. At just about everyone. And I was mad at you for kicking me out. I was in a rage, you understand. It's not an excuse, but I'm not really myself when I drink. I wanted to hurt someone and you were my target. I decided to turn you in for harboring illegal aliens. So I think I called Homeland Security."

"You *think* you called them?"

"Well, I tried to find immigration in the phone book but I couldn't. I remembered that it's part of Homeland Security, so I think I called them. I'm not really clear on what I said. In fact, I thought it was a dream until I found the napkin with Homeland Security on it with the phone number."

Myla moaned. Was this a bit of irony the Universe was tossing her way: a reformed drunk with a memory problem turned in by a drunk with a memory problem.

"You did this on Thursday?" Myla asked. "Why didn't you tell me right away? What if they had come here yesterday?"

"I figured I'd see you tonight and tell you," Cathy said. "I can't imagine they work on the weekends. They're the government. Come on. I'm really sorry. They probably figured out I was drunk. I bet nothing will happen."

"I can't take that chance!"

"If they come get Ernesto, Maria, and Lily, they'll just send them back," Cathy said. "They'll get a free ride home."

"They'll get a ride to the border," Myla said, "and have no way to get home. And for your information, if Maria goes home, she risks getting raped—again—by her uncle. How could you be so thoughtless? Especially after we tried to help you."

"I said I was sorry," she said.

"That doesn't make it all right! You're a spoiled selfish woman with a great son and way too many squandered opportunities. Then you shit all over everyone else who hasn't had any of the breaks you've had."

"I don't deserve to be talked to in this way," Cathy said. "You're the one breaking the law."

"You don't know anything about what I've been doing," Myla said. "And now it's all over. Because of you. How powerful you must feel now! I hope you get the help you need, but I want you out of my sight."

Cathy started to say something. Then she turned and left the house. Myla stood in the middle of the kitchen.

Now what was she going to do? She would have to get Lily, Maria, and Ernesto off the Old Mermaid Sanctuary before Monday. She hoped Cathy was right about one thing: *la migra* wouldn't come out on Sundays.

David returned to the house with Lily, Stefan, and Ernesto.

Myla gave Lily a big hug and asked if she was ready for bed. Then she took her into the room where Maria slept. She helped her undress and put on her pajamas, then tucked her into bed. Myla crouched so that her face was at the same level as Lily's as she lay in bed, her head resting against her left hand.

"Is Mama all right?" Lily whispered in Spanish.

"Yes, Lily my Lily," Myla said. "She told me about leaving you alone in the desert. That must have been very scary."

Lily nodded.

"She knows that was wrong," Myla said. "She won't do it again. She's just been feeling very bad. She loves you very much. And so do I. If you ever feel frightened, you can come to me or to David Crow. We'll protect you."

Lily nodded. "I know. The Old Mermaids told me that too. Can you tell me a story?"

"Tonight it will be a short one," Myla said, "so that we don't wake up your mother. Okay? All right. Once and again forever the Old Mermaids loved a little girl named Lily my Lily. And so did Myla Alvarez. The end."

Lily scrunched her eyes together. "That isn't a story."

"It'll have to do for tonight," Myla said.

"Do all mermaids have tails?" Lily asked.

"That's an interesting question," Myla said. "When the Old Mermaids left the Old Sea, they didn't have tails for a while, not that you could see. Not that they could see. It was such a shock leaving the Old Sea. They missed the sea and they missed their tails—they missed who they had been. Grand Mother Yemaya Mermaid told them, 'As long as you swim within the sea of your true selves, you are always Old Mermaids.' So they made their lives here and created beauty and love, and they came to know who they were again—and they found their tails again. Oh, maybe not like before. For one thing, legs are much more practical on

251

land. But sometimes in the right light, they could see their tails, and you could see their tails."

"Could anyone be a mermaid then?" Lily said.

"I think that might be true, Lily," Myla said. "When a person knows who she really is, once she understands her true wild oceanic self, she discovers her Old Mermaid self—and that self includes her mermaid tail!"

"Myla," Lily said, yawning.

"Yes, dear."

"Everyone keeps asking you what happened to the Old Mermaids," she said. "What do they mean?"

"They want to know why they went away, why they aren't here any more."

Lily closed her eyes. "That's silly. They didn't go any place. They're still here."

Myla kissed Lily's forehead. "See you in the morning," she said.

She quietly left the room and went out into the kitchen where David, Ernesto, and Trevor sat at the table. Myla sat with them.

"Well, Ernesto," Myla said. "I'm sorry to say this, but we're going to have to find somewhere else for you, Lily, and Maria to stay. I've learned that someone may have called immigration and reported me."

"Who would do that?" Stefan asked.

"It doesn't matter," Myla said.

"It was my mother, wasn't it? She is such a—"

"Stefan," Myla said. "It doesn't matter. A lot of things have happened this week that seem to indicate maybe closing the sanctuary is a good idea. This latest thing just stamps 'the end,' on it all, I'm afraid. Before this no one had any inkling of what I was doing—nobody in authority, as far as I knew. If someone has reported me, we can't ever be sure it'll be safe."

"There were some loose tiles on the patio," Ernesto said. "I never got a chance to fix them."

"That's all right," Myla said. "You did enough. Besides, the important thing is that you're feeling much better."

"I can go back to the place where I was staying before I got sick," Ernesto said. "I am almost like the old Ernesto. I could be cook to them for a while. Until I find work."

Myla nodded. "We'll take you in the morning," she said. "It's late. You might as well get a good night's sleep here."

"I'm sorry, Ernesto," Stefan said.

"You did not do it," Ernesto said. He shrugged. "That is just the way it is. Maybe I will go home. I miss my wife."

"What about Lily and Maria?" David asked.

"I don't know," Myla said. "I'll figure something out."

Stefan looked heartsick.

Ernesto got up from the table. He put his hand on Stefan's shoulder. "Time for sleep. I have more jokes for you before I go."

Stefan stood.

"Remember he's a boy," Myla said.

"He is *hombre* enough for my jokes," Ernesto said.

"Don't worry," Stefan said. "I don't understand half of them. Though the hand gestures help a bit." He smiled wanly.

Ernesto and Stefan walked down the hall. Ernesto put his arm across Stefan's shoulders.

Myla looked back at David.

"He's a good influence on Stefan," she said. "He'll be all right."

"Stefan or Ernesto?"

"Both, I hope," she said. "I found out what has been bothering Maria. Lily is not Juan's biological daughter. Her uncle raped her and Lily was the result. He's been sniffing around Maria—and Lily—since Juan left, so Maria felt she had to come look for

Juan. She also left Lily out in the desert. That's why Lily runs around with that orange rope. She wants to make certain she doesn't get left again."

"She left her?" David asked. "To die?"

"No," Myla said. "She wanted someone to find her."

"She didn't want Lily? Lily?"

Myla nodded and blinked away tears.

"Oh man," David said. "What should we do? Is Lily safe with her?"

"I don't think she'd hurt Lily," Myla said. "She might hurt herself. But I could be wrong. I wouldn't have guessed any of this. I wouldn't have guessed Cathy would call Homeland Security."

"I'm sorry this is happening," David said.

"I am too," she said. "I hope you don't get in trouble. I'll tell them you don't know anything."

"Myla, you don't have to protect me," he said. "I'm not that quiet young man you knew ten years ago."

"No? Then who are you?"

"I'm the quiet older man you know now," he said. "But that doesn't mean I can't take care of myself. Tell me what you need, and I'll do it."

She looked at him. "You've always been kind. I know you can take care of yourself. I just don't want my mistakes to hurt you. Not again."

"Again?"

"I know it wasn't all your fault ten years ago," Myla said. "I did care about you. I wasn't able to admit it then. My pride got in the way. I didn't think I could take you rejecting me on top of what my ex-husband did. I'm sorry I was so drunk when we made love. I wish I remembered."

"Do you remember any of it?"

254

"I remember laughing," Myla said. "I remember feeling free. Mind you, I thought I was remembering making love with George. Not that I see his face." She closed her eyes. Then opened them again. "Or yours. I remember feeling as though I was swimming in an ocean of love. Yes, love and ecstasy. As if I were finally myself. I hope that doesn't hurt you, that I don't remember your part in it."

"I don't think I had anything to do with it in a way, from your perspective. Maybe that night, despite the alcohol, you were able to feel free of your old life."

"I don't want to trash Richard," Myla said. "He is who he is. But I felt regimented when I was with him. He had a time for everything. He had a place for everything. For instance, if a friend of mine stopped over for a visit and it was time for dinner, he'd just send them on their way. Because the schedule was important. Otherwise people and their problems would run you over. That's what he used to say. And he was right, I suppose. But what kind of life is that? We got a lot done together. Well, we got the business going. But it wasn't much of a life. When I think about it, I don't know why I was so upset that we broke up. I should have been relieved."

David smiled.

"What are you smiling about?"

"Because you were wrong when you said I didn't know you and I couldn't love you now. You were wrong. You are wrong. I love listening to you talk. I love the way you sigh. I love the way the way your forehead crinkles. I love your crow's feet."

Myla laughed.

"See," he said.

"Is this how you seduced me last time?" Myla asked.

"I wasn't the seducer," David said.

"Oh no! That's what I was afraid of."

"You didn't let me finish," he said. "I wasn't the seducer the *first* time."

Myla laughed again. Light flashed outside the window. They turned and looked. Another flash. Lightning.

"Is it supposed to rain?" Myla asked.

"Up in the mountains," he said.

"We could use a little rain here," she said. She put her face in her hands. "I've got a lot of things to do tomorrow—figure out what to do about Lily and Maria, for one. Do you think I should call the owners, warn them I might be arrested?"

"No! You don't know that's going to happen," David said. "For one thing, if Ernesto, Lily, and Maria are gone, what would immigration arrest you for?"

"That's true," Myla said.

"You should sleep here in the house tonight," he said. "In case Lily or Maria needs you."

"I don't want you out on the couch again," Myla said. "I'm not as mad at you today as I was yesterday."

"Then I'll sleep with you," David said. "I promise I'll stay on my side of the bed."

Myla laughed. "Yes, well, I don't think we know each other well enough for that."

"I beg to differ," he said.

"Good night, David," Myla said. She stood and stretched. "Nice try, though. I'll sleep by myself in your bed."

He reached for her hand. She leaned over and kissed his forehead.

"Myla, I'm not Stefan," he said.

"And I'm not the woman of your dreams," she said.

"I don't think I'm in a dream," he said. "I'm talking about right here and now. Or later. I'm in no hurry."

"Apparently not," she said. "Since I haven't seen you for ten years."

She gently took her hand back. Then she went to David's room, closed the door, and got into bed.

Twelve

All the wisdom of the ages can be distilled into one suggestion: Be.

Mother Star Stupendous Mermaid

Myla woke just after dawn. She got up and walked the wash alone. It was a damp and chilly morning. Dark clouds floated above the Rincons. A coyote walked across the wash. She stopped and looked at Myla. They stared at one another. Then the coyote continued on her way. Myla went back to the house and started breakfast. She sautéed onions and shitake mushrooms in olive oil. As they sizzled she put oatmeal in a pot of boiling water. She sprinkled in a bit of cinnamon. Ernesto loved her oatmeal. She could not imagine why—probably had something to do with the almonds, cashews, bananas, and maple syrup he poured over it. She cracked egg after egg into a bowl. Two eggs for each of them. She broke the yokes with a fork and whisked them. The metal tines hit the inside of the bowl as she stirred them faster and faster, turning gold into more gold. As she poured the eggs into the pan with the mushrooms and onions, she thought, "This is the last breakfast I'll be making for the refugees at the Old Mermaid Sanctuary." She liked to think that the migrants came to the sanctuary as refugees but left as pilgrims. It was such a difficult decision to leave one's family and country—a desperate decision. How terrible then to be left in the desert to wander or die alone—or together with others as lost as you are.

Myla stared at the scrambled eggs as they began to set. She was glad she had dreamed of the Old Mermaids. It didn't really matter if she had originally dreamed of the Old Mermaids because of the mermaid tile or because she had seen David painting the mermaid. It didn't really matter if the Old Mermaids had been the voice of the Universe speaking to her. What mattered was that she had gone into the desert and helped people who needed it. In turn, they let her be a part of their families—their lives—for a time.

How could she ever have doubted the importance of that?

She turned the eggs gently.

"Can I help?"

She jumped slightly and looked over her shoulder.

"David. I didn't hear you," she said. "I thought you were still snoring away on the couch. Yes, make the toast."

"Good morning," Stefan said. "Can I help?"

"Yes," she said. "Set the table."

Lily came running into the room, her arms outstretched. Myla knelt and opened her arms. The girl and woman embraced. Myla kissed her on the cheek. Lily wiped it away. Myla laughed.

"Help Stefan set the table, Lily my Lily," Myla said.

Ernesto stepped into the kitchen and came over to the stove.

"Oh, your oatmeal! Marvelous."

"The syrup is in the refrigerator," Myla said.

Maria came into the kitchen last. She smiled at Myla, then

walked over to Lily and kissed the top of her head.

"You sleep well, *mi niña?*"

"*Sí, Mama,*" Lily said.

"Anyone else want oatmeal?" Myla asked.

"Lily will have a little," Maria said.

Stefan put the plates on the table; Lily followed him with the flatware: a spoon here, a fork there. When Myla glanced their way, Stefan said, "It's like art. Very eclectic."

She laughed. "Okay, breakfast is ready." She glanced outside and saw Gail getting out of her car.

"David, can you serve?" Myla asked. She hurried out the kitchen door to Gail. "Is everything all right?"

"With me?" Gail said. "Yes! Theresa called me this morning. Cathy told her what she did, calling Homeland Security. She knew you'd be looking for a place to stash Maria and Lily. I'll take them. They can stay with us for a while."

"What about your husband?"

"What about him?" Gail said. "We've got plenty of room in that big old house."

"I don't want to get you into trouble," Myla said.

"Hey, I'm offering. Don't look a gift horse in the mouth."

"Why is that?" Myla said. "I've always wondered."

"Because it'll bite you," Gail said. "Actually I think it had something to do with assessing the age of the horse. But who cares?"

"Come have breakfast with us," Myla said. "Don't say anything about taking Lily and Maria. I haven't had a chance to tell Maria that they'll have to leave."

Myla and Gail went into the house.

"Good morning, everyone," Gail said. "I couldn't stay away."

Myla and Gail sat at the table with the others.

"Dig in," Myla said.

"You haven't said grace," Stefan said.

"Oh, I'm sorry," Myla said. "Maria, would you like to say grace?"

Maria's face flushed, and she looked down. "Uh, I am grateful for Myla and David. I am glad to find this Old Mermaid place out in the desert where we almost died. Thank you for saving us. I hope to be worthy of your kindness. Thank you for this meal and all the others."

"You are already worthy," David said. "Just live a good life. Take care of your daughter."

"I'll second that," Myla said. "Come on, now. The eggs are getting cold. Where's the salsa? Oh, thanks, Stefan. Peach salsa? Who bought this?"

"One of the Old Mermaids must have left it," David said. "But I kind of like it."

"I should have guessed it was you," Myla said. "He's such a desert novice."

"Aren't we all novices of the Church of the Old Mermaids?" Stefan asked.

"That's true," Myla said. "By the way, you and Trevor did very well with the stories yesterday. That was fast thinking on your part. The Old Mermaids may have deserted me—or I deserted them, whatever—but you boys did good."

"Speaking of which," Stefan said, "Trevor and his dad just drove up. And Theresa and Luisa."

"The gang's all here," David said.

"It's the crack of dawn," Myla said, looking outside.

"We wanted to get started on the art project," Stefan said. "Can we still do that today? I mean with Ernesto leaving and everything."

"Sure," Myla said. "But finish your breakfast."

"Ernesto is leaving?" Maria asked.

"Yes," Myla said. "I had hoped to talk with you about this

before, but something has happened, and everyone is going to have to leave the Old Mermaid Sanctuary. Someone may have called immigration."

Maria looked panicked.

"Is *la migra* coming for us now?"

"No," Myla said. "It's all right. I don't even know if they're coming. But to be safe, we thought we should have you leave. Gail has offered to house you and Lily if you like. Ernesto will go back to his old place."

Lily stopped eating. "Does Gail live here?"

"No, honey," Gail said. "I live across town. But it's a nice house."

"Are the Old Mermaids there?"

"Well, it depends on—"

"Knock, knock," Theresa opened the door and came inside, followed by James, Trevor, and Luisa.

"Come in," David said. "Find a chair. We've got some left-overs. Coffee? Tea?"

James laughed. "Didn't mean to come so early, but Trevor said the kids wanted to work this morning."

Lily started to cry. She held her arms out for Myla. Myla leaned over and picked her up. "Oh, Lily my Lily," Myla said, carrying her away from the kitchen. "It'll be all right."

Maria followed them into the bedroom. Myla sat on the bed with Lily on her lap.

"I'll come see you," Myla said. "I promise."

"What about the barn?" Lily said. "They were letting me help with the surprise."

"Sure," Myla said. "You can help them. You don't have to leave this second or anything."

Lily wiped her eyes. She held up the end of the orange rope. Myla took it.

"You promised," Lily said.

"I'm not leaving you," Myla said. "You are just going to another house. We'll see each other all the time until your mother decides what she's going to do next. All right?"

Lily nodded.

"Why don't you go finish your breakfast," Myla said, "and then you can go out to the barn with the other children."

Lily slipped off Myla's lap and left the room, sniffling.

"Myla, please, you should take Lily," Maria said. "She will be better off with you."

"She is your daughter," Myla said. "That's the end of that. You've got to decide who you are, Maria. And you need to decide now. Are you a victim of that man or are you Lily's mother? That man is a speck on the landscape of your past. He certainly isn't Lily's father. Juan is. Whether you ever see Juan again, he loves Lily. And you love Lily. You are her parents."

She took Maria's hand as she stood. "We need to finish our breakfast. It's good for us."

Maria smiled and nodded.

The four children went out to the barn when they finished eating. Myla stood at the kitchen window watching Lily run after the three older children, twirling the orange rope. Luisa looked back at Lily and held out her hand for her. Then they went into the barn together.

"Shouldn't we get going?" Gail asked as she came up behind Myla, "in case they come today."

"Just a little longer," Myla said.

"I'm so sorry about this," Theresa said. "I really feel like it's my fault."

"It is," Myla said.

"What?"

Myla glanced over at her and smiled. "You wanted it to be

about you, didn't you? So I'm giving you that gift."

"Very funny," Theresa said.

"I'll go make sure I have everything," Maria said.

"What's going on?" James asked.

"Ernesto, Maria, and Lily are leaving today."

"Oh," James said. "I'm sorry to hear that."

"I've got everything," Ernesto said. "Do I have time for a few minutes in the spa?"

"I turned it on before breakfast just for you," David said. "It should be hot enough about now."

"*Gracias*," Ernesto said. "Call me when you're ready."

Myla stared out the window for another minute. Then she said, "How about one last walk in the wash? With all of us. Everyone is always bugging to go with me. Let's do it now!"

Gail said, "All right. Get your trash bags."

"I'll get the kids," James said.

They all went outside. James called to Trevor, and the children came running out of the barn. Myla went into her apartment and got the ruby colored bag, a plastic bag, and her gloves.

"All right," Myla said once she was outside again. "You know the rules?"

"Everyone has their own way," Stefan said.

"And?" Myla asked.

"Watch out for prickles," Lily said.

"That's right," Myla said.

"Can we keep whatever we find?" Luisa asked. "I mean, what if I find a diamond ring?"

"If you find a diamond ring," Myla said, "it is yours. If it's just what you need."

"I don't know if I need a diamond ring, but it would be fun," she said.

"Don't pick up anything if you don't know what it is," Theresa said.

"That's always a good rule," Myla said. "And even if you do know what it is you might not want to pick it up."

"Are we talking or walking?" Gail asked.

The group began walking through the wash. Lily put the end of the rope in Myla's fingers. The teenagers walked behind them, Gail and Theresa walked with James, and Maria and David brought up the rear.

"This is like having a party in the wash," Stefan said.

"Oh, look at that branch," Luisa said. "That might be good."

"We'll pick it up on the way out," Trevor said.

"What are you all concocting in the barn, anyway?" Myla asked.

"It's not in the barn exactly," Luisa said.

"No?"

"No," Stefan said. "It'll be bigger than that."

"Bigger than a barn?" Myla said. "That'll be something to see."

"I don't know that it's bigger than a barn in scale," Trevor said, "but in scope it's big, it's really big."

"Boffo," Stefan said.

"I'm getting sand in my feet," Gail said.

"I just pulled a cholla out of my shoe," Theresa said. "Those buggers hurt."

"Well, I—" Gail began.

"I'm never bringing you out here again if you don't stop complaining," Myla said.

"I'm not complaining," Gail said. "It was a statement of fact."

"Me, too." Theresa.

"Now!" Lily said.

They all stopped. Lily closed her eyes. Myla did the same. She breathed deeply. When she opened her eyes, Lily looked at her feet. She leaned over and picked up what looked like a thin curved white stone. She held it up to Myla who crouched next to her.

"Lily my Lily," she said. "Do you know what this is?"

The others gathered around them.

"A pretty rock," Lily said.

"It's part of a sea shell," Myla said. "This is quite a treasure. You know what this means?"

Lily shook her head.

"If you find a sea shell—especially one in the desert—it means a mermaid just found her tail."

Lily smiled and nodded. She folded her fingers around the stone. Then she skipped forward. Myla let go of the orange rope.

They continued walking. Then Myla stopped. She closed her eyes and breathed deeply. When she opened them, she looked to her left. Beneath an old palo verde, where an animal had probably dug, she saw a flash of silver. She moved closer to the tree. The bottom branches lay on the ground with a huge pack rat pile built over them.

"I bet we could find stuff in that pile," Trevor said. "Pack rats are great collectors."

"Thus the name pack rat," Theresa said.

"I think it was the other way around," Gail said. "What do you see?"

Myla pointed. It looked like a squat chalice. Or a dog dish.

"Excuse me, palo verde," Myla said as she walked closer. It would be difficult getting to it, whatever it was. If she leaned forward, the silver piece under the tree would still be out of reach.

"We could crawl in there," Stefan suggested.

"I have an idea," Myla said. "Run back to my apartment and get the shovel by the door, then get the hooked poker by the fireplace in David's house, and duct tape, which is in the laundry room."

Stefan nodded, and the three teenagers ran down the wash.

James and David crouched to get a better look.

"I see the silver," James said.

"It looks like it might be a light," David said.

"What does it matter?" Gail asked. "You could leave it there. It looks like it's lodged pretty tight there."

"You think it belongs to the pack rat?" James asked.

"Looks a little big for a pack rat," Theresa said.

"Unless it's a really big pack rat," David said.

They all stood up straight and looked around. Myla laughed.

"Just leave it," Gail said.

"It is what Myla does," Theresa said. "She picks up treasure in the desert."

Maria and Myla looked at one another and smiled.

The teenagers soon returned with the requested items. Myla had Luisa hold the poker against the top part of the shovel handle, which Trevor held. Then she wrapped duct tape around the handle and poker to keep them together. She tested it for strength.

"I think this will do," she said.

David held the branches open and Myla stepped closer to the tree. She pushed the hook of the poker under the tree, trying to snag whatever it was. She didn't hook it, but it tipped and they could see it better. It was some kind of big light bulb.

"Maybe if you push it that way," Theresa said.

"Pull it towards you." Gail.

"Maybe from the other side." James.

"Lily could probably crawl in there." Luisa. "No. Might get pricked."

"I'll do it if you want." Stefan.

Myla couldn't get it from this angle. She walked around to the other side of the tree. David came with her. Using a fallen branch, he held the cholla away from her and she bent and pushed the light forward.

"We can see it," Luisa said.

"It's almost out!" Theresa said.

Myla pushed gently. This was more effort than she usually exerted to get something in the wash. She didn't want to break the light. Then the creatures who used the tree might get hurt on the glass.

"I wonder how that light got there," David said. "Stuck way underneath that tree. Must have been quite a flood to get this far up out of the wash."

Myla pushed a bit harder.

"It's out," James said.

Now she saw something else.

"There's two," Myla said.

"This reminds me of that expression," James said. "How did it go? She's hiding her light under a tree."

"I think it's 'she's hiding her light under a bushel.'" Gail.

"What is a bushel?" Stefan.

"A unit of measure, I think." James.

"Hey, Myla, does this mean you've been hiding your light under a palo verde tree?" Gail asked.

Myla pushed the second light.

"Apparently she's been hiding two lights," Theresa said.

Myla pushed the second light again. She breathed the dusty air. Everything suddenly felt timeless. As though she had been with this group of people forever. And ever. They would always be together no matter what happened. She was vaguely aware of David standing behind her and the others on the other side of the tree, the sound of the metal poker tapping on the glass, distant thunder.

If it could only be like this always...

The tree and earth gave up the light. It moved forward.

Go with the flow...

"We can reach them both now," Trevor said.

Myla straightened and stepped back from the tree and the cholla.

"Thank you," she said to David. They went around the tree as Trevor picked first one light out of the dirt and tossed it to Stefan and then the other. Stefan held the dusty lights out to Myla.

"They're halogen lights," Myla said.

"Probably like the floodlights on the barn," David said.

"How on Earth did they get under that tree?" Myla asked.

"I'm wondering how you saw them under there," James said.

"It's the Old Mermaid way, Dad," Trevor said. "Do you need them for the Church of the Old Mermaids or can we use them?"

Myla shrugged. "You can have them." She handed the lights to Trevor.

"We're going back to the barn now," Trevor said.

The teenagers turned around and took a left fork out of the wash that went behind the house to the barn. Lily followed.

"I need to get back home," Gail said. "So maybe we should get going."

Myla nodded. They started walking back to the house, their feet slip-sliding on the sand. They walked in silence for a few minutes.

"It's really raining in the mountains," Gail said. "I heard it on the radio. There are flash flood warnings."

"Gee, thanks for telling us," Theresa said.

"What do you mean?"

"We're standing in a river bed," she said.

"Oh yeah," Gail said.

"Maybe we better get out of the wash," Myla said. "Just to be on the safe side. I've seen this wash flash before. It can come fast."

She pointed behind her. "Let's go back and take the path the kids took."

They started walking.

"What's that noise?" David asked.

They stopped.

In the distance was a kind of dull roar. The sound of many hands slapping. Or water lapping.

"Come on," Myla said, her pace quickening.

The adults hurried up out of the wash and onto the path.

"Let's make sure the kids all went to the barn," Myla said.

"What's wrong?" Maria asked.

"Stefan!" Myla called, hurrying down the path. "Lily!"

Myla ran past the back of the house. "Trevor! Lily!"

Suddenly she was at the barn.

"What?" Stefan came running out, followed by Trevor and Luisa.

"Where's Lily?" Myla asked.

"What's that sound?" Trevor asked.

"She was just here," Luisa said. "Two seconds ago."

The sound got louder. Myla looked toward the wash. Gray water cascaded between the berms, back and forth, rushing forward, logs and branches flipping up and down. Myla ran toward the wash which was now a river, a foot or more deep, churning like water in a washing machine, getting deeper every second.

"Lily!" Maria called.

Myla stood on the berm. She leaned forward, looking in both directions. She saw water and desert.

Then she saw color. Orange. On the other side of the wash, partially submerged in water, caught on a prickly pear pad, was the orange rope.

Her heartbeat quickened.

"Lily," she called. "Lily." She whispered. "Lily," she screamed.

Myla had to get to the other side. Had to get to Lily. She leapt into the water...

...And the water knocked her on her ass. Instantly. She did not have a chance. She flailed and grabbed onto a palo verde branch. The palo verde bent but held her. She couldn't stand. The water pushed against her. It stung, full of desert. Prickly.

David called her name. And James. Trevor. Stefan. All of them were screaming at her. She looked for the orange rope. It was down the arroyo. Still on the other side. Myla tried to pulled herself up, but the branch dipped further into the water every time she moved. Trevor and David were ahead of her. David held onto Trevor while he held onto the shovel and poker and reached it across the wash to the orange rope. Caught it. Held it up. Lily was not inside it.

The water slapped Myla. Her butt scraped the bottom. Then the current turned her around. There was Maria. And Lily next to her. Dry. Safe.

Oh, Lily my Lily.

Oh, Lily my Lily.

She wanted to clap with joy. Maria was crying. She could see it. Her arms around her daughter. Lily waved. Water was all Myla could hear.

Go with the flow.

This was how people died.

Or lived.

She couldn't stay here forever. She waved to Lily and let go of the branch.

The river took her down. Away. She held her breath. The Old Sea was not what it used to be.

Neither was she.

Thank goodness.

Thank something.

She reached up. Grabbed a hold of the first thing she touched. Held on for dear life.

It was a poker at the end of the shovel. Good thing she had

wrapped that duct tape three times around the shovel handle. She thought this as they pulled her up out of the rush of water. She wasn't able to help them right away. Her tail got in the way. She laughed as they lifted her.

"Wait," she said, "I don't have my land legs yet."

Then she closed her eyes and rested her head against David's shoulder.

For only a moment. Then her feet hit sand and she ran toward Lily.

Lily held her arms out and Myla ran into them.

They held each other tightly.

"I saw your tail," Lily said. "See. I told you the Old Mermaids were still here."

"Where were you?" Myla asked.

"I heard you calling me," Lily said. "You told me to get out of the wash."

Myla frowned. "How did the orange rope get in the water then?"

"I threw it back into the wash," Lily said in Spanish. "I didn't need it any more. That's when I heard your voice. Or the voice of the Old Mermaids. I get them mixed up. I was standing in the wash with the orange rope. I left it and I went in the house to look for you. I followed your voice. Ernesto was there, so I sat with him and waited for you."

Suddenly, Myla's legs began to buckle beneath her.

"You might be bleeding," Gail said. "Let's get you cleaned up."

"Who's that?" David asked.

Myla followed his gaze. A white truck was coming down the drive. She had seen that truck before, hadn't she?

"I think it's the Border Patrol," Myla said.

"Maybe if they ran," Theresa said.

"Not a good idea," David said.

The truck dipped into the new river, whose water seemed to be receding, and came back up. It stopped beside Myla and the others. No green stripe. Maybe it was not Border Patrol. Myla leaned against Gail. Her legs throbbed.

The driver's door opened. Ruben Morales stepped out. He was not wearing his Border Patrol uniform.

"Myla Alvarez," he said. "What happened to you?"

"She tried to become a mermaid," Gail said. "Who are you? What do you want?"

"He's a friend," Myla said. "Welcome, Ruben. You scared us. How'd you find me?"

"The bookstore," he said. "I convinced someone named Pietra that I was a friend. I've brought a surprise."

The passenger door opened. Another man stepped out. Myla recognized him immediately. Maria began weeping.

"Papa!" Lily cried. She ran toward him. He crouched and scooped her up into his arms. Maria went to him, sobbing, and he put his arms around his *familia*.

"I'm sure there's a great story to this," Gail said. "But we need to see whether Myla needs to go to the hospital or not."

"David," Myla said. "Can you take care of our guests?"

Myla leaned on Gail and Theresa and limped toward her apartment. Once there, they stripped her and put her in the shower. Then she sat on the bed and they looked over her body. No cuts. A few scrapes. Bruises.

"How is that possible?" Gail asked.

"It's the Old Mermaid way," Theresa said.

"Did you hear what she said out there to David?" Gail said to Theresa. "Can you take care of 'our' guests? Geez. You'd think she was queen of the castle already."

"She is," Theresa said. "She always has been."

"Ain't it the truth," Gail said.

Myla got dressed, and they went back to the house. Lily sat on her father's lap. Maria sat close by. Everyone else stood around them. Juan looked a bit overwhelmed.

Myla tapped Ruben's arm and pulled him aside.

"Where'd you find him?" she asked.

"In El Paso," he said. "He was homeless. What's funny is that I wasn't even looking there. Too big of a city. But I passed this bar with a mermaid on the logo. I don't remember what it was called. I stopped, thinking wouldn't that be funny if I found Juan there. I went inside. Didn't see him, but a block down the street was an empty lot with a bunch of homeless migrant workers. I called out his name and he answered. I asked him why he hadn't called home. He said he'd been too embarrassed—he hadn't found work and he didn't have any money. I took him home to Mom. She fed him, made sure he cleaned up, and lectured him about his responsibilities. She says hello."

"Thank you, Ruben," Myla said. "And hello right back at her." Then she said loudly, "All right. All of you. You're like a bunch of vultures. Leave them alone."

Someone knocked on the kitchen door. David glanced at Myla. Was this *la migra*? They walked to the door together. Myla opened it.

"Yes?" she asked the man standing there.

"Home and Land Security, ma'am," he said. "Someone called about your wanting more security because of illegals in your area."

"Home and Land Security?" Myla said.

"Yes, ma'am," he said. "We put in alarm systems. I called the number the person left, but no one answered. I was in the area today so I thought I'd stop by."

Myla started laughing. "I'm sorry to have troubled you," she said. "You got this call a couple of days ago?"

"Yes, ma'am."

"A friend of mine was playing a practical joke on me," Myla said.

"She did sound a little drunk," he said.

"Sorry for your trouble," Myla said.

He shrugged. "Let me know if you change your mind." He held out a card for her and she took it.

Then she closed the door and looked back at everyone.

"Apparently *la migra* is not after me or any of you!"

"We don't have to leave?" Maria asked.

"Not right away," Myla said. "This can be home for a while longer."

"Let's go work on the art project then," Luisa said.

The boys followed Luisa outside. A few moments later, Myla heard Luisa calling her name. She leaned outside.

"You've got to see this," Luisa said. "You'll never believe it!"

Myla stepped outside. David and the others followed. She walked to where the children stood, at the edge of the wash.

The river was gone, or nearly so. A few rivulets still ran through it. They would be gone in minutes, Myla figured. Strewn through the wash were branches, small logs, and pieces of concrete here and there—and scattered between it all in glittery pastels were seashells, some big, some little, most in-between. The shells went for as far as Myla could see on either side, until the wash disappeared in curves.

Lily came to stand on one side of her, David on the other. Each took one of Myla's hands in theirs.

"Myla," Lily whispered. "I think every mermaid in the world just found her tail."

"I think so too, Lily my Lily."

Thirteen

The rest is...mystery.
Sister Faye Mermaid

Myla did not walk the wash Saturday morning. The children had declared it off-limits until the opening of the first Old Mermaid Sanctuary Found Art Show. That was what they called it. So Myla set up the Church of the Old Mermaids on Fourth Avenue early. She put out her wares, cigar box, and sign. She had plenty of treasures to display. The children had not used much from the boxes she had given them for their art installation. Trevor said, "In case you changed your mind and wanted to go to the Church of the Old Mermaids one more time. Or two more times."

Pietra brought her a chair. Red bought her a limonada.

"Oh, this is the most comfortable chair I have ever sat in," Myla said. "And this limonada. It is even better than usual."

A woman came to the table and picked up the broken marble and said, "What is this?"

Myla said, "What does it look like? It's a marble, of course. A broken marble. I can't be certain, but I believe this is the same marble that Sister Sheila Na Giggles Mermaid and Sister Sophia Mermaid used to play a practical joke on Sister Bridget Mermaid. You know how stuffy she can sometimes seem. They tried to convince Sister Bridget Mermaid that it was the lost eye of the old one-eyed mountain lion who wandered the wash. Sister Bridget Mermaid knew that wasn't true, but she pretended she thought it was. She told them that she knew a chant that could restore the eye to the mountain lion. She chanted up a storm, so to speak, while the Old Mermaids watched. With a sleight of hand, she exchanged the marble for a green olive. She held it up for Sister Sheila Na Giggles Mermaid and Sister Sophia Mermaid to see. She didn't let them get too close, just close enough to fool them. They started wondering if maybe Sister Bridget Mermaid knew more than they did. Just then Sister Ursula Divine came running into the kitchen where they were and said the old one-eyed lion was outside and he was angry because he knew they had his eye and he wanted it back. Sister Sheila Na Giggles Mermaid and Sister Sophia Mermaid got up and went to the window to see. All the other Old Mermaids began laughing. Funny thing, that old one-eyed lion did show up the next day, so Sister Bridget Mermaid left the broken marble in the wash for him, just in case."

The woman folded her fingers around the marble.

"A sense of humor," she said. "I could use one of those."

Myla smiled. It was nice to be back.

Gail picked her up a little earlier than usual, and they returned to the Old Mermaid Sanctuary. As soon as they got out of the car, Luisa came over and held out her arm to Myla.

"Sister Myla Mermaid," she said. "May I escort you to the Old Mermaid Pool?"

278

Stefan held his arm out to Gail. "Sister Gail Mermaid, may I escort you to the Old Mermaid Pool?"

"Charmed, I'm sure," Myla said. She put her arm through Luisa's.

They went into the house, through the kitchen and living room, and out to the pool. Everyone else was sitting around the pool—except Cathy who was now in rehab, and George who told Myla he was going to be scarce around the Old Mermaid Sanctuary for a while. Luisa took Myla to a chair next to David. Myla smiled at him. He took her hand and kissed it. Lily came and sat in her lap. Nearby Juan and Maria leaned against one another. Theresa, Ernesto and Del Rey sat with their feet in the spa. Del Rey waved. Myla smiled and waved.

Trevor, Stefan, and Luisa stood next to the pool in front of the adults, each holding onto index cards. Luisa motioned to Lily, and she got up and went and stood with them.

"*Buenos días*," Luisa said. "We stand here on the border."

Trevor, Stefan, and Lily pointed to the pool and then to the audience. Lily watched the boys to see what they did and then she copied them.

"This is the in-between place," Luisa said. "One step could take us into the water, for ill or good. Or onto the patio, for ill or good."

Trevor said, "The Old Mermaid Sanctuary is a border place. Like all borders, it is also a threshold. Pilgrims, refugees, artists, storytellers, those who are betwixt and between are welcome."

"The Old Mermaids themselves are betwixt and between," Stefan said. "Observe our pool mermaid. Is she woman or is she fish?"

"Imagine all the lines are erased," Luisa said. "We get to decide whether we step into the Old Sea where everything is possible. And the possible is everything. We are travelers, all of us."

She glanced down at the cards in her hand. "And today, we seek the truth of the Old Mermaid Sanctuary."

"This means we have to ask the right question," Trevor said.

Lily looked up at Luisa. Luisa nodded. Lily walked over to Myla.

"Sister Myla Mermaid," Lily said, "before we can go into the wash, they want you to tell them what happened to the Old Mermaids."

"Yes, that story is for this day," Myla said. Lily crawled up on her lap again. The three teenagers sat at her feet.

"It's not a big secret or anything," Myla said, "what happened to them. Like many things, it ended suddenly and slowly and not unexpectedly. The Old Mermaids finished their beautiful house and studio. Wildlife roamed freely. The Old Mermaids grew much of their food. They had good neighbors, and they all worked together. They had their problems. Everyone has their problems. I told you about some of them. But they had a good life here for a long time. Then one day someone came and told the Old Mermaids that they did not own the property, and they would have to move. The Old Mermaids didn't really understand. After all, the Old Sea had been their home. When it dried up, they were left here. What other place could they call home? The man with the papers was insistent. They had to leave. Sissy Maggie Mermaid said it was all a mistake; they shouldn't worry about it. Mother Star Stupendous and Grand Mother Yemaya Mermaid talked with people who should know about such things, and they did not know what to do. The law was the law, they said. It doesn't appear as though you own the land, they told them. You can't live there any more. 'Does someone else need the land?' the Old Mermaids asked. 'They are welcome to live here with us.' 'No,' the people who knew such things said, 'that is not how it works here.'

"One day the man returned and tacked a paper to the house.

The Old Mermaids gathered round to read it. They had thirty days to get out. They were being evicted. Since the house was made from the land, the paper said, the Old Mermaids could not take it with them. Everything had to stay. The neighbors encouraged the Old Mermaids to take everything they could with them and leave before the thirty days were up. If you don't take it all, they will bulldoze it, they said. All that beauty destroyed.

"The Old Mermaids walked around the Old Mermaid Sanctuary. They waved to Rocky the Crow up in the evergreen. They listened to the great horned owls awaken in the palm tree. They watched the cactus wrens and gila woodpeckers. They listened to the wind coming down from the mountains. They howled with the coyotes. They stalked the day with the mountain lion. They dug in the dirt with the javelinas. They looked at the painted walls of their house and wondered if they could walk into them and disappear into those beautiful worlds. They stood in the wash and wondered why the Old Sea had deserted them.

"Mr. Hunter came down the hill and offered to get his bow and arrow and go after the man with the papers. The Old Mermaids said they didn't think that was a good idea. He was just a man. Someone else offered to burn down the house when they left so that the new owners would not benefit from their work. The Old Mermaids said they hoped someone would benefit.

"The thirty days were up. The man showed up with the law. They were prepared to force the Old Mermaids out. Instead, the Old Mermaids walked into the wash. They didn't take anything except the clothes on their backs and the vegetables from their garden. Then they went up the hill. Mr. Hunter and his wife said they could stay with them for a while. The Old Mermaids stood on the hill looking down at the Old Mermaid Sanctuary for most of the day. As the sun went down, the Old Mermaids began to hum. Everything around them seemed to hum with them. Or tremble. And then they began singing. Their siren songs. The Old Mermaid Sanctuary vibrated with their songs. The Old Man and Old Woman of the Mountains stopped what they were doing and listened. All the flora and fauna near and far listened. Or so it seemed. People came from miles around just to hear the Old Mermaids sing. Tulip and Poppy stood by the Old Mermaids and hummed along with them. Some say the song lasted for days, years. It made some people cry, some laugh. Everyone agreed it was beautiful and true.

"When the song was finished, night came. The Old Mermaids slept on the floor of Mr. Hunter's house. The next morning they got up and gazed down at the Old Mermaid Sanctuary. People with machines came in and didn't seem to see all the beauty the Old Mermaids had created. The Old Mermaids grasped hands as the machines rolled over the cholla and prickly pear. They stood right up over there, all in a line." Myla pointed.

"One machine went toward the house. And just like that, it pushed the walls over. The first wall was the prairie wall. The next one was the mountain wall. Then the valley wall. The ocean. All their worlds came tumbling down. This was hard for the Old Mermaids to watch. Some of them sobbed. Some of them cried quietly. Some of them yelled at the machines. But this did not stop the destruction of the Old Mermaid Sanctuary. Grand Mother Yemaya Mermaid turned her back on the destruction. Then Mother Star Stupendous Mermaid did the same. Soon they had all turned away. After a while, they walked down into the wash. They embraced each other as they stood in the Old Sea. Then they walked away from one another, each singing their own siren song, each walking in different directions, except for Sister Dee Dee Lightful Mermaid and Sister Bea Wilder Mermaid who would never separate and Grand Mother Yemaya Mermaid and Mother Star Stupendous Mermaid who remained together too. The story goes that some of the wild creatures went with the Old Mermaids, certain that if there was no place for the Old Mermaids here then there was no place for them. Those left behind howled or sang or roared their grief. Some say the Old Man and Old Woman were so displeased that the mountains rumbled. Needless to say, the place has never been the same since."

"But what happened to the Old Mermaids?" Luisa asked.

"I have heard—although I can't say for sure—that they each established a new Old Mermaid Sanctuary in different parts of the world," Myla said, "to help those who were in need—to remind those who had forgotten how to live in the world with hope, with reverence, with love. And each one swam in the ocean of herself and her world for her whole life."

"Did they ever see each other again?" Stefan asked.

"Well, that's the interesting thing," Myla said. "I can't be sure about this part, but I've heard that they used to meet once a year. Some said it was every five years. They took turns going to each new Old Mermaid Sanctuary. They liked seeing what they were all up to. For instance at Sissy Maggie Mermaid's sanctuary, a lot of lonely men and women found solace."

Everyone laughed.

"For some reason a lot of failed comedians ended up at Sister Sheila Na Giggles Mermaid's sanctuary. And Sister Ursula Divine Mermaid took care of endangered animals. Sister Bridget Mermaid looked after poets and healers. Sister Faye Mermaid helped out mystics, shamans, and caretakers who got tired or burned out. Grand Mother Yemaya Mermaid helped those who were working to clean up the oceans. Sister Ruby Rosarita Mermaid did a lot of work around food. She had a great restaurant at her sanctuary."

"What about Sister Lyra Musica Mermaid?" Trevor asked. "She had a lot of trouble adjusting when the sea first dried up."

"That's true," Myla said. "But she did just fine. She wrote about the Old Mermaids. And she was the one who got them all back together finally. Yes, some time later after they had gotten their new sanctuaries up and running and other new Old Mermaids were out setting up their sanctuaries, Sister Lyra Musica Mermaid arranged for the Old Mermaids to come back together here. After the buildings on the Old Mermaid Sanctuary were bulldozed, no one came to live here. Apparently the owners just didn't want any squatters on their land. Eventually they sold the land, so the Old Mermaids returned—or so some believe. Maybe they did come back, maybe they didn't. Some people say you can see them walking in the wash some nights, especially when the moon is full."

"Does that mean they're still here?" Theresa asked.

Myla shrugged. "I'm just telling you what I heard."

"I think we can answer that question," Luisa said. "Come one, come all. This way."

Trevor opened the back patio door. Luisa led Myla and the others outside. Myla reached her hand back and David grabbed it. They followed Luisa and Lily down the path until they stopped in the middle of the wash.

Myla laughed and clapped her hands. Along the side of the wash was a mermaid shaped out of the bones of the desert. Her hair was black desert brush, with bits of sea shell in it. Her eyes were stones. Her breasts were the halogen lights. Her tail was made from prickly pair pads.

"This is Sissy Maggie Mermaid," Trevor said. He walked down the wash a bit and Myla followed. "And this one is Sister Bridget Mermaid."

Another Old Mermaid! She, too, was made from logs, twigs, string, seashell. The old shovel was part of her backbone. The orange twine was her hair.

All up and down the wash, Old Mermaids swam in the sand. Sister Laughs a Lot Mermaid had a giant smile. Sister Lyra Musica Mermaid's eyes, nose, and mouth were made from the broken mermaid tile. Bottles became Sister Bea Wilder Mermaid's arms. Sister Sophia Mermaid's tail was part tree bones, part animal bones.

"I tried to tell everyone," Lily said. "The Old Mermaids are right here. Now you can see them."

"These are beautiful," Myla said. "Really extraordinary."

They all walked slowly down the wash and past the house until they had seen thirteen Old Mermaids.

"There's more, ladies and germs," Trevor said. He directed them toward the barn with a wave of his hand.

In front of the barn was a dresser. It was shaped like Myla's old oak dresser, but it did not look anything like it. Each side of it was painted in a different scene: an ocean, mountain, river, desert.

"It's like the scenes from the walls of the house in the Old Mermaid Sanctuary," Stefan said. "We all did some of it. Everyone here. David coordinated it all. We wanted to thank you for all you've done for us—for helping us find our siren songs."

Trevor opened the top drawer. It was filled with the black journals Trevor brought to the Church of the Old Mermaids every Saturday.

"Your journals?" Myla asked.

Trevor lifted one out and opened it.

"These aren't my journals," Trevor said. "I've been writing down your stories for years. My dad told me ones he remembered that I didn't. I asked other people too. Every story I could get is in these journals."

"David told us that you two have been talking about starting a kind of school," Luisa said, "for art and story. The Old Mermaid School of Telling Tales and Finding Art. You'll need money.

Maybe these stories can help with that."

"Or you could have the students go into the wash with you," Stefan said, "and find stuff to sell at the Church of the Old Mermaids to raise money. They could even help with the stories, like Trevor and I did. That would be the 'telling tales' part of the school."

Myla took the journal from Trevor. She opened it and started reading. She nodded. "I had forgotten this one," she said. She flipped the pages. "Oh, that Sister Sheila Na Giggles Mermaid. She is funny." She looked up at the others. How could she have ever doubted the Old Mermaids—or herself? These stories were her siren songs. And her relationships with these people were her songs, too.

"Trevor, I am so touched. I had no idea! James, you kept this a secret all these years? And this dresser. It's incredible. It can be the first piece of furniture for the new school. David, why don't you tell them the other news."

He nodded. "I'm going to buy the house from my parents," he said. "This is where the school will be. Or whatever it turns out to be. We'll do something else with these corrals besides put horses there. We've asked Juan, Maria, and Lily to stay here with us, and they've agreed. They'll take over Myla's old job, once we get their immigration status figured out. We'll all live together for a while, and expand the living spaces. Make Myla's old apartment bigger. Something. We don't know how it'll all turn out, but we're going to try it."

"That's great," Theresa said.

"So you two are together together now?" Gail asked.

"We're working on it," David said.

"Took you long enough," Gail said.

"The children have more to show us," James said.

"Yes, now, for the last piece of our art installation," Luisa said, "we require your help. Boys!"

Trevor and Stefan opened the middle dresser drawer and began pulling out pieces of colorful fabric and tossing them into the air.

"Catch them!" they called.

Myla grabbed a red one and held it up. It was a mermaid tail.

Del Rey held a blue tail in his hand.

"What am I supposed to do with this?" he asked.

"Wear it," Luisa said. "We're all mermaids tonight. The Old Mermaid Sanctuary is alive with mermaids!"

"Yeah, you've got a gun and you wear a badge," Theresa said. "We know. And now you're a mermaid."

"Well then, let's party!" Del Rey said.

They all put on their tails and wrapped themselves in shiny fabric. Then they went to look at the mermaids in the wash again.

David put his arm around Myla's waist.

"Will you respect me in the morning?" he asked.

She looked at his dark blue tail. She laughed. "I'm not sure I respect you now, darlin'. Ask me tomorrow. See if I remember."

After dinner, most everyone sat down for a card game of Old Mermaids.

"I win!" Luisa said, showing five colorfully decorated Old Mermaid cards.

"How can this possibly work?" Del Rey said. "We can all see which ones are the Old Mermaids."

"Just revel in the beauty of it," Theresa said.

"I'll tuck in Lily," Myla told David. Juan and Maria had already gone to bed. They were sleeping in the master bedroom for the time being; Lily was in David's sister's room. Ernesto and Stefan stayed in their old room. Myla and David were bunking in her apartment.

Lily tugged on Myla's hand. Myla leaned over. Lily whispered in her ear.

"I want to show you," she said.

Myla let Lily lead her out the front door into the dark and chilly night.

"Honey, let me get you a coat," Myla said.

"Shhh," Lily said. She exaggerated tiptoeing until they were standing on the berm. The wash flowed into the darkness to their left and right. Above, a full moon shined. The sand was snow-colored.

"Now!" Lily said. She began humming softly.

Myla closed her eyes and breathed in Lily's song. When Lily stopped humming, Myla opened her eyes; she looked to her left and then to her right. There. Someone was crossing the wash. Several someones. Shimmering in the moonlight. Did each of them wear a ghost of a tail? One of them waved. Myla recognized her, didn't she? From her dream so long ago. Myla waved. She blinked. The wash was empty again. The night was rich with moon beauty.

"I told you I knew where they were," Lily said.

"Yes, you did," Myla said. "What do you suppose they were doing in the wash tonight?"

"Looking for treasure," Lily said.

"We better get you in the house then," Myla said. "You're my treasure and I saw you first."

Lily laughed. "You're silly."

Myla crouched down next to Lily and gave her a wet kiss on her cheek. Lily wiped it away.

"Oh! You don't want my kisses, eh? You know that kiss is on your hand now, so if you want it back, you can just touch your cheek any time."

Lily put her hand against her cheek and smiled.

288

"It's cold out here," Myla said. "Time for bed."

Lily reached for Myla's hand, and they walked back to the house.

"Do Old Mermaids have to brush their teeth?" Lily asked.

"I think so," Myla answered.

"Do they have to eat their vegetables?"

"Gladly."

"What about school? Do they have to go to school?"

"Probably. I think it's called the School of Fishes."

"Nooo!" Lily said. "There's no School of Fishes."

"There was," Myla said. "That was one of the things the Old Mermaids missed when the Old Sea went dry."

Myla opened the door, and Lily went inside.

"Do the Old Mermaids have to eat their oatmeal?"

Myla followed Lily inside. "Only with nuts and fruit and maple syrup. And maybe a drop or two of sea water."

"Why?"

"Why? Because, Lily my Lily, that's the Old Mermaid Way."

Acknowledgements

I'd like to thank the first readers of *Church of the Old Mermaids* who so enthusiastically embraced the novel: Lloyd Antieau, Mario Milosevic, Michael Bourret, Joanna Powell Colbert, Charles de Lint, Catherine Kerr, Patricia Monaghan, and Terri Windling. I want to thank all the readers who wrote to me about the stories I wrote and posted on the Church of the Old Mermaids blog. I felt so tender about this novel and these characters and your encouragement helped me continue to champion the Old Mermaids. I especially want to thank Joanna and Cate who opened their hearts so early to the Church of the Old Mermaids. Your words have meant so much to me, especially when I doubted myself. I am so grateful to Delia Sherman, Ellen Kushner, and Terri Windling for creating a beautiful sanctuary out in the desert where the Old Mermaids began telling me their stories. I don't have adequate words to express how much this sanctuary means to me and how it has saved my life on more than one occasion. I am also grateful to Emma Bull and Will Shetterly for being such great stewards of this place and for welcoming us back every year. I thank you all and send you oceans of love. May you all dance and swim in beauty.

About the Author

Kim Antieau is the author of many novels, including most recently *Ruby's Imagine*, *Broken Moon*, and *Coyote Cowgirl*. She and her husband Mario Milosevic swim in the Pacific Northwest and Desert Southwest. For more information about the Old Mermaids dive into www.oldmermaids.com. Contact Kim or any of the Old Mermaids at kim@kimantieau.com.

CPSIA information can be obtained at www.ICGtesting.com
Printed in the USA
BVOW031836120612

292481BV00002B/55/P